UNDER THE RADAR

Stories by

Rosalia Scalia

For my children---Richard, Erin, and Antoinette- their partners and their children.

ACKNOWLEDGEMENTS

Gratitude to the journals that previously published versions of these stories:

Under the Radar, *Evening Street Review; Sweet Tree Review*

Maneuverings, *Hawaii Pacific Review; SLAB*

All the Small Joys, *Loch Raven Review*

Bridges, *Euphony, Big Muddy*

Static Electricity, *moonShine Review*

Butterfly Moments, *El Portal*

The Two Anthonys, *Oklahoma Review*

Henry's Fall, *Silk Road Review*

Patent Leather Sandals, *Loch Raven Review*

Practicing in the Dark, *Furious Gazelle*

Home Beautiful, *Blue Lake Review*

Daddy's Shoes, *Evening Street Review; Eckleburg; Door is A Jar Magazine; Loch Raven Review*

A Nut Job, *Loch Raven Review*

Training Wheels, *Rougarou*

Nothing Falling Apart in the House, *North Atlantic Review*

Doorways: Entrances and Exits, *RiddleFence*

BoomBoom Becky's Bakery Rises, *Green Hills Literary Lantern, Menacing Hedge, Swamp Ape Review*

Pirate Burger, *Brief Wilderness*

ACKNOWLEDGEMENTS

Thank you to all the journals that first published these stories.

For their inspiration and insights, I'd like to the many people who offered their support in a myriad of ways, tangible and intangible, but especially to Susan Mauddi Darraj, Kenya Griffin, and Carla du Pree.

For proofreading, website management, and much more, I'd like to thank everyone at Writer's Relief, whose deadlines to submit new work motivated me to keep writing. No one felt sadder and more disappointed when this fine company closed its doors in 2024. It served as a writing anchor for me since the inception of my writing career in 2003. I'm grateful to everyone at The Writer's Studio in New York City, especially the excellent and inspiring workshop instructors and to Philip Schultz for his dedication to persona narrator and to helping aspiring writers to understand it better. Also, thank you to Tom Jenks, editor of Narrative Magazine (online) for teaching me to improve my writing craft, a lifelong endeavor; thank you to all the writing instructors and teachers along the way for emphasizing the power of sentences and the art of storytelling.

For keeping me young at heart and aligned with all that's fresh and new, for bouncing around with me on an array of adventures, good and bad, and the poverty line until I could get established as a professional, I'd like to thank my family: kiddos—Richard I, Erin E. and Antoinette M. Levon—and their families. I thank my parents, the late Joseph A and Philomena R Scalia, without whom I never would have been able to write anything more than a grocery list.

Finally, for taking a chance on me, for editorial guidance, exceptional talents, precision, and patience for getting this book made at the height of unrest in Portland, Oregon, and through the challenges of a pandemic, I'd like to thank the Unsolicited Press team: Esme, Summer, Giuliana Woods, Robin Ann Lee, Katie, and Kristen Marckmann.

STORIES

Under The Radar	1
Maneuverings	11
All The Small Joys	16
Bridges	29
Static Electricity	42
Butterfly Moments	52
The Two Anthonys	64
Henry's Fall	85
Patent Leather Shoes	102
Practicing in the Dark	105
Home Beautiful	118
Daddy's Shoes	135
A Nut Job	138
Training Wheels	148
A Beautiful Death	157
Chocolate Learns Marketing	178
Nothing Falling Apart in the House	203
Doorways: Entrances and Exits	211
Boom-Boom Becky's Bakery Rises	222
Benjamin Came Home	232
Pirate Burger	256

"Goodbyes are only for those
who love with their eyes.
Because those who love with
their heart ad soul no there is no such thing as separation."

Rumi

UNDER THE RADAR

UNDER THE RADAR

Kenny. I can talk about him now. I can still see how he looked at the airport when he came home from the rig job that first time. The job required six months on, then six months off, but it paid a bundle, so he took it to pay off school loans and to save up for our wedding and his dream restaurant, the next step to our destiny, he'd said. I can still see his inky-black eyes sparkling under the backward orange-and-white Orioles baseball cap, his long hair, in a knot, poking through the cap's size gap in the back, hair he usually stuffed into the pipe section of his toque blanche, his chef hat. Back then, everyone wore long hair and wide sideburns that looked silly by today's standards. Kenny hated those mutton sideburns and stayed clean-shaven but did wear hair bigger than mine, something we often laughed about. I can still see his jaunty walk, his wide bell-bottom jeans, his sexy, slender waist with his stomach muscles poking through the lightweight T-shirt. I can still see how his biceps and triceps strained his shirt sleeves. How surprised I was by those taut muscles, something that came from his stint on the rig. Something had to fill up his time when he wasn't working, he said, and it was the gym, for lack of anything better to do. I'd teased him about having the same physique as the Tasmanian devil but secretly felt thrilled he'd started exercising. Mistakenly, when I saw him looking so defined, I thought we'd jog and work out together during his time off the rig. That never happened.

Whenever I think about him, it's his radiance, of him looking muscular and fit, his complexion glowing, his eyes flashing, his smile wider than the horizon as he came toward me that day at the airport, filled with high energy, rather than the emaciated and frail way he looked when he died. I'd anticipated hearing all his stories about rig life and sharing mine about nursing life. At that point we'd been together for six years, engaged for two. When he proposed, he'd hidden the most gorgeous, ridiculously large jade-and-diamond ring in the middle of a chocolate mousse pie—my favorite—and slipped it on my finger, telling me to never take it off, pudding clinging to the gold and obscuring the diamonds' shine. The ring, he said, had belonged to his grandmother. His family and mine met up at his parents' house for dinner to celebrate, and while Kenny cooked up a special dinner, his mom dragged out his baby pictures. I gazed at those photos, wondering what our own children would look like—if they'd have his wide-gapped smile and inky-black eyes or maybe they'd be a combination of both of us. His eyes, my smile. Or my green eyes, his big hair, his smile—the possibilities felt endless and our future exciting.

I cherish the ring, still. Even when we were engaged, I never wore it to work. It seemed too outrageous at the hospital, too delicate with the constant handwashing. Kenny's nieces will get it after I'm gone. To be honest, I'd felt some uncertainties about us before he left for the rig, something I'd never mentioned to him. I didn't want to hurt him. Kenny and I rolled along together, ticking all the boxes of the steps we were expected to take.

"Hope, darling!" he yelled, waving his free arm, flashing his gap-toothed smile, holding his luggage in the other, setting it down when he saw me.

I ran to him and threw myself into those muscled arms. He oozed exuberance and crushed me in a fierce hug, nearly squeezing the breath out of me. We kissed like any other long-separated couple. He picked me up and swirled me around in a circle!

"Look at you," I said, squeezing his biceps when he finally set me down. "Rig life agrees with you!"

He laughed. "It's boring as fuck. They sometimes run movies in the big theater. Not much to do but work. And go to the gym." He flexed his biceps. "Finally exercising. I hate every minute of it.

"You look maaaaaarvelous!" he sang as he swooped me up in his arms. We'd waited six months for this moment.

Back then, before Wi-Fi and FaceTime, before text messages and WhatsApp, we chatted by pay phone every few days at odd hours in the allowable six-minute intervals we had, always in the middle of the night. I waited for those calls and felt as if the world had tilted the wrong way if he didn't call. Walking toward the airport garage, holding each other by the waist, we caught up. I told him about working at the medical center, and he talked about rig life: the galley staying open 24/7 for the two hundred people living on it and a team of chefs and sous chefs working in shifts. He described the danger for the men working the drill and how monstrous and frightening it felt during violent storms and hurricanes.

"It's a harbor, an airport, a hotel, and a refinery rolled up in one," he said. "My roommate's from the UK, but we never see each other. It's like living with a ghost," he said. "But opportunities to advance can't be beat."

On the ride home he told me his ideas for fusion food, equipment he wanted to own in his dream restaurant, and I told him how it felt to lose a patient, even when the loss was expected, and how more men have entered nursing, many former military corpsmen or men who simply had felt the call.

"I submitted a menu proposal for the company's next annual meeting. It could mean a huge promotion if they like it."

"Brilliant plan," I said. "Would that mean you'd have to extend your contract?"

"It would. Just a year. Babe, I can't turn down that kind of money," he said.

"That would mean our first years of married life, we won't be living together," I said, trying not to cry. "I started looking for a gown. We just need to set a date."

Kenny and I met at Tattoo's, a now-defunct joint downtown. He'd worked in the kitchen while I waitressed to pay for nursing school textbooks and lab fees. A scholarship paid for everything else. In those days, everyone but us smoked a little weed, got a little drunk, got a little high. Kenny and I both came from tough, working-class backgrounds, which meant neither of us could afford to party. We worked, and at Tattoo's we were the only sober people in the joint at the end of our shift, and that's how we started talking. Tattoo's had been the second place he worked after chef school. Not wanting to pay him a salary that matched his degree, the first place fired him after he created a menu and taught everyone how to cook it. We'd already been seeing each other pretty regularly when Tattoo's did the same thing, and that's when we moved in together.

"Did you miss me?" I asked.

I'd missed him, longed for him, thought about him every minute of every day—the first thought in the morning, the last thought at night. I waited for him to notice how I'd kept his old beastie in good shape, having the tires rotated and oil changed on the schedule he set before he left. He drove. Like a wild man, so happy to be in control again. He held my hand as he maneuvered around corners too fast.

"Of course, darling!"

He kissed my hand, sending my heart into loopy swoops.

"You can work in the rig dispensary. We'd be together," he said.

I shook my head. "I want to stay here. Lots of hospitals and the chance to see all kinds of medical conditions."

"It'd be temporary," he said. "The work might be interesting enough—rig life is dangerous. You'd see some trauma and some routine stuff."

I promised to think about it. Although we were supposed to get married during the next break, every time we passed a bridal or florist shop, or a caterer or a photographer, or a gown shop, he failed to latch onto any of the hints I tossed about setting a date. I asked him directly when we'd tie the knot, though he pretended not to hear me. Something felt wrong. Despite all the anticipation and longing to be with him, despite satisfying sex we enjoyed in the first few days after his return, despite his affection, warmth, care, and love, something I couldn't name made me anxious. The sex diminished, our emotional distance increased, and I started snapping at him.

We visited our families but Kenny spent increasing amounts of time with his friends, and I felt neglected yet guilty for snapping at him all the time. He could at least spend my off time with me, I yelled at him over the phone one night after I'd worked a twelve-hour shift and came home to an empty place. He could have at least prepared dinner for me, I shouted. The following Sunday, when he was cooking us a fancy breakfast, the uncertainty got the best of me, and I exploded, demanding to know what the hell was going on, demanding that he break up outright if that's what he wanted to do.

"I don't want to talk about it," he said, looking straight at me, his eyes focused like a laser on mine.

"You better start talking about it or I'm leaving you." Those words tumbled out of my mouth before I could take them back. I didn't mean them.

The aroma of his French toast with coconut cream stuffing, of bacon and shrimp with grits, intruded, came between us like a wall. I wasn't hungry. In my soul I knew he was dating someone else, maybe someone who spoke his language of roués, spices, and sauces and not someone who smelled like disinfectant, rubbing alcohol, and medicines, of sickness and death.

"I'm not stupid. Who is she?" I shouted, afraid of the answer, my arms crossed.

"Are you insane?" he shouted. "There's no other woman. I promise you that."

How dare he make a fool of me. "I don't believe you."

He took both of my hands and squeezed them and I threw them off. I didn't want him to touch me since he had stopped being intimate with me weeks ago. Undaunted, he crushed me into a deep embrace, reassuring me repeatedly there was definitely no other woman.

"You seem to have plenty of time for all your friends but none for me. It's worse than when you're on the rig because here, you have a choice, and you're not choosing me," I shouted.

I burst into tears. A long silence followed.

"Kenny, whatever it is, you need to come clean. Are you on drugs?"

"Please sit down."

He faced me and held both my hands.

"We're not getting married. There will be no wedding." His voice sounded gentle and timid.

"What are we doing then?"

"It's not you."

"Really, Kenny?"

"Hope, I love you. I love our lives together. But it is me. That's the truth."

Another silence between us. He continued holding my hands.

"I think I'm gay. I keep my head down and my mouth shut on the rig because of the feelings I'm having for other men. I'm sorry."

I wept. I loved him. That kind of thing—people didn't discuss. What I had been unable to articulate smacked me in the face. His innate goodness, his sense of humor, his work ethic, his sense of fun and play, his sexiness; how could I hate him after years of loving him? Or be angry at him for wanting to be himself? Or consider him a sicko or criminal?

"It's okay," I said, stroking his arm, unable to stop crying.

There'd be no wedding, no children, no growing old together. Just unbearable loss. He could have married me and hidden the truth. Relief and peace flooded his face, as if a giant boulder had been lifted from his shoulders. That day we spent the most wonderful hours together, and I witnessed him flower, his true self finally blooming with a radiant loveliness and light.

"I was afraid you'd reject me. I don't want to lose you. I want you in my life."

"What's going to happen with your job?"

"I can't afford to lose my job. We can't tell anyone."

I pulled off the engagement ring and handed it back to him, freeing him of any obligation toward me. He refused to accept it. He put it back on my finger.

"You promised to never take it off," he said.

"Things between us … will never be the same, Kenny."

We hid the truth from our families and, thereafter, kept up appearances, each sneaking around with other lovers as if we were cheating on each other instead of protecting his status. We moved into a larger, two-bedroom apartment, brushing off incessant questions about a wedding date. Kenny extended his rig contract for another year while making inroads on national food shows, doing cooking demos and guest appearances on new cable shows in his off time, laying the foundation for his post-rig career in New York City, far from family pressure. He cut his hair, grew an amazing mustache, developed a sophisticated European style, and became part of the NYC gay scene. He no longer wore bell-bottoms with raggedy hems when I picked him up from the airport. Finally, when the contract ended, we told our families we broke the engagement, blaming it on differences of where we wanted to live. While Kenny didn't hide his gayness, he didn't flaunt it either and never officially came out to his family.

"It's really none of anyone's damned business," Kenny told me over the phone one night. "Why should they know anything about me? Or my life? I don't go asking people if they're having an affair or who they're fucking." He sounded indignant.

"Why rob your family of the chance to prove themselves?"

"They're strict and stifling. They'd tell me I'm damned to hell for eternity."

Our strong bond surprised us both, as did our candor, care, and the love we shared as we each dated others, advanced our careers, and even after I met the man I married. Kenny served as a witness in our wedding since my husband had accepted him and our relationship early on without reservation.

"People make public pronouncements every day," I said. "Isn't that marriage in a nutshell?"

"Not for people like me. We're stuck flying under the radar, considered criminals in a lot of places."

"Maybe things will change. Everyone loves the Village People," I said.

"You still tell bad jokes," he said.

A few years later, HIV/AIDS emerged as a mysterious disease, one then without a name afflicting gay men, one that incited fear in my colleagues, some of whom refused to treat patients with it. I began interrogating Kenny about his choices until he finally told me to stop. But I couldn't. He didn't see the hysteria, the protocols for double gloves, goggles, and face masks, the opportunistic infections killing people, the derision and panic among my co-workers, the slow, torturous deaths. The fear.

"I'm doing everything with everybody, Hope honey. This is not a dress rehearsal. This is my life. If I ever need a nurse, I'll call you first," he said.

"Now who's telling bad jokes?"

He did call me first, but only after he couldn't hide being sick anymore and lacked the energy to work. Kaposi sarcoma lesions covered his upper back. His doctor told him to get his affairs in order. My husband and I moved Kenny into our home, transforming the den into his room with a hospital bed. Our families scolded us, told us we were endangering our sons, but how could I turn my back on my best friend, a man I'd loved for so long? My husband, knowing the stakes, embraced kindness, saying our sons would learn more by what we do than what we say. Kenny's family helped, though I doubt they connected the cancer to HIV/AIDS, or maybe they chose not to know.

Kenny. I can talk about him now. Sometimes, when I'm alone, when my husband and now adult sons are out, when the radio and television are off and silence drapes the house, a cardinal with its red beak, its black mask under its silly, feathery crown, flutters outside the windows of the den. Kenny's presence fills the room with the joy he radiated when he was alive, and endless waves of a deep, abiding, unconditional love wash over me, paralyzing me to the point of tears. It comes at the most unexpected times with no logical explanation to account for the sensation of bliss that overcomes me.

MANEUVERINGS

We all sit on the floor in a house in Northern Virginia eating roasted goat, curried vegetables, and steamed rice during the Festival of Lights party. Next to me, Soros, who came to America almost a year before I did, eats with his fingers like back home. I use a plastic fork provided by the host, a white American lady whose name I can't remember or pronounce. Wanting to embrace new ways in America, I practiced using a fork and knife before coming to the party. She worked in my country as a veterinarian in the Peace Corps, and now back home in America, she stays connected to people from my country by hosting holiday parties for newcomers, and everyone who's attended in the past is invited. A lady from my country lives with her, but something doesn't add up with them. They hold hands sometimes in the house, but not in the same way ladies hold hands at home. The lady from my country should already be married, but she's here in America going to school when she should already be a mother.

All the traditional foods from my country cover the buffet table, cooked by ladies who have been in America for a while, and I can't stop eating it. It tastes like home. I don't realize how much I miss these dishes until I'm eating, and the tastes and variety cause a rush of memories to crash into my brain. I put the plastic fork down and begin eating with my fingers, like at home, and lick the sauce from them.

I came to the party with a friend of a friend of a friend, a guy I met for the first time tonight, who's lived in America almost forever, long enough to own a fancy car, stylish clothes, a beautiful house, and an American nickname, Max.

Max looks like a movie star, with cowboy boots and his hair slicked back. He and the hostess talk in the kitchen, where she passes out hard candies to Americans who find the food too spicy-hot. Tears run down their cheeks from the hot chili powder that's in every dish. The candies counter the fire of the chili powder. Americans use plastic forks and knives because they don't know how to eat with their hands, how to form the rice into a bite-size ball, grab some vegetables and meat, and plop the ball into their mouths.

While we eat, Soros tells me about his pizza delivery job, a dream-come-true kind of job. Soros says he's earning three hundred dollars every day he works, delivering pizzas to people so lazy they can't drive in their own cars to the pizza store to pick it up themselves. He works seven days per week, twelve hours a day. I want to be like Soros and earn money from lazy rich people who pay others to do things for them. Like pick up pizza.

Back home, people work a whole year to earn three hundred dollars. I can't even imagine how long it would take to earn twenty-one hundred dollars back home where it's beautiful. I miss the thick green jungles, the loud rivers gushing down from the mountaintops at breakneck speed. I miss the crackling, crisp air and the sky thick with puffed white clouds. Everywhere you look back home, you see the mountains, and the moon appears close enough to stroke. The giant third eye of the Buddhist stupa watches over the city closest to my village, but the eye is blind to the hungry bellies, to the small children working by sweeping dust off streets to earn a few coins, to the starving, ignored, bony dogs, roaming around searching for food. The rich suffer a lot less than people like my family, and my secret stays locked inside me: The name on my visa papers is fake, but I'm real.

I can tell by his last name that Soros belongs to one of the higher castes. Back home, he wouldn't be speaking one word to me, much less sitting on the floor next to me, and certainly not eating from the same dishes. The strange harshness of America, where only a few others look like us and even fewer speak our language—the differences magnified back home vanish here. The minute we return to our country, the barriers rise without fail, like the sun. When people here look at Soros and me, they see two brown men, foreigners. They see all that makes us similar and fail to see the divisions inherent in our surnames. My fake name is of the highest caste. I smile inwardly, remembering that back home, I'd have to wipe off my seat when I leave it before someone like Soros could sit down. I wonder if Soros would sit next to me on the floor of this white lady's house if he knew the truth about me, obvious in my real last name, which he'll never learn. People told me that America has no castes, but people everywhere divide themselves. We're new here and can't see it yet. When Soros sees Max in the kitchen holding a beer, his expression changes.

"Look at that asshole Manos with his fake American nick. We came together when he was still Manos."

"You mean Max?" I ask.

"Max in America. Manos back home. Married a white lady to stay in America legally, and then divorced her one month after he made citizenship. I know he didn't pay her. He cheated her. Did you know that?"

I didn't. Nor do I care. Was he judging Max for his fake marriage, his fake American name, or for his legal status as an American? Soros's status stopped being legal months ago. If Soros knew the name on my papers is fake, would he judge me, too? I know with certainty that back home, Soros would be expecting me to wipe my seat before he sat down, and he wouldn't be drinking or eating out of the same serving bowls.

America has seduced me with indoor toilets and hot showers; with orderly streets and cars that stop for red lights; with fast-food drive-throughs, big-box stores larger than whole villages back home; with its streets empty of animals—no cows, no pigs, no monkeys, no goats roaming around, shitting wherever they go. Or fucking when they're in season.

"What do you need for this pizza job?" I ask.

Soros laughs. "A driver's license, a car, and insurance."

"Sounds easy enough," I say.

He smirks. "It's not. It's tough. I had to do some maneuvering to get the proper documents for the driver's license. That's the hardest part. Especially when you have no papers. But even in America, everyone has a number."

I laugh inside. My whole life back home requires maneuvering from one bottom rung to another bottom rung. What do they call us? *Dalits.* Untouchables. The name itself robs us of our humanity. Knowing this, I take Soros's empty paper plate and bring it to the kitchen to throw into the trash bin. Interrupting Max, I speak to the hostess, thank her for having all of us at her house, and introduce myself as "Bill." She knows this isn't my true name and asks what it is. I wink and smile at her.

"In America, I'm Bill." I don't tell her that in America, I'm also bold, now with two fake first names.

I bring Soros a fresh plate with more rice and vegetables, more goat, passing it to him with my untouchable hands, and inside I'm dancing. Of my father's three wives, I'm the youngest son of six children born to the third, the only one who could have children. No money, no status. No car. No refrigerator. No glass in our windows. No stove. We collect water at the village well and carry it home in metal pots, careful not to spill a single drop onto the dirt floor. My family maneuvers every day to survive. I maneuvered myself into a visa and passport with a higher-caste name, and I maneuvered myself to America.

"Some maneuvering?" I ask Soros, wondering if other newcomers in the room are like me and Soros—here to stay, regardless of all obstacles. I imagine myself maneuvering this and that, just like back home, except here in America, I'll eclipse both Soros and Max. And all the other newcomers too.

ALL THE SMALL JOYS

"Denise better not cause commotion at Mama's viewing tomorrow or at the funeral. Why does she always mess things up?" Kathy asked, not wanting an answer.

"You've got to admit, it's a half-brilliant plan. Coco did sleep at your mother's feet for the past fifteen years—and they *were* inseparable, even if she was Denise's dog," Frank said. "Maybe your mother died because she missed the dog too much. I mean, the dog went, and then she went. Just saying." Frank stifled a smile.

"Seriously, Frank?" Kathy said, sounding cross. "It's not okay. Not remotely okay. Denise shouldn't have asked. She's not going to bury that stupid dog with Mama."

Kathy breathed deeply to calm herself. She disliked Coco, a persnickety, temperamental animal with wiry fur that appeared as if it had been run through a wash cycle too many times. The feeling was mutual, considering Coca stared and growled at her whenever she visited Mama, who always referred to it as Denise's dog. Now home after a painful day, Kathy felt drained.

She and Frank had rushed to the hospital at the butt crack of dawn after Mama's next-door neighbor called, saying she'd found Mama collapsed outside. Eva had already called an ambulance. They sped to the hospital, the wheels of the car jumping the curb of the ER parking lot ramp. Kathy didn't realize she'd left the car door open before rushing through the automatic doors until she heard Frank shutting two doors. He followed her inside and they both stopped at the check-in desk to ask about Mama. Kathy immediately called Denise, who said she'd come after work. Annoyed, Kathy dropped her phone into her purse.

"Denise?" Frank asked.

Kathy held up her hand and shook her head.

They waited for hours until a skinny doctor with a beard, a ponytail, and tired eyes led them into a room where he told them Mama had died. Kathy's eyes watered from the shock and then she couldn't stop weeping. Mama was going to vacation at Cape Verde. She couldn't be dead! Mama was going to be a foster grandmother now that Kathy and Frank completed the training.

"Aneurysm," the doctor said. "We did our best ..." he added, his voice trailing off.

On the ER gurney, Mama's candy-red hair—a pop of color against the white pillow and against her now gray, waxy skin—radiated from her head like a halo. Kathy touched Mama's face and shoulders. She looked like an empty shell. Holding Mama's hand, Kathy was shocked that her warmth had quickly evaporated. Where was that spark that animated her? All she could do was weep.

She called Denise, who began howling on the other end of the line, insisting she couldn't possibly come to the hospital. Kathy then dialed the undertaker who took care of their father.

The next day, Denise joined them in the undertaker's cluttered office, where they discussed funeral details. Kathy seethed as Denise, who never asked about money and took over the planning process as if she was paying for it until Kathy exploded in fury.

"Why don't you want a limo?" Denise asked, undeterred.

"There's us and Frank!" Kathy said. "Fuck the limo. Who's going to be pallbearers?"

"The three of us can ride in the limo behind the hearse," Denise said.

"No limo," Kathy said, looking at the undertaker. "We need pallbearers."

"Why are you being so damned cheap?"

Denise chose a pearl-pink metal casket with angel figures in the four corners and rectangular bas-relief plates of the Last Supper all along the sides. Kathy said nothing about the extravagance, but she did nix the schedule Denise wanted that stretched the viewing and funeral to three days and instead opted for two viewing times on the first day and a simple prayer service at the funeral home before the interment on the second day. After Kathy gave the undertaker the down payment from Mama's checking account, they went to the cemetery to purchase a grave site. Kathy paid for the grave space, the requisite concrete wall, then later, at the florist, for the casket spray. Now finally at home, Kathy lacked an appetite and her bones ached.

"They're both dead. Who cares?" Frank said from behind a newspaper. He was sitting at the kitchen table, annoying Kathy by breathing. She wished he'd just shut up already.

"And the dog's already cremated in a nice-looking box. You got to admit, Denise did pick an attractive box. Maybe your mother would like some company." He appeared amused by the idea of the dog cremains in her mother's casket.

"Don't be ridiculous," Kathy said, sounding irritated. *Why is Frank colluding with Denise?* she wondered.

"It's a feasible plan to put Coco's cremains in your mother's casket," he said.

"No, and no, and no again," she said. She slammed the palm of her hand on the kitchen counter. "Shut up about Denise and that stupid dog," she shouted. She imagined hurling a tomato at Frank. "Show some respect. Dammit."

Kathy pulled cucumbers, tomatoes, lettuce, and other salad fixings from the fridge. At the sink scrubbing the cucumbers, Kathy smiled about the word "Mooooooooooooom," the way Mama signed emails and notes to her and Denise for fun when they were in school. But now Mooooooooooooooooooooom was gone. Tears rolled down her face.

"The undertaker did say he could slip the box in by her feet, and no one would be the wiser. The cemetery won't charge extra for the dog if no one says anything. It's a nice gesture, don't you think?" Frank said.

Kathy scoffed and rolled her eyes in a way that Frank wouldn't see.

Putting that silly box with Coco's cremains into her mother's coffin represented just one more of Denise's indignities forced on their mother. Kathy bristled at the thought. Mama was gone now. After everything was done, she'd never see Denise again. Kathy paused. *Mama's gone.* She allowed the concept to sink into her brain and ricochet around her body. Grief snuck up on her when she least expected. Twice now she'd reached for the phone to call Mama before remembering she was gone. She wondered if missing Mama would characterize the rest of her life.

Kathy wiped the tears escaping down her cheeks. She wanted to wail and scream. Instead, she focused on preparing the salad for dinner. She set the knife down on the cutting board and scraped vegetable peels into the sink. She reached for her cell phone and dialed Mama's number just to hear her voice on her voicemail and started sobbing at the sound of it. Kathy buried her face in her hands still wet with cucumber bits. Damn brain aneurysm!

Frank hugged her from behind and rubbed her shoulders. "Imagine all the foster children we'll have soon. Maybe we'll be able to adopt one," he said, whispering in Kathy's ear.

After dinner, Frank decided to stay home, enabling Kathy to take her time with choosing Mama's funeral clothes. Relief flooded Kathy because Frank's focus on the dog in the casket irritated her. Denise declined helping to select Mama's clothing, saying she was too overwrought.

At Mama's house, Kathy inhaled the spicy aroma—garlic, ginger, basil—that smelled like home. A full coffee mug sat on the kitchen table next to a newspaper, the feature section pages open. A frying pan sat atop the front burner; two eggs in a small bowl, the olive oil spray bottle on the counter beside the stove comprised Mama's uncooked, uneaten breakfast. Upstairs, clothes Mama had bought for her upcoming vacation to Cape Verde filled the open suitcase perched on a chair in her bedroom. Her travel jewelry bag lay open on the bureau. Kathy opened the closet, pushed the hangers first one way and then the other, searching for a suitable dress. She saw a white knit dress, a solid black sheath with a wide red belt, and a royal-blue lace cocktail number Mama had worn to a recent wedding. She held the royal-blue dress up to the light to make sure it was stain-free and laid it across the bed with the others. She pulled a fur piece from under the garment protector, and that's when she saw a large manila envelope taped to the back of the closet wall with the words IF I DIE in large, red, block letters. Kathy pulled it from the wall and opened it, her hands shaking.

The envelope contained all Mama's email passwords and web and mobile bank passwords, the location and amounts of each of her insurance policies. A clear plastic envelope held all her important papers: birth certificate, marriage license to their father, a set of small keys in a plastic bag, and other stuff for Kathy to review. A letter was attached to the plastic envelope.

Kathy, if you're reading this, the plane crashed either to or from Cape Verde. Or something else happened, and I'm gone. Everything you need to know to dispose of my stuff and settle my affairs is in this envelope. A copy of my will is here. Uncle George keeps the original in his office. And please, look after your sister. Take care of each other. I know Denise is difficult. She's a high-octane person—but her heart's in the right place. Most of the time. If you're reading this, then you know that all you have is each other. And Frank, of course. Remember to cherish all the small joys.

Love, Moooooooooooom

Mama's rough line sketches of misshapen cats, high-heeled shoes, and flowers both in pots and floating festooned the note. The envelope contained information on her banking and insurance policies, her will, some instructions, but nothing about what to bury her in. Maybe she thought her body would be left in Cape Verde? Kathy hugged the envelope to her chest and cried before searching through bureaus for new, never-worn pink matching panties and a bra. She found a never-worn slip and was holding it up to the light, deciding if she ought to include it, when the front door opened.

Denise ran up the stairs. "What are you doing here?" she demanded.

"I thought you couldn't make it," Kathy said. "Getting Mama's clothes together."

"You said tomorrow morning," Denise said.

"We have to *deliver them* to the undertaker tomorrow morning," Kathy said. "Find Mama's shoes to match the blue lace dress on the bed. Do you think we should include this slip?" Kathy asked, showing it to her sister.

"You think she needs a slip? Or shoes?" Denise scoffed and picked up Mama's jewelry case. "Why's this out?"

"She was packing for Cape Verde," Kathy said, blinking back tears.

"She didn't say anything to me about any trip," Denise said, her tone sharp. "When was she leaving?"

"Next Wednesday," Kathy said, her voice nearly a whisper.

"Why didn't she tell me?" Denise sounded accusatory. She stared intently at the jewelry pieces in the case, examining the contents and fingering the items in the pouches beneath the plastic. She plucked a pair of good gold earrings out of the case and examined them closely.

Still holding the slip, Kathy stared at her sister, wondering why she showed up at Mama's when she thought Kathy wouldn't be there.

"We're not burying her with jewelry," Denise said, still examining the earrings. "Not even the fake stuff."

"It's hers," Kathy said.

"Why waste it?" Denise said.

Kathy hated Denise at that moment. She'd spent endless hours defending Denise in court for her animal activism, springing her from the city lockup for disturbing the peace, trespassing, malicious destruction of property, and other charges too numerous to list. Denise acted as if she believed she deserved her sister's legal services without a thank-you or payment. After Denise adopted Coco, she abandoned the dog with Mama once the newness of a shiny new puppy wore off and she had to actually care for it.

"If you're not helping with Mama's clothes for the viewing, you can leave," Kathy said, sounding harsher than she meant. "Put the earrings back. We need to go over the will."

"I forgot how you excelled at being a bitch," Denise said, tossing the jewelry case onto the bureau, setting the gold earrings beside it. "Mama died, but you're still an A-number-one bitch."

Denise thundered down the stairs and slammed the front door behind her. After emptying the vacation clothes out of the suitcase, Kathy replaced them with the funeral clothes, including her mink fur stole and a pair of silver pumps to match the blue dress. She dropped a tube of lipstick from the half-packed travel bag into the suitcase and snapped it shut. Kathy pushed the rest of Mama's vacation clothes to the foot of the bed before burying her face in Mama's pillow, squeezing it tight, smelling Mama's scent in the fabric. She sobbed into the pillow. All the plans they made together, she and Mama, who suggested Frank and Kathy take in foster children after she saw Kathy's purple-and-yellow bruises from all those failed IVF hormone injections.

"Why torture yourself when too many children already born need good parents?" she asked. "Do something else. Foster children to adopt them!" Mama said. "Better than that," she said, pointing to the bruises staining Kathy's torso.

Kathy kicked off her shoes and phoned Frank to say she was spending the night and would deliver the clothes to the undertaker on her way home tomorrow. She tossed Mama's vacation clothes off the bed. They sailed to the floor in a cascade of greens, pinks, oranges, blues, and blacks. Kathy climbed into Mama's bed and fell asleep, weeping.

At the funeral parlor the next afternoon, before the first viewing, Kathy heard a row the minute she and Frank stepped inside. Unmistakably, Denise's voice dominated the fray. Kathy forced herself to take slow, measured steps toward the Peach Room. Frank squeezed her hand. Kathy's heart beat ferociously against her chest, and once inside the Peach Room, Kathy stared at the ceiling to avoid crying. The unwelcome sight of Denise and a funeral parlor employee fighting over Mama's fur piece greeted her.

"She's *my* mooooooooother," Denise shouted, stretching the word "mother." Denise clutched a red-and-gold box to her chest—Coco's cremains. Denise and the employee engaged in an odd game of keep-away. The kid, probably the undertaker's son, was unable to capture the stole despite his height.

"You're not supposed to touch the guests after they've been prepared," the kid said, sounding earnest.

"Guests? Is this a fucking hotel?" Denise yelled.

Flowers, plants, and sympathy cards filled the room. Metal tripods with collages of Mama's life flanked the casket, collages Kathy made , unable to sleep, made the previous night. Behind Denise, a strange man shuffled foot to foot, looking confused. In the casket, Mama's glasses sat askew on her face, and a large red splotch on her cheek looked as if a tornado had blown lipstick clear off her lips and smeared it there. Denise's outfit—a flowy black pantsuit—sported a garish-looking golden lion that appeared to encircle her body from foot to head so that its printed, large lion face stared from her shoulder. As Denise moved and the fabric shifted, the giant lion print appeared to be climbing her petite frame. *Where on earth did Denise find that awful outfit?* Kathy wondered. Rivers of black mascara streaked Denise's cheeks under her plastic, bug-eyed-framed glasses.

"Get out!" Denise yelled, but the kid stood his ground.

"You gave them this fur?" she screamed at Kathy. "She's not being buried with this fur. Or red lipstick."

"It's not about you," Kathy said, working to keep her tone even.

Kathy found herself wishing Denise would have had the aneurysm instead of Mama. Denise sucked in air and sobbed, sounding fake. Kathy glanced at Frank, their signal for "crazy." Kathy extended her hand to the confused man in the hideous vest. "Katherine. Denise's sister. I don't believe we've met. Frank, my husband," she said, nodding toward Frank. "Denise didn't introduce us to her new boyfriend," she said, irked that this stranger would be present.

"Correction. Herb is *Mama's* boyfriend," Denise said between fake sobs.

Why would Denise know an important fact like this? Kathy wondered.

"Berry said you both treated her like her mothers-in-law," Herb said. "She thought neither of you would approve."

"How do you know Denise then?" Kathy asked, wishing she'd looked more closely at the IF I DIE file.

"Accident," Denise said, sniffling. "I came early, and he was here."

"Doing what?" Frank asked.

"Avoiding them," Herb said, pointing to Denise and Kathy. "I wanted Berry to have something special."

Kathy studied the man, disbelieving Mama would hide a lover.

"Now let's wait a New York minute here," Frank said, stepping in front of Kathy and Denise. "Where's the proof? Just because you say you're Berry's boyfriend doesn't make it true."

Denise honked into her tissue. Kathy squeezed Frank's fingers in gratitude. Her brain had been foggy since Mama died.

"Mama never mentioned a boyfriend," Kathy said.

Herb's face crunched in disgust as if he was eating a lemon. "I was going to propose again at Cape Verde." Herb smiled, but Kathy remained skeptical. "I wanted to slip the ring on her finger," he said, holding up a gold ring fished out of his pocket.

"NO!" Kathy and Denise shouted at the same time.

"I don't need your permission," Herb said, sounding indignant.

"Mama wouldn't want to be buried with valuable jewelry," Denise said.

Just then, the undertaker entered the Peach Room. After a glance at the casket, at Mama's glasses askew, at the blotch of lipstick on her cheek, her mouth crooked, the undertaker erupted in fury.

"Who did this?" he thundered, glaring at Denise.

"No fur or that awful red lipstick," Denise said.

"She can do both," Kathy said, as if Mama could exercise a choice. "No dog cremains in the casket."

"What about what Berry wants?" Herb asked, but no one paid attention.

"Why do you get to decide everything?" Denise asked, wanting to argue.

The undertaker bent over the casket to assess the damages.

"Stop being ridiculous," Kathy said.

"Ridiculous? Red lipstick and a mink fur stole are ridiculous," Denise yelled, holding the stole.

"She's not being buried with dog cremains either," Kathy said, her voice rising. She snatched the red-and-gold box of dog cremains from Denise, holding it away from her in the same manner that Denise held the stole. "It's not about you, Denise!"

"Mama always liked you best!" Denise roared, rushing Kathy to reclaim the gold-and-red cremains box. She accidentally pushed the undertaker into the casket, pushing it off the bier, the casket bottom hitting the floor with a loud bang. The casket's crown struck Kathy's hands, jerking the cremains box into the air, its loose lid allowing Coco's cremains—a coarse, gray dust cloud—to rain on all of them, covering them, the two peach-striped sofas, and the peach rug. Her face filled with rage, Denise tackled Kathy. In that odd lion suit, it appeared as if a lion were mauling her.

"Stop it!" Herb yelled, but no one listened or heard.

He pulled a referee whistle from his vest pocket and blew it for three solid minutes, his face turning crimson as he kept the long, loud, obnoxious tone. Everyone covered their ears until the whistle stopped. Frank helped Kathy stand while Herb pulled Denise to her feet. The casket hung off the bier, and the man and the kid worked to right it. In the casket, a slit cut into the zipper area of Mama's lace dress exposed her back and her new pink underwear.

"This because you two can't decide which dead animal can be buried with your mother?" the undertaker said, each word staccato with anger. The undertaker grimaced as he surveyed the ruins of the Peach Room and Mama's dust-stained face. Coco's cremains polluted everything in the room.

"Give me the stole, the box of cremains—what's left in it," the undertaker said. "No time to fix things. It's a closed casket."

Kathy opened her mouth to speak, but the undertaker held up his hand.

"Not a word. From either of you," he said.

The undertaker wrapped the fur piece around Mama's shoulders as if he was swaddling an infant. He arranged the gold-and-red box in the leg portion of the casket and situated Mama's body in the center of the casket before gingerly shutting and locking the lid. Denise sobbed.

"I can't put this ring on her finger?" Herb asked.

The undertaker shook his head. Herb wore disappointment on his face as he pocketed the ring and the whistle. Kathy glimpsed Herb's disgust before he turned to welcome Mama's friends at the Peach Room threshold, all of whom knew him and greeted him with warmth.

BRIDGES

They left Baltimore before dawn, before the sun rose, and while the moon and stars of the night sky still bathed the city in a diminishing, speckled light. The dappled light cast shadows along the roofs of the city's rowhomes, and those shadows clung to the homes and the streetlamps as the first delicate rays of sunlight appeared in the east, bouncing off the Middle Branch segment of the Patapsco River, dancing across the river as if it had been draped in crystals, mesmerizing Jade as she and her mother crossed the Hanover Street Bridge. Jade drove, her first long trip since she got her driver's license, the weight of the responsibility pressing her assuaged only by the calm voice on her phone's GPS Wayfinder. She would not get lost. She glanced at her mother in the passenger seat, staring out the windshield with focus that Jade knew came from the fact that she sat behind the steering wheel and not her mother.

"You don't have to white-knuckle the chicken handle all the way to OC," Jade said.

Her mother nodded but continued squeezing the grab handle, her face resting on the bicep of her raised arm, her red lipstick the brightest thing on her face under her Jackie O sunglasses. Jade noticed that her mother's hair had just begun to grow back, returning as gray curls, now barely hidden under the brunette, bobbed-style wig she wore only outside the house. The wig, crooked on her mother's head, looked nothing like her real hair. Her hair had cascaded around her shoulders like an unruly mass of thick, tangled, chestnut curls like Jade's. The wig's chin-length, straight bob cut looked as if her mother embraced a new and different persona when she wore it. Her father had teased Jade's mother the first time she modeled it, saying it made her look sexy, but Jade knew he said it to cheer her up.

"Not too bad," her mother said, frowning as she inspected herself in the mirror, trying to adjust how it sat on her head. *Not too bad*, her mother said on the mornings she made it to work before putting on the face mask her doctor required her to wear on the thirty-minute metro ride to downtown Baltimore, where she worked as a graduate-level university administrator helping foreign doctors get their paperwork and credentials in order to matriculate into specialty programs. The face mask protected her while her immune system was under assault, the doctor explained. Self-conscious in it at first, she announced that she'd wear it after cancer because everyone on the train left her alone. "If I'd known the power of a little face mask, I'd have started wearing one ages ago!"

Her mother's co-workers outdid themselves, pooling funds and gifting her mom with a special car service to transport her to chemo, after which either Jade or her father brought her home.

"She's a fighter," her father said one day when her mother, sick from chemo, was puking in the bathroom. Despite the chemo, despite the cancer, Jade's mother still looked like a youngish forty-seven with a wide smile and bright eyes. *Except for the kerchiefs and hats, she hardly looked sick*, Jade thought. Jade drove because of "chemo brain," and when she glanced at her mother, she sighed, glad her parents trusted her to drive.

Orange, pink, and violet streaked the dawn sky as the sun struggled to wake the still-sleeping city, blanketed in silence. Sparse traffic made it seem as if Jade and her mother comprised the handful of people on the road at dawn; the fast-food restaurants, tire stores, electronics stores, big box stores, and car dealerships along both sides of the highway remained shuttered to the hustle and bustle that awaited them. They appeared unremarkable, and Jade marveled how everything unremarkable now felt remarkable and new, as if she was seeing them for the first time. Everything changed since her mother became sick and forced Jade to assume a different role in the family. Jade, no longer carefree, skipped meeting up with friends. Instead, she picked up more chores, straightened up and cleaned the house when her mother's nausea and fatigue prevented her from doing so. She made grocery lists and stepped up the supermarket trips and prepped dinners her parents could no longer manage. She kept her younger brothers on track, picked them up from school, helped them with homework, ensured that everything ran smoothly so her mother needed only to focus on getting well. Jade delegated chores like a boss, taught her brothers to do the laundry and to vacuum, saying that now they all belonged on the same team.

What Jade hated was mopping the floor and her mother asking for a glass of water, and she always had to have a straw. She refrained from voicing complaints, though guilt overcame her for having them. How could she get mad at her mom for being sick? Yet sometimes the simplest request enraged her. Though, after, she'd make up for being angry by being extra responsible. She hated losing friends who didn't know how to treat her since her mother's diagnosis. They treated her differently, as if cancer was contagious, and then, not knowing what to say, said stupid things like "I'm sorry," as if they caused the cancer, or her mother died, before ghosting her. *Idiots,* she thought.

Jade spent her friend-free time researching anti-cancer foods, slowly substituting everything in the pantry and in the fridge to adhere to the anti-cancer diet she put the family on without their notice. She tossed white flour and replaced it with whole wheat, almond, or chickpea flour. She tossed sugar and sugar substitutes and used dates and raisins to sweeten desserts. She bought less chicken, no beef, and more fish. She added fresh greens into every meal, made gigantic salads and hearty soups. No one complained about her new foods, least of all her mother, who sometimes ate and sometimes didn't. In fact, for this trip, Jade filled the back seat with all the anti-cancer foods possibly unavailable at the beach: the almond and chickpea flours, jars of spices, a box of steel-cut oats, low-salt vegetable broth, and an array of items to keep her mother on track so her cancer would diminish, fade, and never return.

"How are your grades?" her mother asked, shaking the sleep from her face, though she continued to clutch the chicken handle.

Jade shrugged. "Nonexistent. Summer vacation," she said, holding back that she barely passed the previous year by the slimmest margin, that she was lucky to now be a senior. Before, her mom would have inspected her homework and report cards, met with teachers, helicoptering in Jade's and her brothers' lives with strict precision. Now she couldn't keep track of something as simple as the beginning and end of the school year, or things Jade considered important, like missing the junior prom. What pulled Jade through junior year was realizing that focusing on school allowed her to put her mother's cancer out of her mind for a few hours. She knew she'd have to focus better as a senior to get into a decent college.

"Oh, that's right. I'm sorry, honey. I forgot," her mother said. "This is temporary," she added. "I *am* healthy. I *am* healthy. I am cancer-free," she repeated aloud, sending her intentions into the universe, she explained, firm in her faith that positive affirmations and a positive attitude would absolutely heal her, would vanquish the cancer. Then her mother punched the radio buttons, turning it on, the volume already blasting from the last time Jade drove.

"We'll listen to your favorite. Which one?"

"It's already on," Jade said, happy the music would break the silence.

Her mother decreased the volume and surprised Jade by humming along with the tunes.

"They played the radio on the oncology unit," her mother said. "This station, too. I like it." She smiled at Jade.

Jade wasn't sure about the usefulness of her mother's affirmations, but they seemed to propel both of them into a happier mood, a victorious mood that comforted Jade. They rode with the windows up, the air conditioner blasting, ineffective against her mother's hot flashes, a side effect of chemo-induced menopause. Blasting the air conditioner did nothing to evaporate the beads of sweat that periodically formed on her mother's forehead and streaked down her face before her mother blotted them with a cloth that she kept handy. She also kept a penguin pillow handy, but the heat of her mother's body turned it into a heating pad instead of a cooling pad. Jade wondered if the Jackie O sunglasses and red lipstick masked the war being waged inside her.

Once the sun rose, chicken hawks circled the cerulean ocean of the sky dotted by billowy white clouds edged in gold by sunlight. It took three to four hours to drive to Ocean City, depending on the traffic, especially in summer, and at least forty-five minutes to reach the Chesapeake Bay Bridge. They sped toward their week-long, girls-only vacation near the healing, salty sea waters, happy to leave her brothers and father behind. Jade worried about taking care of her mother, worried about what to do if she suddenly took a turn for the worse, despite all those positive affirmations her mother believed and daily sent into the universe.

Summertime traffic approaching the Bay Bridge usually slowed to a stop-and-go pace—mostly stop—miles ahead of the toll booth. But the early morning hours translated into the absence of parking-lot traffic, the main reason for their predawn departure. With traffic slow but manageable, they paid the toll and reached the first set of the bridge's gray towers. Neither had yet eaten breakfast, and Jade could hear her stomach growl. Jade's mother pointed at the almost invisible snowy owl sitting above the safety rail of the second tower, far from its Arctic home and unusual this far south in Maryland. Jade could only glance at the giant bird because she concentrated on driving across the spans, her stomach an anxious knot due to the bridge's breathtaking height above the choppy bay waters, where Jade feared nurse and bull sharks would attack and eat them if she made a single driving error, afraid an accident would hurl them both to certain death. She kept her eyes on the road, her hands at four and eight o'clock on the steering wheel. But she remembered the TV newscasts reporting the owl's rare presence, so she couldn't help glancing at the bird. Stark against the gray tower with its white feathers and black speckles, the bird appeared smaller than Jade imagined it, although she realized the distance of the tower's cap made it look smaller. In a glance at the bay below, she saw white sailboats dwarfed by commercial cargo ships with large red or green stacked bins. Sunlight danced along the whitecaps. Far above the owl, a colony of gulls soared and dipped in large arcs, their keow *ha-ha-ha-ha*'s faintly audible in the car. Jade wondered if the owl—perched like a watcher—considered them prey.

Her mother suggested they could stop, use the restrooms, and eat breakfast someplace on Kent Island. Jade nodded, wanting to be sure that her mother ate properly, chose the right anti-cancer foods. She worried about the weight her mother had lost over the past year. Although the trip was her mother's idea, Jade welcomed it. Next summer would be different with her parents driving her to college in August, the hope that this cancer war would be over. Her mother sifted through her purse for her phone and began fiddling with it.

"Let's stop at a place called Bridges. It claims to have great views," she said. "Pause your GPS so that we can follow mine," she said, tapping the restaurant address into her device. "I'll call ahead so they'll be expecting us."

Jade worried about eating at a restaurant, worried that her mother would be seduced by foods other than the anti-cancer ones, but she obeyed. In the restaurant parking lot, her mother straightened her wig and reapplied her lipstick.

"How do I look?" she asked.

Ridiculous in that wig, Jade thought, but instead said, "You look great," because, in fact, her mother did look great under the stupid wig. She looked healthy and younger due to her new, slender figure. Her mother's deceptive appearance, her clear complexion and bright-green eyes, gave Jade great hope her father's prediction would come to pass: that they'd look back on this time with relief.

"I'll look even better when I get my new boobs," her mother said, laughing. "No more awful drains or skin extenders, or these horrible hospital-wear tops. I'll be sexy again! Woohoo!"

Jade's face flushed, embarrassed by her mother's desire to look sexy.

Sitting on a bluff just before the Kent Narrows Bridge, three walls of the restaurant's dining room consisted of ceiling-to-floor windows overlooking the bay, which resembled an ocean with seagulls flying around the outside deck and pink herons swooping in to land someplace nearby. Her mother gazed at the windows, openly awestruck by the beauty of the view.

"How magnificent! Aren't you glad we stopped here?" she asked. "I'm starved."

Jade nodded. The hypnotic swirl of the waves, the sun sparkling on the surface, the keowing of the gulls produced a calming effect on her. Much to her surprise, her mother ordered a large breakfast—eggs, bacon, pancakes, sausages, orange juice, coffee, toast.

Jade winced. Her mother could skip the cancer-causing bacon and sausages. "Maybe we should stick to oatmeal," Jade said. "It's healthier."

"No way! I'm going to eat a decent breakfast for a change."

How was Jade going to keep her mother on track with the anti-cancer diet if she began eating recklessly? A long battle lay ahead with the forthcoming radiation treatments. Jade ordered oatmeal and fresh fruit. When the waiter served their food, it smelled delicious. The waiter forgot the toast. Jade's mother took a bite first from the eggs, then moved to the bacon and sausage, one bite of each item she ordered before setting her fork down.

"I still can't taste anything," she said. "Everything tastes tinny. Where's that toast?"

Her mother unsuccessfully tried to flag the waiter's attention. "Do you mind switching? I don't want all this to go to waste. The toast and the oatmeal will be fine for me."

Relieved, Jade agreed, resolving to cook her mother flavorful and spicy foods, smoothies sweetened with raisins or dates, brown rice, and fresh vegetables when they were at the beach, things that could break through the tinny taste.

"Live on to battle another day," Jade said as she pushed the oatmeal toward her mother.

"Battle? I'm not at war," her mother said.

"What about the cancer?"

"Not a battle, not a war, Jade. It's an unexpected situation that I'm handling. I'm going to keep handling it like everything else, and soon I'm going to wear my high heels and short skirts again."

"It looks like a battle to me," Jade said. "It feels like one, too."

"If I die from this, will you hold it against me, believing I didn't fight hard enough to beat it, Jade? Will you be mad at me for losing the battle?"

Jade didn't respond. She believed if she made everything at home operate smoothly, her mother wouldn't have to worry about mundane tasks; if she was good at home and at school, then she'd do her part of the battle. She believed her mother would regain her health. Jade wanted everything to return to normal.

"We cannot control anything," her mother said. "Except how we react to what life throws at us. It's always a choice, Jade. Remember that."

They ate in silence, watching the bay swirl toward the island's marshes and shores. They listened to the keowing of the gulls, saw pink herons swoop toward the marshes on the other side of the restaurant's structure and the sun paint everything with a golden light.

Her mother tried again to flag the waiter's attention. Then, without warning, she banged her hand, palm open, on the table.

"What do I have to do around here to get my fucking toast?" her mother shouted. "Do I have to stand on the table and dance a jig to get anyone's attention? Does it take an act of God to serve the toast we ordered forty minutes ago? What the fuck is wrong with this place?"

The angry woman, screaming at everyone and no one, beating the table with both fists to punctuate every word, shocked and terrified Jade, so unlike the woman she'd known her whole life. Other diners stared at them. Jade wanted to shrink into the size of her thumb and disappear from their gaze. She didn't know her mother at that moment. Their waiter appeared with a plate of toast, apologizing for the oversight. Jade's mother stood, her wig askew, and fled, leaving behind her purse, her Jackie O sunglasses, and Jade. Her stomach in a knot, clutching the car keys in her pocket, Jade remained at the table as the restaurant door shut behind her mother, knowing her mother couldn't go anywhere.

Ten minutes later, her mother returned, crying with a puffy face. She apologized to the wait staff, to the other diners, saying she'd been under a lot of stress lately. She paid the bill and hugged the waiter, still apologizing. She reapplied her red lipstick and put on her Jackie O sunglasses.

"My turn," her mother said, getting into the driver's seat.

Jade shook her head, afraid the confusing incident inside the restaurant indicated that chemo brain kicked into a higher level.

"Give them to me," Jade's mother said, holding out her hand.

"No."

They glared at each other, a standoff, until Jade capitulated and set the keys in her mother's waiting palm.

Jade's mother drove for an hour before pulling into the parking lot of a box store.

"Time to switch," she said.

She turned off the car. "Sometimes I'm mad at God. At cancer. At the world. It leaked out when I least expected it. I shocked myself. I'm sorry."

"So much for choosing your reactions," Jade said, her voice monotone.

They glanced at each other and burst into laughter. Jade drove the rest of the way to Ocean City, through all the small towns, noticing the verdant woods, the extensive corn and soy fields. They chased the top-40 radio stations, singing hits as loud as they could. Her mother suggested they take a break, and Jade stopped at a farmer's market, where they bought a fresh cantaloupe, a small watermelon, and some fresh peaches that looked juicy and sweet. Jade's mother poured some bottled water over a pair of peaches and handed one to Jade. They leaned against the car on the side of the road and bit into them.

"Is it sweet?" her mother asked. "I still can't taste anything."

Jade nodded her head. "Sweetest one all summer."

"I'm going to pretend to taste it," Jade's mother said, closing her eyes, biting into the fruit and looking as if she savored each morsel. "I can't think of anything else I'd rather be doing now than eating this delicious peach with you on the side of this road, surrounded by farmers' fields, trees, and blue sky."

Jade knew her mother couldn't taste the peach.

"I'm happy being a traveler on this road with you, Jade."

Back on the road, Jade's mother removed the wig and flung it into the back seat. "Scraggly-assed wig," she said. "It's too freaking hot for it."

Jade laughed, preferring the curly, gray, fluffy down covering her mother's head.

* * *

Two years later, as Jade's freshman college year closed, newscasts reported that the snowy owl left its perch on the bridge tower and had not returned. And her mother died. Jade wondered if her mother, like the snowy owl, simply traveled someplace else where Jade couldn't see her. Whenever Jade was alone, she recalled their week-long trip to the beach. She remembered walking along the surf with her mom, her mother's positive affirmations for good health, the universe deaf to them, her joy, gratitude, and appreciation for all that she saw and experienced in the moment: the various bird species, the cottony clouds, the fragrance of the salty sea, the sound of crashing waves, colorful stones and the rare, bluish sea glass they found, even noxious odors and annoying people.

"When I was little, your granddad once told me that I could catch a bird by sprinkling salt on its tail. I spent many hours running around the yard with a salt shaker, trying to catch a bird," her mother said when they were eating one of Jade's eggless vegetable quiches that looked pitifully unformed on the plate and tasted terrible.

Jade laughed. "He probably wanted to nap."

"I believed him," her mother said. "I still believe in miracles, the power of Light and Love."

For many years Jade raged at God, at the universe, and at cancer for robbing her of her mother until she finally realized the gifts her mother had given her that week.

STATIC ELECTRICITY

My twin sister Raisa and I are in our childhood home. Overstuffed with clothing, furniture, drapes, toiletries, and all kinds of things that our mother loves and uses daily, the room feels empty even with us in it. On each of her closet doors, an elephant garland with vibrant colors, bells, and beads jingles every time Raisa opens and shuts them, the garland a remnant of Mom's days as a hippie. I'm sitting on Mom's bed, above which hangs a giant portrait of our grandmother—Mom's mother— painted by Mom's ex-boyfriend Tim when Grandma was struggling with Alzheimer's and spent most of her time in a hospital bed installed in the living room.

We're going through Mom's stuff, deciding what to bring to the hospital, and while we both find comfort in touching her things—as if doing so would change the situation back to normal, back to the way it was just the day before or last week—it's a colossal waste of time. We should have stayed at the hospital. Raisa believes it'd be a good idea to clean the house before Mom returns, but it's busywork, a way to stay frenetic, which is how Raisa deals with things. The house is already tidy and clean, but Raisa likes to submerge herself in frenetic activity, whereas I prefer to observe and study things before taking action.

Mom kept the masking tape labels posted all over the house from when Grandma first moved in, labels identifying what things could be found in the drawers and what things were named—useful until Grandma lost the ability to read them. In Mom's large block letters in black marker, the labels are everywhere: "mirror," "bathroom," "underwear," "linens," "door," "window," "spoons," "spices," "pots," and an array of other words. Raisa wants to remove them, but I veto that, reminding her that it's not her house.

Raisa rolls her eyes. "It probably never occurred to her to take them down. She's always so oblivious."

"It's her house," I say.

"Like she'll even notice they're gone?" Raisa says, but leaves the labels alone.

As she packs things for the hospital, I'm jittery, wanting to return as soon as possible. Older by two minutes, Raisa always tried to boss people around. She's already switched off Mom's waterfall wall in the hallway, saying it makes too much noise reverberating throughout the house; unplugged the aromatherapy diffuser, saying it stinks; and stuffed her refrigerator with chicken and bacon, knowing Mom, a strict vegetarian with a "Meat is Murder" bumper sticker on her car, has avoided bringing meat in the house for ages. When I turn the water wall and the diffuser back on, Raisa shuts them off. I don't want to fight with her.

"We should call Tim," I say, changing the subject.

"No," she snaps. "Her phone number hasn't changed in the last hundred years. He's the one who should be calling us. Or her."

"Maybe he hasn't seen the news …?"

"Maybe if he lives under a rock," she says.

I text Tim anyway. Raisa leans over and pulls a small suitcase from under Mom's bed then moves the curtain. Outside, people approach the house with arms full of flowers. Some carry teddy bears and others lighted candles, large handmade posters, and mementos of all sorts. Not wanting to see the spectacle, Raisa shuts the curtains abruptly, but I'm comforted seeing Mom's positive impact at the school having value to others in our town.

"We should just go," I say. "She doesn't need anything from here."

Raisa insists on completing the packing.

I don't remember consciously thinking of myself as a twin, and Raisa and I never treated each other like twins, although, growing up, others often confused us. We always acted like sisters. Born two minutes earlier, but smaller, Raisa fought for her life and perhaps never graduated beyond the initial drive to survive. Raisa tosses Mom's underwear into the suitcase. Her robe, her slippers. She tosses in perfume, cosmetics, sundries as if packing for a vacation instead of the hospital, overpacking useless items. I want to leave so I hurry her along.

Raisa points to the portrait. "Grandma at her best. Not as the demented, diapered old lady who failed to recognize any of us," she says.

"I've always loved it," I say. "And Tim, too. What a good egg."

Raisa rolls her eyes. "Such an annoying man!"

Raisa says the same thing about my husband, Tony—that he's an annoying man. From day one she's disliked him and created tension between them. He prefers to avoid her when she's in town. When we were newly engaged, she'd implied he was too lazy or dumb to go to medical school, which is why he became a physical therapist, and smashed an egg on the top of his head. We were all shocked. She called it a joke and accused us of lacking a sense of humor.

"Now I know the reason you can't keep a boyfriend and will never marry," Tony told her while sopping the egg off his head. "It sounds like 'rich.'"

"Something you'll never be," she said.

Tony stays at home with the kids, and it's okay because she doesn't ask about any of them. We're thankful that our kids attend the school where I teach math in the next town over. He and I chatted before he put the kids to bed last night, ourselves numb and dazed that this happened so close. I stayed with Raisa at Mom's house.

Neither Raisa nor I could focus on anything else and obsessively watched the news about the shooting: the timeline of events, interviews of the parents of dead or wounded children and teachers, and vigils that we skipped because we didn't want to talk to anyone. We didn't want to be present watching all those people who lost nothing chasing their fifteen minutes. We looked through Mom's photo albums, laughing at all the crazy things we remembered from the photos—when Grandma danced and sang with a wooden spoon microphone; when our father, still alive, planted the gardens that continue to bloom around her house in waves of colors as the seasons change; when Tim and Mom painted the delicate and beautiful strands of green ivy still circling the top of each doorway; when Raisa and I were dressed in identical clothing, but in different colors, doing different things.

Also in the photo album are shots of Grandma, Mom, and us in front of Capital Police Headquarters where they took Mom after she was arrested for protesting Corcoran's cancellation of the Mapplethorpe exhibit. In the photo with us, she holds her sign

CENSORSHIP IS OBSCENE. NOT ART. Angry that politicians could cancel an art exhibit because of a bunch of unenlightened prudes, she participated in the group that projected Mapplethorpe's work on the walls outside the museum. We were too young then to appreciate her courage. In all the photos, including the ones after she was released from police headquarters, Mom's perpetual smile stretches across her face under her serious-looking, black-plastic framed glasses.

In the drab trauma waiting room, parents and family members of those injured in the school attack drape themselves over the chairs, pace, squeeze their hands, stare at the TV without actually watching it, or sit cross-legged on the floor. Worried, weary, clutching cell phones, water bottles, brown bags, snacks from the hospital cafeteria and vending machines—they, like Raisa and me, wait. Good news. Bad news. Any news. The principal approaches us and tells us Mom's a hero. He says she yelled "Shooter! Shooter! Protect the students!" at the top of her lungs soon after the gunman entered the building and the havoc began.

"She ordered her aide to hide her students in the windowless room with her art supplies and to barricade the door after she left the room," the principal said. "She grabbed a fire extinguisher and ran down the hallway toward, instead of away from, the gunman, and then aimed the fire extinguisher at the shooter and sprayed him with the foam," he says.

The white foam caused the gunman to cough uncontrollably, disrupting his progression through the hallways for a short time, he told us.

"Without actually seeing her, the shooter turned and shot her, hitting her first in her leg, then in her gut. She sprayed him until the extinguisher was empty. Then she hit him with the canister, and that's when he shot her a third time. She tried to stop him," he says. "She succeeded for a minute."

The principal sounds as if he's told this story one hundred times with the same level of disbelief and shock. He takes my hand and envelops it in both of his—his eyes shiny, bloodshot above the puffiness beneath them. "I'm sorry."

He tries to envelop Raisa's hand but she pulls away.

"How did this monster get in?" she yells, her voice shattering the uneasy silence of the waiting room. "You only said those things to avoid a lawsuit. How the fuck did you witness this interaction without helping her, and where the fuck was the security guard when Mom was confronting the gunman by herself? Alone."

No answers. The other families shift their gazes between Raisa and the principal. They, too, want answers that aren't forthcoming. I thank him for telling us as he backs away. He looks at Raisa with eyes as large as tangerines while Raisa says nothing, shredding the tissues in her hands.

I picture Mom's school building, try to imagine the altercation between her and the gunman. How incongruous it must have been for her amid the brightly painted walls, the bold blues and greens, the happy yellows and cheerful reds that fostered positivity and learning. Mom's middle school students' colorful lanterns—fashioned from empty gallon milk jugs and LED lights—hang from the ceiling in the school's corridors like a luminous, aerial, 3-D cross-stitch. Her students' life-sized self-portraits—their outlines traced onto paper, cut out and decorated as mini-mes—line hallway walls leading to her classroom. Outside her classroom door, tombstone etchings of the town cemetery grace the wall—a project of her older students. Her mission as an art teacher, she once said, meant helping her students see beauty in the world around them, even in the most routine things. Yellow police tape now surrounds the property, an active crime scene, and I wonder if blood spatter now mars those beautiful lanterns, self-portraits, and etchings.

A nurse in blue scrubs enters the trauma waiting room and calls our names. Raisa and I hold each other's arms as we follow her into a trauma bay where Mom lies connected to tubes and machines. A ventilator breathes for her, and I imagine the long recovery ahead as I watch the machine inflate and deflate her chest. The nurse stares at us. I know she's puzzled by the fat and thin versions of the same face and body type standing before her. She holds a clipboard but doesn't speak for a long time. Usually one of us speaks first, explains that we're identical twins, but this time neither of us does that. Mom appears small and breakable, her face pale as a waning moon, and her body is surrounded by tubes and beeping machines. We fail to notice the nurse leaving.

I swallow a wail that fights to escape my throat because Mom looks so delicate, so fragile, amid the tangle of corded machines. We flank each side of the bed and hold her hands. Raisa leans over and whispers into her ear. "Don't worry, Mom. We're here!"

"People in a coma can still hear," she tells me in her know-it-all voice.

When the doctor comes, she tells us that they did everything possible, that the ventilator is the only thing keeping Mom alive, that her brain has ceased to function, that she's not going to improve. She asks about Mom's advance directives, if she has a do-not-resuscitate directive, because if she doesn't have one then we must decide whether it's time to turn off the life support system. Neither Raisa nor I know, and it dawns on me that neither of us knows much about Mom beyond her role as our mother. We don't know why she and Tim parted ways, why she never remarried after our father died, why she chose to teach art rather than work as a medical illustrator like our grandmother—far more lucrative than teaching. Suddenly, all that I don't know about her feels like a gigantic hole, a chasm of loss, a treasure stolen.

"Is your mother an organ donor?" the doctor asks.

"How premature. And insensitive," I say, my turn to be indignant and accusatory. As I watch the machine inflate and deflate my mother's chest, my math brain concentrates on the numbers of breaths a healthy person takes for granted: sixteen breaths per minute, 960 breaths an hour, 23,040 breaths a day, 8,409,600 a year. If Mom were to live to be eighty, she'd take about 672,768,000 breaths in her lifetime, and it kills me that my children are being robbed of seeing their grandmother take in and expel all those breaths. I imagine all my children's milestones and all their activities she'll miss: birthdays, graduations, weddings. And mine, too.

"No response in the brain or the stem," the doctor says in a matter-of-fact voice.

Hope clings to me like static electricity. Maybe time will restore her responses. It's only been three days since the shooting. Miracles can happen. I believe in miracles.

I look at Raisa, her face identical to mine—but mine's gone soft and full from pregnancy and motherhood, whereas Raisa's remains sharp and thin. Her hair, thick chestnut sheets, falls just below her shoulders in a sexy bob, while mine, cut short, exposes my ears. We could pose for before-and-after photos for a weight loss advertisement.

"We did our best." The doctor says the words slowly as if we are idiots who cannot comprehend.

I know they can't turn off the ventilator until everything about organ donation and withdrawing life support is laid down, signed in triplicate, settled.

"Rumian, she wouldn't want this," Raisa says.

"She's not dead yet," I yell.

Raisa takes the clipboard from the doctor and signs away Mom's organs as if she were signing over the title to her car. I leave the room.

A stony silence fills the car on the ride back to Mom's house. Raisa's driving. Wishing with every cell in my body that she was shot instead of Mom, I peer out the passenger window to avoid looking at or speaking to her. I want to put distance between us—to drive home to see my kiddos and Tony. I want to take a break from her—from this awful situation.

"She's still on the ventilator," Raisa says, as if that makes a ton of difference. "We have a lot to do," she adds in that know-it-all voice and begins ticking off a to-do list beginning with "make arrangements."

"Shut up. Shut the fuck up," I say, my words venom darts. "You're going to turn her waterfall wall and diffuser back on. And you're going to be polite to Tony and my kids when they arrive."

Raisa stares at me with disbelief on her face.

When we turn into Mom's driveway, a large object covered in thick brown paper tied with twine leans against the front door. Without speaking, I unlock Mom's door, drag the package inside, cut the twine, and tear off the paper. I immediately recognize Tim's work. It's a companion piece to Grandma's portrait, capturing Mom in her youthful glory: Filled with energy, her eyes appear flashing behind those large black-framed glasses, her hair wild, curly, large, untamable. Love shines from her face as she smiles at us, her arm encircling Raisa and me, our young faces identical but slightly different with our heads forming the top slopes of a heart; her elbow, the point, and her forearm closes the circle.

BUTTERFLY MOMENTS

Pearl always marched in antiwar demonstrations, plastered MAKE LOVE, NOT WAR bumper stickers on her car, and said she'd die a million deaths before her child would join the military over her dead body and go off to some God-forsaken place to kill babies. So when her only child, a son Mitchell, obsessed with being a Marine since forever, skipped college and enlisted in the Corps without her blessing or permission the minute he turned eighteen and then got himself killed during Iraqi ground attacks during the earliest days of the Gulf War, Opal kept an eye on things. She happened to be at Pearl's place when two smartly dressed, somber-looking Marine officers knocked on the door, and as soon as they stepped into the living room, their shiny black shoes, loud, dark puddles against the soft tan rug, and before they uttered a single word, Pearl began screaming, "Don't say it! Don't say it! Don't say it!" as if not hearing the words would make their news untrue. Mitchell had been killed by friendly fire shortly before his twenty-third birthday. The words sounded so unreal to Opal—"friendly fire," an oxymoron like "jumbo shrimp," except lacking in any kind of humor—that she wondered if it were a terrible joke.

True and real, Opal also mourned her nephew, a sunshiny, joyful boy whom she doted on, not having had any children of her own, but feared that she'd lose her sister, too, leaving her alone in the world. She never thought to remarry after her husband, Sam, suffered a heart attack when they were both still young enough to have children.

Opal drove Pearl to Dover Air Force Base in Delaware, a two-hour drive, so that they could both witness the arrival of Mitchell's flag-draped casket and to bring him home. Pearl had already arranged for a local undertaker to travel to the base. For the duration of the trip, Pearl's mouth formed a straight line on the bottom of her face, and she sat silent for the entire trip with the exception of asking to stop to use a restroom an hour into the drive. Opal fiddled with the radio dial, looking for stations playing music she knew Pearl liked before finally settling on the white noise of a classical station before turning it off when they drove out of the signal. A comfortable silence enveloped them in the car, though Opal didn't allow herself to sink into any reveries so as to keep an eye on Pearl.

At the Air Force base, Opal allowed Pearl to lean on her, cried with her, and held her upper arm to support her. She wondered how different it felt to lose a child from losing a husband. She recalled feeling as if someone sucker punched her in the stomach when Sam died, going through the motions of the tedious job of living when all she wanted to do was sit somewhere and cry. She watched Pearl lean over and embrace the casket that held her son, and she stood with Pearl, tears slipping down both of their faces, as the Marine pallbearers in their smart dress uniforms loaded it into the hearse for the trip home. When the Marines folded the flag, their hands encased in crisp white gloves, then handed it to Pearl with a salute, their faces were even younger-looking than Mitchell's.

She gripped Pearl's hands when the chaplain informed her on the tarmac at Dover that she was not allowed to open the coffin to look at her son's body—something that made Pearl bristle—and Opal took notes when the chaplain handed Pearl a sheaf of papers to apply for death benefits. They followed the hearse back to Baltimore, both of them weeping for the entire two-hour ride.

A few months later, Pearl railed when she learned she owed the Social Security Administration some $150 related to Mitchell's funeral expenses, incredulous that the government would have the gall to request or expect any sort of payment, saying it owed her a lot more since it murdered her son. She made new protest signs, shouting their slogans—NO BLOOD FOR OIL, and THIS WAR IS NOT FOR DEMOCRACY! and STOP WAR NOW, BRING OUR TROOPS HOME—for the antiwar protests she planned to attend.

"What's the point of protesting?" Opal asked. "None of that will bring Mitchell back."

"Ask Dr. Martin Luther King Jr. that," Pearl snapped. "Did you forget? Mitchell died by friendly fire—assholes who just didn't give a good flying fuck about anyone but themselves."

"Or maybe someone made an honest mistake. An accident," Opal said. "They're all so young."

"Exactly. And not for any noble cause. The government stole my son from me."

"Mitch joined up," Opal said. "He was where he wanted to be."

Pearl planned to join the antiwar demonstrations taking place in Washington, D.C., but, in truth, never made it out the door with her signs. Opal watched her ping-pong between rage and inertia, and when Pearl started questioning the point of living anymore, Opal took action. She dialed the number to the state's chapter of the Gold Star Mothers, recently resurrected after having become inactive after the Vietnam War ended, chauffeuring Pearl to a meeting where other mothers whose children died in the military talked about their fallen sons and daughters, their fallen children's honor, sense of duty, their ultimate sacrifices, and the terrible costs of freedom. Pearl walked out halfway through.

On the way home, Pearl stared straight ahead, her face frozen. "I don't need some bitches in white telling me my son is 'fallen' when he was murdered. There's no glory in that," Pearl said, gripping the hand rest above the passenger seat. "It seems like a cult."

"Maybe they're coping the best they can. We don't have to go back for a while, but maybe another time," Opal said.

"Pfffffpt. Don't count on it."

It had been more than a year of that. Of shepherding Pearl though the paperwork, of emptying portions of vodka bottles after Pearl began sucking them down like apple juice, of listening to her endless regrets about not opening the coffin—Why was she so obedient to the damn government? Why couldn't she say a proper goodbye one last time?—questions Opal understood but had no answers for. She wondered what kind of proper goodbye Pearl had in mind since Sam's heart attack hadn't afforded them time for any sort of goodbyes. The year also had included fielding weekly calls from Mitchell's fiancée, Molly, whom Pearl detested and blamed for Mitchell's decision to enlist.

"Let's go to the ocean for the weekend," Molly suggested to Opal on the phone. Birds filled the May sky, and fragrant buds weighed down the tree branches lining the streets. Mitchell would have been home a week had he not been killed. Since his death, Opal got to know and like Molly during their weekly phone calls and came to understand what Mitchell loved in her. They had dated all through high school and continued to date after Molly went to college and Mitchell left for the Marines. Neither Pearl nor Opal knew that Mitchell had proposed until his funeral, when Molly showed them the ring he'd given her, a sizable stone, a ring that he must have saved all his earnings to buy. He'd proposed before he left for Iraq.

"Molly invited us to the beach," Opal said.

"For what?" Pearl asked.

"A change of scenery." She didn't mention that she'd told Molly that she was worried about Pearl's state of mind.

Pearl said nothing.

"Mitch made his own decisions," Opal said, breaking the silence. "That girl didn't kill him. He loved her. He asked her to marry him, which means she is as close to a daughter-in-law as you're ever going to get."

"You'll never understand. You don't know the hell it is to lose a child," Pearl yelled.

Opal collected her purse and left, slamming the door behind her, the upper glass half vibrating in its frame. Driving home, she wept. For Mitch. For her husband, Sam, who died too young. For the children they never had. At that moment, she wanted to shake and slap Pearl. She remembered Sam—how he smelled, how he made her laugh, and Opal worried about the fact that she could no longer picture his face as a whole, but only in fragments. The way his mouth looked when he laughed, the pristine whiteness of his straight teeth, his wide nose, his black eyes, watery and shiny on their wedding day. She worried that she was slowly losing him a second time since, in her mind's eye, she could only envision aspects of him. His fingers, but not attached to his entire hand, his hand, but detached from his arm, as if Sam were tiny pieces of a Byzantine-stained glass window.

Opal decided she'd drive, and collected Pearl first and then Molly. Pearl sat in the passenger seat staring straight ahead as usual, like a mannequin, unblinking, unsmiling. It reminded Opal of how defiant Pearl had been as a child, badgering their mother to end any punishment she gave Pearl, regardless of how deserved it was, Pearl always pushing back, objecting to any consequences. Molly flashed a wide smile when she climbed into the backseat, placing her black-and-white weekend bag on the seat next to her. Pearl refused to acknowledge Molly, forcing Opal to keep up the conversation, the girl explaining that she was about to graduate with a pharmacy bachelor's and was excited to be going to pharmacy school in the fall.

"Mitch and I would have been getting married next month after graduation," she said. "It would have been a banner year."

"You're still here. Still breathing. A banner year," Pearl said, finally acknowledging the girl with a sharp tone.

"You're not the only one who lost Mitch," Molly said, her tone matter-of-fact.

Through the rearview mirror, Opal saw the girl's face framed by her black curly hair flush red, her fingers clutching the handles of her weekend bag, her knuckles white.

"I'm his mother. No one else counts," Pearl said.

Opal gripped the steering wheel, wondering what possessed her to think that being at the beach with Molly and Pearl would be a good idea.

Then Molly laughed uproariously.

Her laughter sounded like music; a sound Opal hadn't heard since Mitchell died. Opal glanced at Pearl, who also looked surprised at the girl's uproarious response at Pearl's attempt to pull rank. After spending so much time handling Pearl like a hothouse flower about to wilt under the wrong conditions due to the loss of her only child, Opal secretly felt relieved by Molly's response. Opal missed her nephew, too, missed his dimpled smile and silly sense of humor, missed his clever wit and funny stories about things that took place overseas that he wrote to her in short emails and recounted via Skype, missed the fact that he simply walked in joy, happy to have found the thing he wanted to do in the military with the Marines. Mitch seemed happy. She felt detached from his death, too, filled with an inexplicable certainty that his essential truth as a being, as a child of God, lived on in some other dimension where they could no longer see him, but he could see them, and maybe he spent his time hanging out with Sam. She never told Pearl that she'd dreamt of Mitchell about six weeks after he died. In an unforgettably vivid dream, he looked fit and healthy, excited and happy, saying he was returning from a spectacular vacation, that he'd recovered well, and was now going home. He was wearing his dress uniform, and she understood that "home" did not mean to her and Pearl. And then it was over. She awoke with the feeling that the dream was more real than sitting in the car with Molly and Pearl, and it occurred to her at that moment that the three people Mitch loved most in the world occupied the same space, Opal's car, together, heading toward the sea.

At the condo, Opal watched Pearl sitting on the condo's deck facing the ocean, drinking vodka openly from her flask. She suggested that Pearl move inside to watch their belongings while she and Molly unpacked the car. Mostly, she didn't want Pearl outside on the deck unattended. Molly checked her watch as she put away the groceries they brought when the doorbell rang and flew toward the door like a Preakness filly nearing the finish line.

The girl apparently expected the FedEx delivery. She carried it into her bedroom and opened the cardboard box. She withdrew a large, beautiful white box decorated with ribbons of scarlet and gold and the Marine insignia. Atop the white box in beautiful script, Opal saw the inscription, "In Loving Memory of Mitchell Raymond Stone," with lines of two dates, one of which Opal recognized as his birth and death dates.

"What's the other dateline?" she asked Molly, keeping her voice low, not wanting Pearl to hear. Molly hugged the box to her chest, her back to Opal, and seemingly in her own world. But Pearl heard anyway, despite Opal's low voice, and stepped quietly into Molly's room in front of Opal.

"It would have been our wedding date," Molly said, her voice quavering, her cheek against the top of the box. "We had just booked the venue when the news came."

When Molly, her eyes moist and watery, turned toward Opal, the sorrow and grief on her face became one of surprise at the sight of Pearl there in the room. Opal noticed that Molly regained her composure, her face shutting down any expression as she busied herself replacing the white box into its delivery container.

Without thinking, Opal stepped forward to embrace Molly. They decided that dinner on their first night would be at a restaurant Molly had chosen, and Opal observed that Pearl agreed without a fuss. Molly seemed to know plenty about the area. The restaurant's open windows allowed a sea breeze to waft into the dining room and offered a gorgeous view of the ocean from where it sat on a long pier. Opal could see the dusk sky, its ribbons of salmon, orange, and gold streaking across the horizon, blending into the darkening blue of the ocean below. It took her breath away. She noticed that Pearl stared out the window at the sky, too, and she wondered if its splendor was lost on her.

"This was our place. We came here all the time," Molly said, her voice sounding reverent. "He proposed to me at that corner table by the window."

Opal glanced at Pearl, who looked up at the girl then and registered something as close to an interest in anything outside of herself and her grief for the first time since Mitchell died. Molly looked directly at Pearl.

"I invited you here this weekend—aside from the change of scenery—because I and some of Mitch's friends planned something special. I hope you'll join us tomorrow at the Seaside State Park, where Mitch and I camped out frequently before he died."

"Why now?" Pearl asked.

Molly shrugged. "Why not?"

"We'll be there," Opal said. "We wouldn't dare miss it."

Opal saw Pearl's eyes flash, but decided to ignore it. Opal decided that Pearl was going whether she preferred to or not.

"To Mitch, wherever his journey takes him," Molly said, raising her glass of iced tea.

Opal raised her glass to the toast, while Pearl ignored it. They ate dinner in silence, each seeming lost in their thoughts, until Molly broke the silence with a hilarious tale of how everything went wrong on her and Mitch's first visit to the state park campground where they'd be going the next day. How their air mattress sprang a leak in the middle of the night, how it rained nonstop after that, despite the forecast predicting a sunny weekend, how their flashlight stopped working, and how they ultimately checked into a cheap hotel for the rest of their weekend. Opal watched Pearl as she smiled almost imperceptibly at the idea of Mitch trying to save the day and understood that this side of Mitch was not one she would have ever seen as his mother, that of a man trying to protect and provide for his mate. Opal excused herself to the restroom, intending to settle the check, but discovered to her dismay that Molly had already arranged for it to be paid.

At the state park the next day, Molly brought the large white box. Several young people had already arrived, and Molly began introducing everyone. Some of the kids came from Molly's and Mitch's high school, while others came from Mitch's Marine unit. Opal got the feeling that Mitch lived an entire life separate from her and Pearl.

"Mrs. Stone, I loved Mitch like a brother," one young man told Pearl as he hugged her. "He was in good company," he said, noting that eleven other Marines died when Mitch died.

"Friendly fire killed eleven other Marines?" Pearl asked, shocked.

"Yes, but it's not like you think. The Air Force aiming at the Iraqi forces hit us instead."

"Doesn't make me feel any better," Pearl said, anger in her voice sharp and piercing. "Eleven murdered all at once."

"Part of the job, ma'am," he said. "None of us like it."

"Like that's any better?" Pearl said.

"Ma'am," he said, studying her for a long time before turning from her and taking his warmth and any stories about Mitch and his buddies with him.

Opal imagined that this kid suffered far more losses than Pearl had, wondered how Pearl might have wounded him, and wanted to follow him. The battle that killed Mitchell came early in the conflict. She wanted to know every detail about this kid, if he'd spent any final moments with Mitch before the heat of conflict, if he and Mitch did any fun things together when they weren't in combat, what it felt to be in a war zone, any other details that she could recite to Pearl at a later date. But she didn't leave Pearl's side. Opal understood that Pearl's anger made her powerful so as not to appear openly tearful or sad after losing Mitchell and all the losses that came with it: A future now devoid of all the milestones that come with adult children, including grandchildren.

Molly welcomed everyone, explained how this date meant something special to her and Mitch, introduced all present, the cadre of Mitch's fellow Marines who yelled "Ooh rah;" the others from their high school; Pearl and Opal; and the local minister, who led a poignant memorial for Mitch that included these kids telling their favorite stories about Mitch. Opal could tell by Pearl's expression that she hadn't known about any of the incidents, incidents that mothers only discover about their children much later, after they have grown older and everyone can laugh about the things that would have gotten them into trouble. It was as if the group gave Pearl and Opal a sliver of a glimpse of a part of Mitchell's life to which Pearl had not been privy, and Opal couldn't shake the notion, smiled at the idea even, that Mitchell might be orchestrating this gathering from the great beyond. In fact, Opal found that she couldn't stop smiling when she gazed at Molly, or the Marines, or Mitch's former high school friends, taken with their young faces, or Pearl, or the minister, or anyone present, as if seeing them all for the first time through a different lens.

Molly invited everyone to join them in a tight circle in a clearing and, holding the box, she stood in the center.

"Manion wrote, 'To a stranger, you might not mean anything at all. But to me, you are my butterfly whisper, my smile.' Butterflies count not months but moments and have enough time. We aren't butterflies, but we only had a precious butterfly moment together. Today, we release these beautiful monarchs in memory of a man we all love, Mitchell Stone. We're grateful for the moments we had with him and for the promise that we'll see each other again. Soon. Everyone ready?" Molly said in a loud and excited voice.

One of the kids helped Molly untie the double bows on each side of the large box, and another one unzipped the netted container within it. She handed the netted container to Pearl, who didn't know what to do with it. Molly helped Pearl hold it aloft, gently, and together they manipulated the container, freeing a hundred monarch butterflies, orange and black kings and queens taking flight into the great blue sky.

"Mitch and I wanted to do this at our wedding. We already paid for them, so I'm doing this now instead," Molly told Pearl, blinking back tears.

Delighted, Opal watched the butterflies, their wings gracefully flapping their way upward. One alighted in Pearl's hair and stayed perched atop her head like a beautiful barrette. Opal retrieved a compact from her purse and flipped it open so that Pearl could see the butterfly in her hair. For a few minutes, Pearl watched the butterfly in the mirror as it sat still and silent for a few moments longer before it lifted itself and flew away.

THE TWO ANTHONYS

Junior watches Brenda pursing her lips. She's wearing pearl and diamond earrings, the pair he's given her for their fifth anniversary, and a burgundy sheath dress ruched on one side, and he admires how utterly beautiful she is. Her chestnut hair sits at the nape of her neck in a simple chignon, and she wears just a hint of lip gloss.

"Why bother?" She sighs, glancing at him. He turns the car onto the exit ramp and steps on the gas. Junior understands the way she feels. Except it's his father, the only one he has, and something has got to be said for that. He almost lost the old man last year when he would've died if it hadn't been for Junior's kidney, now keeping him alive. Maybe tonight will be different, he thinks.

"Anthony, you know this is an exercise in futility," she says, as if she were reading his mind. "Don't want to see you being disappointed again." Junior shrugs, pushes his hand through his hair, wincing at the feel of his receding hairline.

"He's my father," Junior says, stepping on the gas, merging onto the highway. "He's my father," he repeats, pointing their car north toward his parent's house. He hasn't yet told Brenda or his father or Bev, his stepmother, that he also invited his mom to join them tonight. He wants his mother present when he announces his big news. Junior bursts with energy and excitement.

Junior and his research team won this year's Phillips Times Entrepreneurial Award, with its sweet onetime $10,000 prize for him, and another $50,000 a year for three years to continue his research. Who'd imagine that what began as a quest fifteen years ago to help a kid who lost a leg in a motorcycle accident by creating a better prosthetic would bring such recognition? Elated about this coup, proud of his series of prosthetic leg designs with computer chips that enable amputees to stay active doing all the things they did before losing their legs, Junior basked in the recognition. His device compensates for and adjusts to the user's gait and then attempts to mimic it so that the user doesn't look lopsided or stiff when walking and can go up and down stairs looking natural. The money could advance his work in unfathomable ways. Maybe he can start on computerized arm prosthetics.

* * *

Her father-in-law, Anthony Sr., is in the kitchen in his dress slacks, wearing no socks, shoes, or shirt. His skin sags under his white tank undershirt. Beltless, gesturing wildly, he shouts into the phone. In the other room, the television blares, and Rudolph, Bev's miniature poodle, is barking. Bev can't get any gaudier. Brenda bites the inside of her bottom lip and exchanges a look with her husband, raising her eyebrows as he widens his eyes. Of course, they aren't ready.

"Damn factory wants to raise the price of the rubber green monster toys," Anthony Sr. says to Junior, covering the mouthpiece as if that would muffle his loud voice enough that the person on the other end wouldn't hear him. "Too high, too fucking high; you're killing me," he shouts into the phone. He pulls a small rubber green figure from his pants pocket, rolls it around in his hand, then hands it to Junior. It looks like a Kermit the Frog knockoff in a tux. "Bev!" he calls from the bottom of the stairs, his hand again covering the phone's speaker. "The kids are here already!"

Already? Brenda thinks. She wants to scream.

"We're late," she says, glancing at her watch, keeping her tone neutral. Anthony Sr. tosses more toys at his son, gum ball machine trinkets: plastic spiders, miniature red rubber balls, hard plastic white ovals with eyes painted on them. Her father-in-law, who quit high school two months before graduation and never went to college, owns all the gum ball machines in supermarket entrances on the east coast, and those penny, quarter, and dollar machines thrust him into the stratosphere of self-made millionaires. Insufferable, Brenda thinks. He never allows anyone to forget his success. But money can't buy class, and Brenda had excused herself from their company more than once, when her blowbag father-in-law spouted off about Blacks or lesbians or pick any ethnic group not to his liking being shipped to an unnamed place, so long as it was away. It doesn't take a mental giant to sell vending machine toys to kids at the supermarket. Junior sets the trinkets on the table without looking at them.

"We've got to go, or the restaurant won't honor our reservation," she says aloud to no one in particular. "Can't they just meet us there?" she asks her husband.

Her father-in-law puts his hand over the phone's mouthpiece again and says, "What's the goddamn rush? We're going to dinner at a restaurant. It ain't the goddamn Academy Awards."

Brenda bites deeper into her bottom lip, but says nothing. She'd like to smack the blowhard two weeks into next month. For Junior, it IS the Academy Awards. Junior purposefully kept the reason for the dinner quiet. Brenda fails to understand why

Junior puts so much stock into that old ass-hat. Junior even gave him a kidney, something that irks Brenda considering Junior could likely develop the same condition as his father, except unlike his father, he won't have a ready donor. Selfish bastard. Where's Bev?

* * *

Bev stuffs her wide, puffy feet into bone-colored low-heeled pumps with gold buckles. She dislikes these shoes. They aren't sexy and strappy, but her ankles no longer support higher heels. She examines herself in the mirror, pulls at her thinning hair, and frowns before twisting it into a small knot at the top of her head. She doesn't like what she sees: herself turning into an old hag. She sympathizes with all those women who'd do anything to stay young-looking. She doesn't want to get old. She grabs her auburn, shoulder-length, bob-style wig from its Styrofoam head and places it on her own before adding, then blotting into a tissue, another layer of red lipstick. The reds of the lipstick and wig clash, but Bev doesn't notice it. She notices wrinkles on her face—thick with makeup—that refuse to stay covered by foundation. She still looks youthful at seventy, even if it's with the aid and comfort of Botox and laser treatments, which her husband doesn't know about. Never reveal beauty secrets to a man, she thinks, pushing the wig hair behind her ears so that her chunky gold earrings show.

"Bev, the kids are here," Anthony yells from the bottom of the stairs. She slips a large diamond and sapphire dinner ring onto the ring finger on her right hand and the matching bracelet onto her wrist, admiring the glitter. Grabbing her mink stole and her bone patent leather purse, she heads downstairs, wondering what special occasion prompted the kids' dinner invitation. She wonders if they're going to expect her husband to pay—

something that galls her beyond measure. Though to be fair, she can't remember Junior ever expecting Anthony to pay. Now that she thinks about it, it's always the other way around. Junior gave his father a kidney and made sure his father followed all the dietary restrictions to the point Anthony wanted to avoid him, and has never thrown it up in his father's face. Something's up, she figures, wondering if Brenda's finally pregnant. If so, it's about time. Brenda isn't getting any younger, and her window is about to snap shut. Bev can't help feeling peeved, especially if Brenda's pregnant, because her daughter Romie wasn't invited. What kind of family gathering excludes people? Romie's her daughter, after all, and will be the baby's step-aunt.

* * *

Junior glances at his watch just as Bev enters the kitchen. Bev shouts at Rudolph to shut up. Brenda's staring at Bev's wig, sitting crooked atop her head. His stepmother becomes testy at even the slightest criticism, and he stares at Brenda, hoping she understands. She catches his eye and smiles. He's sweating, he's so nervous.

* * *

Brenda must be shocked at how good I look, Bev thinks.

"Don't you look lovely tonight, Brenda dear," Bev says, though she thinks Brenda looks rather plain without any makeup and tiny pearl and diamond earrings that no one can see. She wonders how much baby weight Brenda will gain. She screams at Rudolph to shut up, but the dog yaps and yaps until Bev breaks down and gives it half a bag of treats, one after the other.

"No wonder Rudolph's so fat," Junior says.

"He's not fat. Just more to love," Bev says and laughs. "So what's the occasion? It's not like we have a habit of going to dinner together," she says.

"Well, Pop was sick for a while, then had to eat carefully; maybe we just got out of the habit," Junior says.

"You can tell that to your dad. I know something's up," Bev says, looking at Brenda. "Brenda, you finally having a baby? Is that what this is all about?"

Brenda's mouth falls open. Bev smirks. Of course, Bev figured it out. She's no dummy.

In the dining room just off the kitchen, Bev opens the top drawer, retrieves a small box of perfume she reserves for special occasions, and douses herself with it. Rudolph, who's circling her feet, gets hit with the spray. Bev scoops the dog into her arms, kisses and pets him.

"I got the best smelling dog around," Bev coos at Rudolph. Now in the kitchen and still holding the dog, Bev sees Brenda's eyes flash.

"Bev, your wig's on crooked. Here, let me fix it for you."

Brenda steps forward and starts to adjust the wig, but Bev drops the dog, yelling, "Stop! I'll do it," rushing toward the powder room. She wants her gold earrings to show, dammit. Why did Brenda touch her wig?

* * *

Brenda nearly gags on the sweet, floral odor permeating the room and sees Anthony glancing at his watch again.

"Dad almost ready?" he asks Bev, who shrugs and shouts at Rudolph to shut up.

"You know your father. Man walks to his own drumbeat." She shouts at the bottom of the stairs at her husband, now upstairs. "Hurry up, Anthony!" Bev turns and flashes a fake smile at her before she asks, "Brenda, you having a baby? Is that what this is all about?"

Brenda's stunned. Baby? Where did that come from? How could Bev have forgotten the shit storm Anthony Sr. raised about Brenda's not wanting children when she and Junior got married?

Brenda ignores the question. But the anger crawls up her spine and she tries to hide it though her eyes flash.

"Since the whole family is present, why wasn't Romie invited, too?" Bev asks Junior, who pretends not to hear it. "She's family, too, you know. Romie should be here, too," she says with a sniff. Junior's face looks pinched.

* * *

"I'm coming, dammit!" Anthony Sr. shouts from upstairs. He's not up for a fancy dinner tonight, but the kids insisted. Anthony Sr. slips into a white shirt with white stripes and decides on a red tie because red's a happy color and Anthony Sr. couldn't be happier. Thanks to Junior, his new kidney has given him a new lease on life, and thanks to his increased energy, he's living every moment to the hilt. He and Bev could win an Olympic medal for doing it. He's making up for lost time, all the time they couldn't when he was sick.

He only regrets that the kidney came from Junior. He wishes he didn't know who donated it, wishes he hadn't been so desperate to get better and waited for someone else's organ. He offered to bring Junior into his business to thank him, but the kid flatly refused, saying he's happy the way things are, but said it as if the vending business is beneath him, even though Junior would earn far more in the business than the chump change he earns at the university.

The kid didn't stop at the kidney; he stuck around for so long, dictating what he could and couldn't eat, like the food police. Anthony wanted to strangle him. Anthony harrumphs. Now Junior and Brenda insist on dinner at one of the most expensive joints around, dictating place and time again. I'm HIS father, dammit. Not the other way around. Dammit!

* * *

Brenda doesn't understand why they just couldn't meet Junior's parents at the restaurant, why he insists they all go in one car. It isn't as if the conversation is pleasant or intriguing. Anthony Sr. hasn't shut up once about the damned factory in China trying to screw him over a penny per item. At the packed restaurant, they've already been waiting fifteen minutes for their table.

"We were late," Brenda says in a matter-of-fact tone when Bev complains about standing too long in what Brenda clearly notices are too-tight shoes. Brenda stares at Bev's hair; obviously, the wig isn't securely fastened on her head, as it keeps shifting. The wig's red and the lipstick's red clash, and Brenda shakes her head, wondering how Junior ever survived his father, much less his stepmother. Thank God for his mother, she thinks. Flora's the normal one!

Her father-in-law complains in his loud voice about the price hike of the green frogs and brags about how he "Jewed" the "Chinks" down. Brenda bristles.

"Pops!" she says. "The word 'negotiate' is better, don't you think? And 'Chinese.'" He looks at her blankly, but clearly he must remember she's Jewish.

When they are about to be seated, Flora arrives, all smiles.

"So sorry to be late," she says, kissing her son and Brenda, offering Anthony Sr. and Bev civil greetings. Brenda is glad to see Flora, but Bev's stony expression says that Bev isn't thrilled. Bev and Anthony Sr. have been married longer than Flora and Anthony Sr. were married, but Bev doesn't seem to appreciate this fact, despite Flora's indifference to her ex. Brenda smiles at her mother-in-law and squeezes her hand, expecting fireworks will ensue. She doesn't wait long.

"Why is Romie not invited? She's your stepsister, Junior."

* * *

Why did Junior go and marry someone just like his mother? Anthony Sr. wonders. Flora always corrected him in public, too, and now here is Flora Repeat, married to his son and seated next to Flora Original. He wonders how long Junior will put up with the know-it-all before he dumps her like Anthony dumped Flora. He's going to pull Junior aside when he can and tell him that he needs to control his wife better or the marriage ain't going to last. Flora Original acts as if they're strangers, with no indication that they'd once been married and produced a son, the one sitting next to Brenda and the one who looks like him, even if he got stuck with his mother's boring-assed personality. Anthony Sr. needs a goddamn drink. Flora's indifference toward him makes him sick. Goddamn know-it-all bitch.

"What's going on, Junior? You assembled all of us here. What's the bad news?" Anthony Sr. is unable to mask his annoyance. "You need a loan or something? Offer still stands to join me in the business," he says.

Junior shakes his head and laughs. "No, Pops. I don't need a loan. I have a big announcement," Junior says, and he's smiling. Since he and Pop can't drink anything alcoholic, Junior orders a large bottle of sparking water for the table and an iced tea for himself and Brenda. Bev frowns when he orders the water. "Feel free to get something stronger if you want. You know Pops and I can't," he says. "Dad, what would you like, some sparkling water? Or anything else? A ginger ale?" His father orders a diet soda. "The sparkling water is the closest to champagne Pop and I can get to these days," he says. Brenda beams at him, but his father seems not to have heard.

"What's the exciting announcement?" his mother asks. Bev doesn't seem to hear either, because she's ordering herself and Anthony Sr. Johnnie Walker Black on the rocks. Junior's stomach twists into a knot.

"Dad, you're not supposed to have whiskey yet. It can compromise your health." His father glares at him.

"I've never felt better, Junior. Stop being a fucking food and drink police. Last I checked, I'm still an adult," Anthony Sr. says.

Junior bristles. "I didn't give you a kidney so you can destroy it."

Anthony Sr. smirks.

"So you're going to lord it over me forever?" When the drink arrives, Anthony Sr. sucks it down like punch. Junior uses a breathing exercise to calm himself. His father isn't going to ruin this evening.

* * *

Know-it-all, tight-assed Junior doesn't react when his know-it-all tight-assed wife insults me, and still is dictating to me what to eat and drink, Anthony Sr. fumes. Anthony Sr. can buy and sell his son and his wife and Flora Original ten times over, and she uses that tone with him. Because of Junior's kidney, this is supposed to be acceptable? Anthony Sr. blows puffs of air out of his mouth and, saying nothing, turns away from Brenda and shoots daggers of hate at Flora.

How many other business men do they know who dropped out of high school and became multimillionaires? Who learned how to fly airplanes and flies his own damn plane? Whose house is so large it requires four distinct heating zones? Anthony Sr. jabs his hands into his pockets, certain this dinner promises to be hell. He appreciates the kidney, and he's grateful, but Junior's insufferable. When the waiter delivers a second whiskey, he throws it back in a single gulp.

* * *

Bev hates sparkling water as much as she hates Flora's sitting at the table, glaring at Anthony Sr. as if he is a crumb under her feet. At home, Anthony Sr. drinks, but Junior doesn't know. She's relieved he's drinking in front of Junior. Kidney donors and recipients aren't supposed to drink, but hell, every once in a while, can't hurt.

Flora raises her glass of sparkling water and says, "To Junior and his big announcement!" Everything about Flora irritates Bev, so she decides to blurt the announcement before Junior.

"To Brenda's baby!" Bev says, raising her glass.

* * *

Brenda squeezes her glass because the alternative is to rip Bev's wig off her head. How Anthony emerged from this family is beyond Brenda's imagination. She's determined that these two buffoons aren't going to ruin the evening.

She emits a fake laugh, "Oh, Bev, you're such a joker!" She turns to Junior. "Now's a perfect time, don't you think?"

Junior nods and announces the national science award, and the purse. Flora jumps up and hugs Junior, gushing over her son.

"Oh my, what wonderful news!" Flora squeals. Tears flow from her eyes, and she's smiling. Brenda beams, too.

"The university is hosting a reception, and he's going to give a lecture about his project," Brenda says, noticing that Flora can barely contain her excitement. Anthony Sr. and Bev fail to react.

* * *

"Chump change," Anthony Sr. says. "You think $10,000 for you and $50,000 a year for three years is something to dance about? It's chump change. You can make far more than that every year if you join me in the business," he says.

"Obviously, you don't get it," Flora says. "Of course, you wouldn't," she adds. "Anthony's research and prosthetic designs serve a greater purpose, can change the world in their own way. Selling trinkets for pennies in supermarket vending machines doesn't impact or change the world, unless you count the pollution of discarded trinkets and their plastic containers," Flora says through gritted teeth. "It's not about the money, but the recognition," she adds.

Anthony Sr. hears the sarcasm in her voice, knows she's mocking him and considers him stupid. Ever since he took Junior out to fly that gas-engine model plane, the first remote control plane ever that he'd seen in his travels and brought home for Junior, things between him and Flora and him and Junior headed south. Junior was only six or seven years old then. The plane was tethered to the remote control gadget by a thin metal wire and could only fly in a wide-arc circle around them. He wasn't paying attention and didn't realize that the trees on their street stood in the plane's flight arc.

The day of its maiden voyage, Junior pointed to the trees and said something Anthony didn't hear. Anthony Sr. insisted on controlling the remote, saying Junior would break it, and flew the plane in a smooth, wide arc directly into the treetop of their neighbor's tree, where it crashed, then dropped to the ground in pieces. Junior knew to calculate the length of the wire at age six. Anthony Sr. painstakingly rebuilt the model, but it never flew again and sat in the basement on a glass shelf. Anthony Sr. held it against him.

* * *

His father and stepmother look at him blankly. "I started working on the prosthetic legs … remember?" They didn't. Junior inhales and continues, hungry for some kind of recognition or spark. None is forthcoming. His father and Bev wait for him. "Phillips Times Entrepreneurial Award," he says, knowing the words mean nothing to them. "My research team and I won this year for the work on prosthetic leg design," Junior says.

"That's nice," Bev says. "Sweetie, Junior won a big award for inventing a kind of fake leg. Isn't that nice? What do you want to order?"

"Hey, did I tell you that we're expanding west, adding twenty new supermarkets—a single chain—in Tennessee?" Anthony Sr. says, changing the subject.

"Who gives a flying fuck?" Flora says. "This isn't about you. Why does everything always have to be about you? Junior won a prestigious national recognition, is considered the nation's top scientist, and all you can say is your stupid vending machine business is expanding into twenty supermarkets? Whoop-de-do! You've raised being an ass to a high art," Flora says.

Anthony Sr. glares at Flora Original. Flora Repeat glares at him. Bev glares at Flora.

* * *

Junior's lips are curled into a barely perceptible smile, and he's staring at the empty plate before him. Brenda knows when he smiles like that and looks downward, he's angry. Brenda's prepared. From her purse, she pulls a folded newspaper clipping and slides it across the table toward her father-in-law.

"Look, Pops! *The Ledger* featured Anthony on the front page this morning." She smiles. The headline in bold letters reads, "Local Scientist Awarded Nation's Top Science Prize."

* * *

Junior mouths "thank you" to Brenda and squeezes her hand under the table. The waiter comes by to collect their orders. Bev asks the waiter endless questions about the substitutions and changes, holding up the process.

"My mother-in-law has reduced her diet to prison gruel," Brenda says with a laugh.

Bev's eyes flash, but she continues asking questions and finally succeeds in ordering something that satisfies her.

* * *

Anthony Sr. reads the headline and the first paragraph of the story and feels his face flush. *The Ledger* never published a story about him, never featured him on the front page. Anthony Sr.'s own father died when he was three years old, and he and his brother had to learn to do everything themselves, from repairing the car to fixing the house. He orders another whiskey.

Bev attempts to soothe things between the two Anthonys. "Oh, it's nothing, Junior. A drink every now and again isn't going to hurt him. Everything in moderation, after all." She plays with her chunky gold earrings to alleviate her nerves. "He just wants to toast your success, don't you, dear?" she says.

"I'm the father, and I damn sure don't need to ask your permission for what I do or don't do." Anthony Sr. gulps the drink, and it feels smooth going down. He raises the empty glass toward Junior. "Congrats on the award, son," he says, meaning it, knowing it sounds insincere. "Let's eat now that that's out of the way," he says, reaching across the table, grabbing the bread basket and tearing off a piece. "They've always served the best bread here, don't you think, honey?"

* * *

Junior's hands are balled up in fists on the table, and Brenda puts her hand over one of them to calm him.

"I forgot how damned good whiskey tastes," Anthony Sr. says. "I'm a new man, thanks to you, son! I can't thank you enough!" he says. "Bev and I are going to get an award for doing it. We're making up for all that lost time from when I was sick." He winks at Bev.

"Oh please," Flora says.

Junior moves the empty whiskey glass from his father's reach and plans to tell the waiter to refrain from bringing Anthony Sr. any more drinks.

"What the fuck?" Anthony Sr. says. "Why'd you do that?" He pounds the table. "Give it here," he says.

Junior shakes his head. "Cutting you off. It's for your own good."

"I'm not a fucking child," his father says.

No longer hungry, Junior moves the shrimp around his dish. In the eighteen months since the surgery, he's never played the kidney card, but now he's remembering the pain he endured. The diet restrictions. The days away from his work. The days away from the gym.

Bev and Anthony Sr. clean their plates. Flora tries to keep a normal conversation flow with Brenda, who eats only a few bites. Anthony Sr. snags his whiskey glass. Brenda winces at her father-in-law's ice-crunching. She wants to ask him to stop, but refrains.

Finally, she snaps, "Pops! Please stop!"

Anthony Sr. asks, "Does she boss you around like this at home? How can you stand it? Reminds me of someone else I know." He looks at Flora. "You married your mother, Junior."

Anthony Sr. crosses his arms and looks smug. "I built a business that bought and paid for Junior's fancy-schmancy education. So in a way, this big award he's gotten also belongs to me. So, how much of that award purse comes to me?" he says and laughs.

Anxious to end the evening, Junior excuses himself and finds the waiter to pay the bill before his father can do it, not that he'd try, but just in case. He discovers the tab is covered. The waiter hands him an envelope from Flora. In the envelope is the newspaper clipping with a note. "Saw it in the paper this morning. Couldn't be more proud of you. You deserve this honor for which you worked so hard. Congratulations!" Back at the table, Flora nods, her eyes gleaming with pride.

* * *

While the waiter clears the dishes, Bev imagines dessert. She imagines chocolate fudge brownie cake with whipped cream. Or chocolate mousse pie. Or some kind of tart with whipped cream and ice cream. She purposefully substituted things to reduce calories in her entrée so she could splurge on dessert. But the waiter doesn't ask if anyone wants coffee or dessert, and instead thanks them for allowing him to serve them.

"The bill's paid," the waiter tells Anthony Sr. after he asks. Anthony Sr. looks as stunned as Bev does.

"What the hell kind of celebratory dinner is this?" she asks Anthony Sr., disappointed that she's robbed of dessert.

"Who paid?" Anthony Sr. asks the waiter.

"Someone who asked not to be named," the waiter says.

Anthony Sr. tells the waiter to bring Bev a dessert menu and to bring him some coffee.

"You can start another bill," he tells the waiter. "Coffee and dessert are on me." Bev orders chocolate mousse pie. "Take your time, dear," he tells Bev and glares at Junior, Brenda, and Flora, who appear as if they are about to jump out of their chairs.

"Perhaps we could get dessert elsewhere?" Flora suggests.

Anthony Sr. shakes his head. "My little lovebird wants dessert here."

Flora laughs. "As you wish." She excuses herself to the ladies' room.

Later, when Anthony Sr. tries to pay for the dessert tab, it's been taken care of.

"Who the hell paid the tab?" he asks the waiter.

"Same person who's covered the dinner," he says. "It's a gift for a celebratory dinner in honor of a big science award."

Bev glances at Flora and realizes that Flora has paid for the evening, but she says nothing because if Flora wants to act as if she's superior, let her go ahead and do it. At least her Anthony didn't have to shell out a penny.

* * *

In the car, Anthony Sr. breaks the silence, "So what the hell was that about back there with your mother, Junior? You rush

80

the hell out of us to go to dinner and then you rush the hell out of us to go home. What gives? That fancy-schmancy award must have inflated your head."

Junior calmly pulls the car over to the side of the highway. He twists his body so he can face his father.

"I'll tell you what gives. My patience," he says. "I wanted this to be a pleasant evening to celebrate something huge. This award is a big damn deal, bigger than your vending business which sells kids crap they don't need and only think they want."

"How dare you talk to your father and me like that?" Bev shouts. "Who do you think you are anyway, Junior?" She adjusts her wig and glares at Junior and Brenda. "He's your father. You're supposed to respect him," she shouts. "Not like you and your mother acting all superior. I know she's the one who paid because she wanted to make your father feel little."

Brenda stares at the clasp of her handbag to avoid looking at her in-laws. A kidney weighs a quarter of a pound. It measures four inches long and two inches wide. Everybody has two. Except Anthony and his pops. They each now have one. Born with two, people can live with one. Brenda considers that the two kidneys between Sr. and Jr. must now weigh a ton.

"What the hell are you smirking at?" Anthony Sr. shouts at Brenda. "This marriage ain't going to last long, Junior. She's a Flora Repeat. She reminds me of your mother, and not in a good way."

Junior feels his heart rate spike. "Leave Brenda alone. She has nothing to do with this. Leave my mother out of this. She has nothing to do with it. Tonight's disaster is all you. I gave you a kidney so you can live longer and be healthier and what do you do? You're throwing back drinks like you're going to run out of alcohol. You insult my wife, and you can't even pretend to be happy for me about anything for once. And Bev is so jealous of mom, her wig should be green instead of red."

Junior knows that his father has been drinking at home. He wonders how long he's been hitting the bottle when he's supposed to avoid alcohol and grapefruit so that the drugs that stop his body from rejecting the kidney continue to work. He imagines Anthony Sr. being noncompliant and wonders if his sacrifice was a waste. He throws the car in gear and speeds to Anthony Sr. and Bev's house.

* * *

Anthony Sr. and Bev exit the car in silence. No one says goodnight. Bev's too-tight shoes are pinching her feet as she limps over to the front door, unlocks it, and pushes it open. Angry with his father, Junior still wants to make sure they both get inside safely before pulling away. He stares at his father, trying to remember good things about him, and he doesn't see Rudolph shoot out the door past Bev in a brown blur. He fails to notice the dog racing around the sides and back of the car, although he hears Rudolph's incessant yapping and imagines the dog's still inside barking on the sofa. He backs out of the driveway and runs over a lump.

"What the hell was that?" he asks. The dog has stopped yapping.

"Believe me, you don't want to know," Brenda says.

Bev's face is contorted in horror, and his father is laughing like a madman, and that's when Junior realizes what the lump is and that his father isn't laughing.

The four of them stare at the inert Rudolph before Brenda retrieves an old blanket from the trunk and hands it to Junior who gingerly scoops the dog, still reeking of Bev's cheap perfume, into his arms.

"It was an accident," Junior says, his voice cracking.

Bev whimpers. "My poor Rudolph."

"Animals keep it simple. They either like you or they don't. They ask no questions and bring no drama. They have no expectations other than being fed and walked and don't even get pissed if you forget to feed or walk them. They're better than people," Anthony Sr. says.

The dog still in his arms, Junior faces his father. "They can't give you a kidney," he says, his tone sharp.

"Don't start!" Bev yells. With her crooked wig, grief-filled face, and smarting feet, she moves like a wounded robin as Brenda leads her limping into the house.

"You never understand anything I say," his old man says, shaking his head. "That's not what I meant. What a fucking disaster of a night!"

For once, Junior agrees but doesn't say so. Despite the late hour, Anthony Sr. helps Junior carry the dog into the house. Without discussing it, they first wrap the body in an old blanket and then seal it in a black trash bag. They erect flood lights to illuminate the expansive backyard behind Anthony Sr.'s palatial house so that Bev and Brenda, both now wearing slippers, can locate the most suitable spot for Rudolph near the rose garden. Admiring her patience, Junior watches Brenda leading a somnambulistic Bev back into the house. His old man must be tired, but Anthony Sr. refuses to quit, surprising Junior by his stamina and their compatibility. Well past midnight, they both smile when Brenda brings them each a glass of sparkling water. Junior knows his father can drop the shovel, walk away, and leave him with the task of burying Bev's beloved pet. But instead, Anthony Sr. continues shoveling and tossing soil in sync with him, as if accomplishing this simple but unexpected chore grants him a long-needed and much-desired succor against an overcomplicated and chaotic world.

HENRY'S FALL

The problem, the way Henry Pinto saw it, began and ended with the pig. He hated the pig with the same intensity that his fiancée, Clara Brumster, loved it. Or the problem, he mused, could be that he loved Clara with the same intensity that she loved the pig. Either way, she loved the pig, and the problem was that Clara loved the pig more than she loved Henry. He wanted the pig gone from Clara's life and, subsequently, his life.

Standing in his underwear at the threshold of Clara's bedroom after a long Saturday spent accruing billable hours at work—a law firm located a mere spitting distance from Clara's house, though not too far from his either—he just wanted to climb into bed next to her and sleep, ending what had been a brutal day. He hated working on Saturdays because it made him feel like a slave, albeit a highly-paid slave. But he was up for partner and Saturday hours came with the territory. He longed for a peaceful night with Clara in her bed, her pillow faintly smelling of roses, lilies of field, and jasmine. Stuck at the threshold, he imagined Clara reading next to him, something she often did long into the night, her right foot gently pressing against his left calf, a way to stay connected, he thought, even if she didn't want to sleep at the same time he did.

On the bed in nearly sheer black lingerie, she flipped through a magazine, oblivious to the stupid pig oinking and squealing at him, giving him the stink eyeball as if he, Henry, rather than it, belonged elsewhere. It oinked and squealed louder with each step Henry took into the room toward the bed. Henry wanted to kick the thing, kick it like a football, this black-and-white pig with an annoying giant red-bow collar, with the utterly ridiculously elevated name, King Charles. But Henry knew that at 360 plus pounds, the pig wouldn't exactly sail across the room. Why couldn't Clara have a normal pet, like a dog? A cat? Or a guinea pig? Or goldfish?

"Clara, do something about the pig," he said, sounding annoyed.

Clara glanced at him and back to her magazine. "You started this row," she said, her voice a sweet soprano. "He wants an apology."

"I'm not apologizing to a pig," Henry said, crossing his arms.

"Why not? You hurt his feelings."

"Since when do pigs have feelings? I smacked his snout for pissing on my rug—and that was two weeks ago," Henry said. "He can't possibly remember."

Two weeks ago, the stupid pig had pissed on his new Oriental rug. Henry, who didn't own pets or want children because of the chaos and mess associated with them, considered a pet pig unnatural. Never mind the stink of porcine urine still assaulting him at home. After soiling his prize Oriental rug, Henry's intolerance bloomed into outright hatred. He wanted Clara to get rid of the pig.

"It has to go," he'd screamed at her while he beat the pig's nose, not expecting her to gather her things and leave in a huff. Things between them have not been the same since.

"King Charles is a smart little piggy," Clara said, baby-talking the pig.

"Nothing's little about that pig. Can't you see this is ridiculous?" His voice sounded whiney—not what he intended.

Oinking, King Charles blocked his way.

Clara went to the pig, rubbed its neck. "He didn't mean it, KC. He's sorry," she baby-talked. "Come on, baby!" she cooed. Henry's stomach lurched when she began singing a Bocelli tune to the thing, leading it into its round bed. He could feel his face reddening, his neck muscles pulsate because Clara should reserve love song lyrics for him, and not a stupid animal; especially not a pig. Once it settled in the round bed, Henry dashed to Clara's bed before the stupid pig noticed. Henry's eye twitched as he watched Clara's tiny, soft hand rubbing King Charles' belly and not his own.

"Can't you put him in another room when I'm here?" he asked.

"He's always slept in my room, Henry," Clara said, climbing back in bed.

Henry grunted, vowing that once they were married, things would change: He'd lay down the law, assuming that he'd sell his house and move into hers. The first change to go would be the towel-covered boudoir chair Clara had placed at the foot of the bed so that the pig could climb onto it and then onto her bed, an open invitation. More than a few times, the pig had edged Henry off of the bed and onto the floor because it wanted to be next to Clara. And invariably, when Henry, bleary-eyed and dazed, struck his toes on the chair's leg, he staggered half asleep to the guest room. Second, he'd banish the pig first to the guest bedroom, then to the kitchen, then to the yard, and then to a farm somewhere in exurbia.

King Charles had strenuously objected when he and Clara became intimate, oinking and squealing his distress, ramming the bedroom door whenever he was locked out. The once-perfect door sagged in the middle from the battering, and Henry resented having to take the pig's sensitivity into account by being extra quiet when he and Clara were intimate. When he'd first met Clara three years ago, the pig slept in her bed all the time, and the round bed under the window became a concession she'd made for Henry, a concession that would lead to others.

Henry snorted. "The pig goes in the guest room—when I'm visiting," he said.

"He's never been alone at night."

"No time like the present," Henry said, believing the pig understood every word he spoke and even could read his mind because King Charles glared at him from his round bed.

"It's giving me the hairy eyeball," Henry said.

Clara scoffed. "You brought this on yourself. He knows you don't like him."

Now that Clara's finger sported the magnificent diamond ring he gave her, it was time to assert his feelings. King Charles belonged on a farm, being prepared for his true purpose as bacon or ham. To Henry, the pig symbolized a salient reminder of Clara's late husband Peter. She and Peter had adopted it as a piglet—naming it King Charles, raising it like their only child for one year and one month before Peter and seven others were killed in a freak beltway accident caused by a tractor-trailer hitting a pedestrian bridge. Peter and Clara had shared more than the pig. They'd shared this house and a career. Peter was a tenor in the same opera company that still employed Clara. After Peter's untimely death, a then smaller King Charles had moved into Clara's bed, Clara holding it instead of Peter, and Henry imagined, crying herself to sleep hugging the pig. Henry believed that the pig channeled Peter from the Great Beyond to interfere with their nuptials. The sight of the pig sitting in the front seat of Clara's car had nauseated him, and when Clara brought the stupid beast to his house when she visited, he imagined transforming it into something useful. Like sausages. Or bacon. Or ribs. Barbequed.

"It's like a retarded kid that pisses rivers and shits boulders, who'll never grow up and leave," he said, making himself comfortable on the bed. "It belongs on a farm, Clara."

"He's a *he* and he's *my* pig," Clara said. "I can't believe you're jealous of a pig! Go home!" She pointed to the bedroom door.

Henry refused to budge. Through her thin, black, lacy lingerie, Henry could see the silhouette of Clara's body, the outline of her thighs, the indentation of her waist, the slope of her breasts, breasts he should be touching if it weren't for King Charles. Why didn't she agree that the pig stay in another room when he visited? Why didn't she just get rid of the thing?

"It doesn't belong here," he said, laying down the law.

Clara pushed him off the bed. "Neither do you. Why don't you just settle it, give him an extra treat, or do something conciliatory? Isn't that better than going to war with a pet? You don't have to win every battle, Henry."

"You're missing the point," Henry said, glancing uneasily at the pig.

King Charles' hooves scratched the wood floors, and squealing and oinking, it rushed him, and Henry dove back onto the bed. When the pig nearly flew onto the boudoir chair and faced Henry, oinking him off the bed, Clara began laughing. She laughed so hard, she doubled over. King Charles squealed louder, butting Henry backward away from the bed, out of the bedroom. Henry imagined bashing its head with a baseball bat. He imagined stabbing the animal in the eye with an ice pick. He imagined all sorts of ways to separate the pig from Clara. King Charles stood in between them, squealing and oinking at Henry until he backed down the hallway, down the stairs, step by step into the living room. Following his descent to the first floor, allowing the pig to humiliate him, Clara laughed uproariously.

"This is no small beer," Henry shouted at the front door. "It's a P-I-G."

Clara sighed. "All he wants is to be loved," she said, handing him his clothes, his car keys, and his shoes.

Henry refused to apologize to a pig that pissed on his rug. Not now, not ever. Grabbing his things, Henry vowed to find another fiancée who wasn't devoted to a pet. But, damn it, he'd bested the keenest legal minds in the city, and he wasn't going to allow a stupid pig to defeat him. He drove down Key Highway around the Baltimore Inner Harbor to his perfectly coifed Canton house. The pig had won a battle, but Henry would win the war.

At home, Henry sulked. A TV chef on the Food Network demonstrated how to prepare salmon, but Henry imagined pork chops instead. He imagined King Charles neatly roasted with an apple silencing his oinking, squealing mouth. He imagined Clara alone, minus the stupid porker channeling Peter, but awoke Sunday morning, still on the sofa, still alone, the television blaring.

* * *

All week, it irked Henry that Clara allowed the pig to oink him out of the house. It irked him that she was too busy to see him any night this week, blaming rehearsals for the new opera season, and it irked him that his boss demonstrated disdain when Henry asked for Saturday off. He wanted to catch up with Clara to settle things. And now that it was Saturday, Clara claimed another rehearsal would run all day. It irked him that he had to invite himself to her house for breakfast since Clara had declined his invitation to meet him at Jimmy's in Fells Point. And now, sitting in her kitchen, it irked him that she poured pig chow into King Charles' purple, monogrammed bowl. She served Henry only a mug of instant coffee. No breakfast, no French toast or pancakes, no eggs, and definitely no bacon. Henry half-smiled at the thought of King Charles eating bacon and ham. Like a cannibal.

"Why couldn't you come to Jimmy's?" Henry asked. He refrained from oinking at the pig. "No breakfast?" He watched the pig chow down.

Wearing a jean skirt and a black sleeveless knit top, Clara slipped into a pair of black flip-flops. Henry admired her killer legs, legs he wanted wrapped around his like snakes on tree limbs.

"I told you already. Rehearsal. You're the one who invited yourself to breakfast," she said. "Why do you think I'm supposed to serve you breakfast when you invite yourself?

I have to walk KC, and then I need to leave for work."

"But I took off today," he said.

"Enjoy your day off!" she said.

Henry wanted them to sit down to a rare Saturday morning breakfast on a Saturday he didn't work, a breakfast that preferably Clara had cooked. And it irked him she tended to the pig like a disciple.

"I'll come," he said, keeping the exasperation out of his voice. He imagined their Saturday and Sunday mornings sans

King Charles. Would they linger in bed over the morning newspapers? Maybe make love again before finally starting the day? Would they stroll over to Mike's in Canton, Jimmy's in Fells Point, or to the South Street Market in Federal Hill for fresh berries and bagels?

Since they have been together, the pig grew from a cute, exotic curiosity to a fat, intolerable pest. The thought of her dead husband using King Charles to interfere with their relationship occurred to him more than once. Henry wondered if he'd hate King Charles if it were a dog, or a cat—God, how he hated sneaky, aloof cats—but then a dog wouldn't have held a grudge against him for a bit of disciplinary action. But dogs are labor intensive. No better. Henry wondered how much the pig would fetch in a sale, certain he could unload it for a tidy sum to Hispanics populating Fells Point. *King Charles, the second main attraction to a quinceañera birthday party*, he thought.

"I'm looking forward to the new season," Clara said. "Maybe you can come to a performance this year," she said as they ambled toward the Inner Harbor.

Preoccupied, Henry said nothing. Instead, he decided he could kill the pig by making it run. Death by heart attack.

"Look at that cute pig," said a woman to a man wearing a straw hat, who approached them. Obviously, tourists. "How adorable is that?" she said.

Baltimore's own Mr. Piggy, Henry thought, his stomach churning.

"May I?" the woman asked, extending her hand.

"Oh, sure," said Clara. "He's a lover—aren't you, boy?" Clara baby-talked the pig, and Henry clenched his fists. The pig grunted, squealed, and appeared to smile as the lady scratched its neck.

"Oh so adorable! What's his name?" the lady asked.

Probably a PETA member, Henry thought.

"King Charles," Clara said with pride.

"Kaycee. Hey, your highness," the lady cooed, petting it. "Wow, solid—what does he eat?"

"Everything," Henry said. "He's a goddamn pig. What do you think pigs eat?"

Clara glared at him. "Pig chow. And treats when he's a good boy." Clara's eyes hurled daggers at him even while she kissed the pig's snout. The woman pulled out a camera.

"May I?"

Clara smiled at the lady and her camera. "Oh, he's such a hambone!" she said, laughing, and the lady clicked her camera.

Henry stomped ahead. More photos of Clara and King Charles graced a mountain of travel picture books than did photos of the *Constellation*, a Revolutionary War ship sitting in the harbor, or any of the city's other historical landmarks. He headed for the Light Street Pavilion, conscious that, once again, this tourist, like the entire parade of others before her, neglected to include Henry in any photos—as if he were the invisible man. Obsessing over the injustice, he sat on a bench opposite the dinner-party tour boat and stared at the bobbing sailboats.

"I hate when you walk away like that," Clara said, the pig beside her, blocking Henry's view. "It's rude."

"Rude is a million people always snapping yours and the pig's photos and never including me," he said, pointing his index finger at her. "The pig has to go." King Charles looked at him, grunted in a way that sounded like a laugh, and fixed a porcine smile on his lips, holding it like a fixture on his snout. "And now he's mocking me!" Henry shouted, his face flushed, furious the pig belittled him.

"Ridiculous," Clara said, rolling her eyes. "You're not exactly Mr. Personable. Especially lately. How will you behave with children? Let's go, King Charles," she said.

"Children?! Who said I want children? They're as messy and demanding as that pig. It's the pig or me," Henry yelled. "I'm damned sick of Peter Pig!"

He didn't know why, but he felt a little joy, confident that the gray look on Clara's face indicated that she'd get rid of the pig; he was winning. He imagined comforting her when she missed the stupid pig.

"Peter Pig?" she asked. She waited for an answer. Then she began walking away.

"You're choosing the pig?" he yelled. Henry sprang to his feet and followed them. She was ditching him for a pig!

After Clara handed him his CDs and clothes, after she thrust a bag of his miscellaneous belongings at him, after she returned the magnificent diamond, he filled Clara's doorway, holding everything in his arms.

"It doesn't have to be this way," Henry said. "A good farm would be best!"

"You don't get it," she said. "He's my pet. King Charles has been with me four whole years longer than you have. He peed on your rug. I paid to clean it, so what's the big fucking deal, anyway? It isn't just the issue of the pig, Henry. It's *everything*," she said.

Clara shut the door with a thud. She didn't say goodbye, wish him a happy life, or thank him for the wonderful times they'd shared.

"You picked a goddamn pig over me!" he shouted through the door. He heard the tumblers of the lock click into place. He walked around to the back of the house, where he heard Clara and King Charles in the yard. From the water streaming into the gutter, he knew that Clara was filling the child-size pool she kept in the backyard for the pig to cool off in. He knew she allowed the pig to play in the water while she dressed for work. Henry clenched his teeth, his jaws, his fists. He would *not* suffer defeat at the hooves of a pig, especially not a pig that laughed and mocked him. Damn him, Peter Pig!

Without work to occupy him, Henry leaned against the bar in the Blue Crab Pub with its owner Rick, a burly, blond, former college football star who'd never advanced beyond his glory days as a Terp quarterback. The Blue Crab Pub overflowed with Terp memorabilia. Steamed blue crab carapaces painted with football scenes dangled from the ceiling on fishing lines. Wanting to avoid being in an awkward position of giving Rick, actually his client, unbillable advice, Henry hardly ever stepped into the Blue Crab Pub. But now, in the pub's dim light, he fingered the engagement ring, a good-size rock in his estimation, repeating, "She picked that goddamn pig over me. A fucking farm animal."

"You're a free man now," Rick said, sliding a draft beer in Henry's direction. Rick pushed his aviator glasses back up his nose and ran his fingers through his thinning hair. "Celebrate!" Rick signaled the bartender to bring another two beers. "On the house," he told the barkeep. "Just keep 'em coming."

They had already killed a six-pack each. The TV above the bar beamed a Terps game, and Rick kept an eye on the play.

Henry surmised Rick was betting on it and winning. Henry had no one else to call. His friends stopped calling him long ago, jealous of his upward trajectory at the firm.

"She dumped me for a pig," Henry slurred.

Rick laughed. "No pig shit for you, my friend!" Rick laughed and slapped him on the back. "Let's toast. To new beginnings!" Rick sounded jovial and proceeded to grow more jovial with subsequent beers, whereas Henry grew more sullen and angry. "We're both free men now. This is great news, my friend!" said Rick, whose third divorce was just final, raising his glass.

"I wish that pig were dead," Henry said.

"Meh. Think of all the babes you can test-drive now."

Henry didn't feel any better. "I hate that pig. King Fucking Charles."

"Give it up, Henry. Terps are up." Rick commandeered two bowls of peanuts. "I've been married three times already, and all three times went south faster than the New Year's Ball at Times Square. Consider yourself spared the pain and aggravation, not to mention the cost of getting divorced. Whoa, touchdown! Yeah, baaaaby!" Rick pounded the bar, yelling at the TV, pushing his glasses back with his right hand before raising it into a victory fist.

Henry didn't care about the game. Nor did he consider himself spared. He wanted Clara to agree with him: that the pig had to go, that he was more valuable than the pig, that he knew what was best for her, for them. He had to convince her.

Henry stumbled off the barstool and threw some bills on the bar. "Hey, thanks, bro," he slurred. "I gotta go."

"Beer's on the house, and the game's not over. Where're you going?" Rick said, shoving the bills back at Henry.

"I gotta convince Clara I love her and that the pig hasta go," he slurred.

"Not a good idea, Henry," Rick said, shaking his head. "Let her and the pig go. Plus you're too drunk to drive."

"Be defeated by a pig? You outta your mind?"

"Let's just wait until the game's over," Rick said. "I'll drive."

Henry could live with that and lost count of the beers that kept coming. Just after midnight, in Rick's silver BMW, Henry directed him toward Clara's house in Federal Hill. A dim light glowed in Clara's living room, a sure sign that she wasn't home. *Where did she go after rehearsal?* he wondered. He wanted her to be home crying, but Clara always demonstrated an unsettling independence—perhaps honed after Peter's death—with an endless list of places to go: plays, movies, art shows, literary readings, nightclubs. Where could she be late on a Saturday night?

Rick glanced at his watch. "She's not here. Let's roll, Romeo," Rick said, slurring.

They both slurred. "Don't you want to see the fucking famous King Charles?"

"Not especially," Rick said.

"The damn pig's probably sleeping in the back."

"Then we gotta get outta Dodge," Rick said, parking the car at an angle in the alley next to the back of Clara's house, an end house before an alley large enough to drive through.

They stumbled out of the car, Henry leaving his door open. Peering through the wooden fence and seeing only blackness, Henry threw himself against the fence with a crash, inspiring the neighbor's dogs to bark.

"King Charles," he called, certain the pig was in the yard. "He's probably afraid of the barking dogs. Clara said dogs and pigs don't mix."

Henry stood on a trash can and heaved himself over the fence, landing with a thud, and opened the gate for Rick from the inside.

"It's not in the yard," Henry said. "Let's go in."

"Are you fucking nuts or something?" Rick said in a loud whisper.

"I'll bring the pig out." Henry said, wanting Rick to see the pig. Henry broke the basement window with his shoe, thrust his arm in, unlocked it, and shimmied in, leaving his shoe outside.

"What the fuck are you doing?" Rick asked through the broken window.

"I'll be right back," Henry said, disappearing into the basement's darkness.

"Where are you, you fat fucker?" Henry called before hearing hooves on the floor upstairs. Henry grabbed the pig chow from the hallway closet and made his way upstairs. "Peter Pig!"

In Clara's bedroom, the pig stood half on the bed and half on the boudoir chair, its beady eyes fixed on Henry. Then on the bag of pig chow.

"Come on, you fat fucker, Peter Pig," Henry said, placing a handful of pig chow on the floor to lure the pig, bite by bite, downstairs and out into the yard, grateful the food distracted the pig from rushing him.

"What a huge fucker!" Rick said, petting King Charles behind the ears. "It's kinda cool. Why do you hate him so fucking much?"

Henry shrugged and didn't answer.

"Okay. Let's go now," Rick said, opening the gate wide.

King Charles dashed out of the yard, faster than Henry had ever seen him go. "Holy shit," Rick said as the pig charged past him into the darkness of the alley behind Clara's house.

Henry, still holding the bag of pig chow, laughed so hard, he couldn't stand up.

"You should catch that pig now. By its toe," Rick said, also laughing uproariously. "Clara's going to be pissed as shit." Rick and Henry roared with laughter, the gate swinging on its hinges.

"Fat fucker won't be going too far. He'll probably be eating something crappy outta a trash can at the other end of the alley or something," Henry said, heaving himself up.

"You got a pig problem," Rick said, trying to catch his breath between guffaws. "Clara's going to kick your ass when she finds out."

"Finds out what?" Wearing a black cocktail dress, a pearl necklace, and stud diamond earrings, Clara glared at them from the back door way. "What're you doing here? Who's that with you? Where's my pig?" she asked.

Henry couldn't stop laughing. The way Clara said the word "pig" struck him as funny.

"Piiiiiiiiiiiiiiiig," he said, the sound of the word coming from his throat instead of his mouth. "Piiiiiiiiiiiiiiiiiiiig," he repeated. "Where's my piiiiiiiiiiiiiiiiiiiiig?" he mimicked her.

"You're wasted," she said.

The last thing Henry wanted was for that damn walking set of pork chops to be found. His head still felt blurry.

"We can get the pig tomorrow," he said, slightly less drunk. "I mean, how hard would it be to find a fucking three-hundred-pound pig in downtown Baltimore? He can't hide anywhere, and every damn body in the neighborhood, in the city, in the whole fucking world knows it's your pig," he said.

Clara glowered. He either helped her find the pig *now*—she emphasized the word by slapping the fingers of her right hand onto the palm of her left hand, as if she were counting out a rhythm—or she'd call the police and report him for breaking and entering. He was an asshole. Pig chow in hand, Henry shuffled down Riverside Avenue, Rick following behind, both merry, calling the pig.

Clara, who had switched into her sneakers, trailed behind them, checking all the alleyways, calling for King Charles in her soprano as melodic as an angel's. They searched Riverside Avenue, William and Montgomery Streets. King Charles seemed to have vanished, and Henry grew happier at the prospect of it being gone. They searched Federal Hill Park, and at the park's north side, Clara began shouting.

"He's in Rash Field!" she yelled, pointing. Clara clutched her gown and ran down steep concrete stairs toward the street, toward Key Highway, toward that damn pig. Rick, more athletic than Henry, bounded down the steps like an unsteady gazelle, and Henry, who gingerly navigated the steps individually, prayed the animal would panic and fall in the harbor. Henry ambled through Rash Field toward the Scupper Restaurant at the end of the harbor's walkway. Ahead, Rick sprinted, making oinking sounds, and attempted to tackle the pig, inadvertently driving it closer to the walkway's edge. Hurrying now toward the pig, Henry was determined to get to it before Clara; he wanted to give it an imperceptible push over the edge. Henry approached the pig from behind, while Rick bellowed pig calls.

"King Charles," Clara sang out from behind, her dulcet soprano reverberating through Rash Field like a gorgeous bell.

"Come, boy, come, come, come. King Charles, come to mama!" Clara held his leash in her hand. The pig's beady eyes searched in the darkness for Clara, avoiding Rick's awful oinking bellows, and edging away from Henry, holding the pig chow bag, toward the walkway's edge.

Henry darted toward King Charles, who had nowhere else to go except over the walkway's edge into the harbor's water. Henry slowed. Standing a foot in front of the squealing, oinking animal, Henry poured pig chow onto the pavement, the disgusting smell of the stuff assaulting his nostrils, while Rick continued the oinking calls.

"Shut the fuck up already!" he yelled at Rick.

"Who'd believe we chased a pig all over Rash Field?" Rick said, exuberant. "This's the best fucking night ever!"

Staring at the pig chow, the pig refused to budge. Hoping to grab the pig's collar, Henry stepped sideways away from the pig chow. With Clara so close, he couldn't push it over the edge and decided to drag it to Clara. Henry gingerly moved closer to the pig just as Clara stepped forward.

"King Charles!" she sang, joy and love in her voice. Squealing, oinking, King Charles turned his entire piggy body toward the musical sound of his mama, and that's when Henry felt it: King Charles's 350-pound porcine ass pushed him over the edge of the walkway.

"Holy shit!" Rick bellowed.

Startled, Henry cursed, "Peter Fucking Pig," as he fell sideways. Panic cleared his fuzzy head. King Charles' curly black-and-white tail was the last thing Henry, who never learned to swim, saw before plunging into the dark harbor waters.

PATENT LEATHER SHOES

It's not the shoes, first, last, or in-between. I can always skip the tying and untying by buying the ones with Velcro straps. I can skip the bending over part, too, by raising my leg up and crossing it over the opposite knee to avoid the rush of blood between my head, feet, and face. It starts earlier—when losses can astonish you, when I'm young enough to still turn heads but old enough to know that when I enter a room, it's not about a dramatic entry but the locations of bathrooms. It starts with compression socks, forced into giving up those Come-Fuck-Me-Pumps, begrudgingly accepting the first indignity of special underwear to catch leakage, only to graduate to adult diapers. It's not the tying and untying of shoes but when the chilled hands of the siblings Age and Death extend their icy fingers through space and time to caress me, a gentle reminder of what's to come, the inevitable.

I shuck off that caress and turn away, beating back those icy fingers, knowing that Death, while a sibling of Age, works hard, much harder than her sister who gradually and lazily waits to take action. Death collects us in youth after massacres of war, after massacres of blistering anger aided by machine guns and assault weapons, after long and short illnesses, after accidents, after collusions like suicides. By the time I get to those Velcro-strapped shoes, I've been at war for a long time, triumphantly beating back those siblings, battle-ready against Age and Death, marred by a history of victories and losses.

Death collected my two babies before they were born. Death collected some of my nieces and nephews from wars and accidents. Death collected my parents from illness. Death finally succeeds in collecting my husband after both siblings ganged up on him, robbing him of energy and vibrancy after his having cheated Death countless times, after 66 years of marriage. My husband left me to battle alone. I know the terrible siblings will win. Not without a fight, I tell them.

Age attempts to best me, clipping my wings so I can no longer fly up the flights, first, second, third, fourth, fifth, of stairs in our apartment building. These flights fail to rob me of my breath. A small win. Instead, they attack my bones. Age makes them stiff with arthritis, frozen with stenosis. Defiant, I take one step at a time. I line my groceries on the step ahead, moving them up each step as I rise. The others in the building hate the sound of cans thumping on the steps, followed by the sound of my feet onto the next, a two-step kerplunk as I force myself up the flights to the fifth. *Why did we never move down floors*, I wonder. *Why did we stay in a five-story walkup in a building without elevators?* Maybe we taunted Death and Aging.

"Why don't you ever ask for help?" an irate neighbor calls from the fourth flight without offering it.

"Then what will I do when you're not here?" I call back, undeterred by the annoyance, and check my impatience. I want to instead shout out for that neighbor to shut up, to mind her own business.

I know I've been dying for close to ninety years. We're dying to live at the same time we're living to die. I know I cannot avoid Death forever. So, I've been playing with her sibling Age, feeling

Age massage my body with her chilly fingers while I sleep. She's attempting to mold my body into the silhouette of a bent tree. Sometimes she's successful. We torment each other, Age and I, because to be honest, I understand how lucky I am to be playing with Age since her sister collects so many before Age wakes up. Also, to be honest, I'm furious with my husband for leaving me alone in the battle, for surrendering the fight and running away with Death.

I visit my anger on everyone I see, especially on those looking happy. What's there to be happy about when fighting a singular battle in a collective war? I arrive on the fifth floor despite my stiff body and step into my apartment, the one I shared with my husband, whose clothes still hang in the closet and whose shoe-stringed shoes still sit in the foyer. In the foyer mirror, I see myself passing by with my bent back, lips covered in candy apple red lipstick, and in shoes on my swollen feet that look like patent leather sandals.

PRACTICING IN THE DARK

It's March and too cold for Delia, who pulls her black wool scarf tighter around her neck and tugs her coat—missing three buttons—tighter around her body. Under the coat, her winter blue-plaid school uniform offers no protection against the chill. She holds a stack of textbooks against her body for added warmth and wishes she hadn't lost her gloves. She longs for warmer temperatures, for spring's kiss on the now-naked winter trees lining the streets. Her father, who has sayings for everything, once told her March comes in like a lion, but leaves like a lamb. Today, the lion roars her to numbness. She reminds herself to remember to sew the buttons back on her coat and to possibly snag her mother's gloves.

On Riverside Avenue, she forces herself step by step toward the Inner Harbor, away from Mary Star of the Sea High School, knowing she must endure the cold for another twenty minutes before she reaches her neighborhood. First a piano lesson, then home to change, and then her cashier job at the grocery store where her mother knows the owner and finagled the under-the-table job.

The stack of textbooks provides some protection against the cold air, but her arms ache from the weight. She sets the stack down on a nearby stoop and shivers in her thin coat until she picks them up again. The books hold her coat shut. A few days ago, she asked her mother for a warmer coat, but winter is nearly over, her mother said, adding that she'd get a new one next year. She also asked her mother to sew the missing buttons, which sit in a small, clear cup in her room, back onto her coat.

"You could do it yourself," Ivy said.

Delia felt guilty for asking. She could do it herself if she knew how to sew. She promises herself that she'll figure it out, sew the buttons on as soon as she arrives home. She wishes she could skip work today, go home after her piano lesson and do her homework. She wishes she could skip work forever, but Bird and her mother arranged the whole thing, and the money pays for the piano lesson, something her mother didn't want to pay for anymore. To her mother, going to work was like going to church, except you get paid, and you didn't skip it unless you were dead. Never mind that Bird gives Delia the creeps.

She increases her pace, reaches Montgomery Street, and foregoes her usual stroll through Fed Hill Park, proceeding instead down the steep hill straight to Key Highway, a six-lane avenue. She plans to duck into one of the Harbor Pavilions to warm up, even if it is overrun by tourists. She could walk through both of them to stay warm for the duration all the way to Pratt Street. Usually, the afternoon sunlight dances over the harbor water causing the surface to glitter, but today's weak sun hides its yellow face behind gray clouds, and the harbor waters appear a dull green. The city's skyline, jagged against the colorless sky, casts shadows that look like dinosaur teeth on the pavilion's faded green rooftop.

In her head, Delia focuses on practicing her Shubert to distract her from feeling cold. She imagines the notes and the rhythms. *Everything is music*, her teacher Lucy told her, and advised her to train her ears. To train her ear, she follows Lucy's instructions of listening to the rhythms of all the sounds around her. She listens hard to the sound of her feet hitting the pavement, but her rubber-soled saddle shoes keep her footsteps quiet. At Key Highway, the orange pedestrian light blinks DON'T WALK, and at the curb near the control box, she listens intently for tones and rhythms around her: traffic horns, tugboat blasts, train whistles, seagulls' cries, children's shouts, car and truck engines whizzing east and west along Key Highway. She shuts her eyes and tries to experience the sounds of the world the way Lucy might, and with her eyes shut tight and with intense concentration, she can hear the whirs and clicks of the traffic light controls. She wonders what different things Lucy might hear and "see" with her blindness. Compared to Lucy's trained ear, Delia knows she misses hearing a lot of stuff and wonders what Lucy misses seeing. A few minutes later, when the whirs and clicks of the control sound again and the sounds of moving traffic stop, Delia knows the light has changed and she can cross. When she opens her eyes, she sees that the cars are stopped at the light. She also sees Bird's red delivery car across the street. Inside, Bird waves to her, and a knot forms in her stomach. What's he doing on Key Highway? What's he doing here? Why's he parked in a no-parking zone, his hazard lights blinking in a steady, unbreaking rhythm?

"Delia, do you want a ride home?" he calls across the street, cupping his hand around the side of his mouth like a yodeler.

She hopes none of her school friends will see Bird waving at her. She's tempted. A ride home would be warmer and faster, but she doesn't want to be with Bird.

"No," she shouts, shaking her head, as she crosses toward the other side, where Bird is parked. She walks past his car. "Thanks anyway."

Bird opens the car door and stands, half in, half out of the vehicle. "Come on, Delia, I'll give you a ride. It's too cold for you to walk," he yells.

Passersby probably think he's her father. Delia imagines breaking into a run, but the stack of textbooks in her arms prohibit that. She continues away from Bird's car.

"Later, Bird," she says.

"It'll be nice and warm in the car," he says, now walking beside her.

"I know," she says. "Thanks anyway."

"I have a little prezzie for you," Bird says, his voice sotto voce, almost conspiratorial.

She stops. She doesn't look at him, though she wonders what could possibly top the diamond earrings that have been dangling from her ears since he gave them to her in the store's office. Tempted, she fights the desire to look and keeps her eyes straight in front of her.

"You can give it to me later, Bird," she says. She begins walking. "I like the walk."

"Come on, Delia. Look."

Bird holds a department store package in his outstretched hand.

"There's another, but you have to come with me to get it," he says.

Delia wonders what's in the box. Her arms are full of textbooks, which are holding her coat shut. She stares at the shiny bag.

"It's yours. Take it," he says, smiling. Then he must realize that she can't.

He grabs her stack of textbooks and trades them for the bag. His eyes shine; he's pleased with himself. Delia imagines him jumping up and down like a small child, but he is standing there holding her stack of books, looking earnest. Behind his lips, his white teeth gleam. He carries the stack of textbooks to the car and dumps them onto the back seat.

"Shit, Delia, you're going to break your back with these books," he says, standing by the car. "Come on, now. Get in and open the bag."

In the car, the hem of her school uniform skirt peeks from beneath her coat. Delia adjusts her coat before fastening her seat belt.

"What the fuck is going on with your coat?"

Delia's face burns with embarrassment when she sees Bird staring at her thin coat with its missing buttons. He says nothing, and frowning, he cranks up the heater, blasting it in her direction. She's grateful to be warm. Eyes watering, tears streaming down her face from the change in temperature, she looks as if she's crying as she pulls a rectangular box covered with black and white paper and a turquoise ribbon from the shiny department store bag. Bird jerks the car out of the no-parking zone, clicks off the steady sound of the blinkers, and merges onto Key Highway in the direction of their neighborhood.

Delia unwraps the rectangle and holds a plastic-wrapped, pale yellow box with gold French lettering "Aromatic Elixir."

"Smell it. You'll love it."

She does. The fragrance enchants her. It smells like a musky combination of flowers and spice.

"Thank you!" she says, meaning it, returning the box and the wrapping paper to the bag.

"Wear it now. Go on, spray some on now. You'll smell grown-up," Bird says.

When he stops at the red light on Calvert Street, Delia notices he's in the wrong lane and fails to turn in the direction of their neighborhood. The knot in Delia's stomach returns.

"You missed the turn," she says, pointing to where the car should be going.

"Don't worry, Delia. I told you there's another prezzie. Part two. We're going to get it. It's waiting for you. Just up the street."

"Part two?"

"You'll see. It's a surprise, though I realize now I should have gotten you something else."

"Here," he says, handing her a brown bag from the store filled with fruit. "That's not your second prezzie. That's in case you're hungry."

Delia grabs a large apple from the bag and bites into it, the sweetness of the fruit flooding her mouth, the crispiness just the way she likes it.

"Let me have a bite," Bird says.

Delia winces. She doesn't like sharing food that's not properly cut. She takes another bite and hands it to him.

"You can have it," she says. Her mother has warned her so many times not to share food or drinks with others because of germs, but Bird apparently missed this lesson because he bites the apple without hesitation. Still chewing, he hands it back to her.

"No thanks. You can have it," she says, pushing his arm away.

Bird finishes the apple, tossing the core out the window and wiping his fingers on his pants. She turns and sees through the car's rear window the apple core bouncing and splattering on the street, the car behind them running it over, obliterating it, and is amazed that Bird didn't wait for a trash can to throw it away.

"You're not supposed to litter," she says.

Bird laughs uproariously as if she's just told a fabulous joke. Delia scrunches her face, wondering if it would've been faster to walk back. Then Bird turns onto Light Street again, except now they are further north but traveling south, homeward bound, and Delia begins to relax until he pulls into the parking garage for the Treehouse Apartments, sliding into a spot near the elevators.

"Part two. Come with me," he says.

"Piano lesson in an hour, so is this going to take long?" she asks.

"Just get out and come with me," he says, slamming his car door.

She wonders what part two is doing in this building. In the elevator, which looks fancier than her whole house, Bird stands too close to her. He tries to kiss her on the elevator, but she averts her face. When the doors open, he squeezes her hand and leads her down a long, blue-carpeted hallway with drab, forgettable posters on the walls and silk floral wreaths on many of the doors. Bird unlocks the door to 1329, and they step inside. With its bare walls, curtain-free windows, unstocked kitchen cabinets, and empty refrigerator, the place looks sad and neglected. A cheap glass-top kitchen table and four plastic chairs occupy the dining room. A scale, boxes of plastic bags, mirrors, and razor blades sit on the table. An unmade full-sized bed fills the bedroom, the sheets stained in areas.

"My secret apartment," he says, showing her around.

* * *

Later at home, Delia's mother Ivy arranges raw walnuts atop a white linen cloth on the kitchen table before covering them with an identical cloth. She leans into the table and with a thick rolling pin begins crushing the walnuts, pressing the pin into the cloth as she rolls it back and forth over the linen. Periodically, Ivy checks on the texture of the nuts, moves them around with her fingers, replaces the top linen, and resumes the rolling.

Delia's mother's black, lacquered hair stands tall in a bouffant, wrapped with an orange kerchief. She's wearing makeup, mostly rouge in two perfect circles on her cheeks and dark red lipstick, her signature look. A faded, flour-dusted apron covers a pair of navy blue sweatpants and an oversized T-shirt, and Delia wishes her mother would pay more attention to how she looks. Measuring cups, a bowl of shelled eggs, containers of already sifted and premeasured flour, sugar, milk, a glass of orange juice, a bowl with two oranges, and a bottle of dark rum sit on the counter next to the mixer. Ivy is baking her usual church bake-sale cake, her famous orange, walnut, and rum cake. Delia dislikes the smell of that cake and wonders why her mother never bakes them something simple and plain, something less fancy than orange walnut rum cake, which Delia dislikes anyway.

On the stairs, Delia holds her coat in one hand and the three missing buttons in the other. A towel wrapped like a turban around her head covers her wet hair, which she will need to dry before leaving for work. She's taken an extra-long, extra-hot shower to clean Bird's smell off her skin, but it lingers.

"Ma, can you sew the buttons on my coat while I get dressed for work?"

"Dammit. You see I'm busy," Ivy says. "You can do it," she says, reminding Delia that she said the same thing yesterday.

"But it's just three—"

"You're not a baby. You can sew three buttons," Ivy says. She doesn't look at Delia. Instead, she focuses on the white linen cloth, on pushing the rolling pin to and fro, on baking her stupid cake. Her mother doesn't have to hide the rum bottle when she makes the orange walnut rum cake. Delia wonders how many swigs Ivy has taken. And she doesn't need Ivy to remind her that she's not a baby anymore, especially after being with Bird in his secret apartment.

"You were late from your piano lesson," Ivy says. "You must tell him you're going to be late."

"I already did," Delia says, lying. "Bird already knows I'm going to be late today." Her mouth doesn't seem to want to work properly, and she forces the words out. Another black mark spreads across her soul, joining all the ones that appeared on it while she was in the secret apartment, and she imagines how they all cover her once stain-free, white soul like an oil slick. She wonders if her mother sees something different about her, a shadow following her wherever she goes.

"Get moving then," Ivy says, eyeing the rum bottle.

Delia remembers when she smoked a cigarette with Francie for the first time. They were sitting on the lower steps of the funeral home, a place they thought was safe from prying eyes, but both their mothers knew what they were up to before they returned home. After that, they weren't allowed to be friends anymore, and Ivy beat Delia with both hands. Delia wonders— if someone saw her and Bird at the Treehouse, or walking to the car in the garage, or Bird driving her back and dropping her off a few blocks away from Lucy's house for her piano lesson—would Ivy beat her again?

"You were probably wasting time with that big oaf Fred. Bird told me that Fred hangs around you. Don't let me find out you were with him after your piano lesson, or you're going to be in trouble." Ivy's voice sounded matter-of-fact.

"Why are you talking about Fred like that? You've known him forever," Delia says, knowing that she met up with Fred before the lesson and not after.

"It's different now. You're in high school, and things happen," Ivy says. "Boys that age want different things, things you don't know anything about yet."

Delia bugs out her eyes and smirks. She wants to tell Ivy she knows plenty. "I wasn't with him after the lesson, Ma. Okay? My lesson ran over."

Delia wonders if she's become invisible to her mother. The diamond and gold earrings that Bird gave her shimmer in her ears like giant billboards, and Ivy has not noticed them. She hid the perfume bottle in the back of her underwear drawer along with prezzie number two, a bracelet matching the earrings.

"Bird barred him from coming into the store," Delia says.

"You'd better not be lying, Delia, or there will be hell to pay," her mother says without even a glance at her. Fred walked her to Lucy's house after Bird dropped her off. He carried her books for her. Delia squeezes the three buttons in her hand but imagines throwing them at her mother, whom she fiercely hates at this moment. Ivy empties the now-crushed walnuts into a small glass bowl by shaking them loose from the linen cloths.

"Do we have any needles and thread?" Delia asks.

"In the flatware drawer. Do you have time to sew them on now?"

"Bird said to get there when I get there," Delia says.

He said exactly that when he let her out of the car. Maybe she wouldn't get there at all today. Through her lesson, Delia contemplated not going to work. In the flatware drawer, she finds a spool of burnt-orange thread with a rusty needle poking out of it. The orange thread will clash with her grayish black coat, but she doesn't care. She wants to be warm. Sitting at the kitchen table with the coat, buttons, needle, and thread, she accidentally pricks her index finger with the needle more than once. She struggles to sew a button onto her coat, yelping softly whenever the dull point stabs her finger and wiping the blood droplets on the towel wrapped around her head.

She imagines the statue at school, the beautiful girl with the long, golden hair who plucked out her eyes rather than marry an older man. Delia can't imagine plucking her eyes out to avoid the sensations Bird made her body feel after school, even if she knows it's wrong. Delia's soul gained a new black mark every time Bird thrust himself in and out because she couldn't stop it from feeling good. Her body transformed itself into a wicked, out-of-control thing, humming, groaning, moaning, betraying her with its urge to meet Bird's thrusts and to wrap her legs around his hairy thighs, wanting him to go deeper, faster as if she didn't recognize herself anymore. A part of her likes the way Bird moved inside her as if he were late for a train. Unable to look at him or keep her eyes shut, she studied the cracks on the ceiling above the bed in the secret apartment, hating her body for the pleasure it felt from Bird's fingers, worrying about the state of her soul, imagining it looking as black as Benny Pokino's eyes. Benny, the boy she loved since third grade until she saw him shoplifting from the store.

In the secret apartment, Bird's face scrunched up as if someone stabbed him in the back. He squeezed her tight and groaned; his weight crushed her as she struggled to breathe, and he kept himself inside her until the last possible minute. Later, all through the piano lesson, something leaked out of her into her underpants. When she showered, the crotch of her underwear looked stained with pale yellow. She washed them with shampoo and blow dried them before dropping them into the hamper so Ivy wouldn't see it.

At the kitchen table, Delia completes sewing the first button, the orange thread shouting from the black button. She picks up the second button and begins the process again. Delia notices that her mother has retreated into her own world, perhaps forgetting that Delia is still sitting at the table. Ivy dumps softened butter from its small container into a large mixing bowl and turns on the mixer. She pours sugar into the mixing bowl, a slow stream of white granules, moving it around with a rubber spatula. Delia returns to the button and then smells rum as her mother pours it into a liquid measuring cup. When she looks up at her mom, she catches Ivy taking two quick swigs straight from the bottle. Delia completes the second button and moves on to the third; she glances up and sees Ivy swigging more rum from the bottle. Delia stabs the needle in and out of the cloth, the orange thread growing taut.

"It's time to put the rum away," Delia says, unable to keep the anger out of her voice.

Ivy, who's startled by the sound of Delia's voice, faces Delia with a murderous expression.

"You don't tell me. I tell you. It's time to get your late-to-work ass out of here before I slap you two weeks into next month."

Delia completes the third button before getting up.

"I quit," she yells, just to annoy Ivy, who must have been swigging rum for most of the day because she's drunk. For a moment, Delia misses the mother Ivy once was, the one there for her always, and despises this odd replacement, an obese look-alike with perfectly round circles of rouge on her cheeks and not a clue about anything else.

"Like hell you did," Ivy shouts, lobbing a rubber batter-coated spatula at her.

Delia avoids the spatula winging its way toward her and splattering cake batter everywhere along its trajectory. She doesn't want to be home with a drunk Ivy without her father, who's working. She doesn't want to go to work because she doesn't want to see Bird again. When she leaves the house, she walks across the street to the church rectory and rings the doorbell. The church secretary knows exactly why she's there and lets her in. She calls the store and leaves a message that she won't be in. She then enters the church from the rectory and heads straight for the piano where she's spent many years practicing in the dark, the area illuminated only by dim lights of flickering candles.

HOME BEAUTIFUL

I know that sound. I've made that sound before. It is the rhythmic creaking of an old bed straining when two people make love in it. The sound follows me like a panting, hungry dog. Again.

When the creaking starts, I turn up the stereo to drown it out. But the rhythmic eek-ee-eek-ee-eek-ee-eek-ee always overwhelms the rock and roll blaring from the stereo speakers, and I can't concentrate on anything else.

Josie lives upstairs with her two sons, Sal and Jake, both in their early 30s. I live downstairs with my two daughters, Rachael and JoAnna. The house, divided into two apartments, mine and Josie's, belongs to Josie's brother, who comes once a month on the seventh to collect the rent. The place, a dump, sits across the street from the projects, across the street that serves as an unspoken border between a good and a bad neighborhood, a safe and a crime-ridden neighborhood. Plaster walls in our house blister and peel like sunburned skin. So does the gas-station green paint that covers every room and hallway, except for the walls in our apartment. I call it "gangrene," and I've decorated around it until the color just made me sick. So I have repainted every room in our apartment with a clean, glossy white. My place looks like a sanctuary compared to the rest of the building, and although Josie's brother has promised to reimburse me for the cost of the paint, I'm still waiting.

JoAnna, Rachael, and I love our neighbors. They don't congregate outside our front door all night long, playing loud music. They don't fight, bang doors, or entertain a never-ending flow of visitors like the roughnecks from our old neighborhood, like the roughnecks across the street. They're quiet. They're old ladies, widows, a trio of them. My parents are gone, and I don't have other relatives. I haven't seen my ex since Rachael was three, and he hasn't sent a dime in child support.

The old ladies and I trade for dinners. I drive them to the Broadway market to buy fish or to the supermarket for groceries or to Highlandtown to the salon where they all go once a week for their "sets, hon." When I can, I take them to doctors' offices and wait until they are done to drive them back, and they babysit for me for free.

They sometimes visit for a couple of hours, telling me stories about the neighborhood. Over coffee or tea and cookies and cakes, they relive special moments when their now-dead husbands were courting them. They repeat the same stories, but I don't mind. They remind me of my Grandma Carolina. Before Grandma Carolina died, she and I spent hours in her kitchen. She taught me how to grate cheese and cook simple dishes, and she let me wear her beautiful red shoes. Grandma Carolina's stories were about how she and Pop survived "the Big War," how food was so scarce even for dogs, reduced to chewing leather shoes they found in the rubble of bombed-out buildings, how Pop had to turn his bakery over to Nazis and deliver by bicycle bread to their camps, how he stole a case of sauerkraut from them, and when he brought it home, how it stank when Grandma Carolina opened the cans, and how they threw it away, thinking it had rotted. Grandma Carolina crinkled her nose at the smell of sauerkraut all those years later, much the same way Mealie crinkles her nose when she sits in my kitchen and the creaking starts.

"Asia, what da hell is dat noise?" She stares at the ceiling as if the answer would suddenly appear in the air.

"Who knows?" I say with a shrug. I suggest we go outside to see if Blondina or Rosa or both of them are sitting on the corner bench. They provide a distraction to the creaking sounds. Better yet, Blondina and Rosa distract *me* from thinking about the creaking sounds. Talking, speculating, or thinking about them is the last thing I want to do, so I get Mealie out of the apartment before the creaking speeds up and before the thump-thump-thump sounds of the old bed banging against the wall start. How in the world would I explain *that* if I couldn't explain the creaking?

I want to move, but I can't because the place is cheap, and still, I can barely make the rent sometimes. So we live with the quirks. Like the creepy creaking. Like the dining room ceiling. Every time the toilet upstairs overflows or Josie's mental son Jake overflows the tub, rust-colored water comes rushing down into my dining room like sea into a sinking ship.

"It's leaking again. It's leaking!" I scream up through the ceiling while shoving the dining room table out of the way of the cascading water and hollering for JoAnna or Rachael to bring a bucket. And I can almost picture that 300-pound demented fool upstairs, grinning like a giant ghoul, his bandana-ed head tilted to the side, clapping his big, outstretched arms, mumbling, "Jesus Christ, son of a beetch, son of a beetch, shit-shit-shit" while watching as the water pours over the side of the tub. I can almost hear him laughing through his nose like a sneaky cartoon character, and when the water leaks, I hate his stupid grin, the menace of him, and his fat cow of a mother.

Why does Josie allow him in there by himself? Why does she allow him to fool around with the spigots, anyway? Couldn't she get it through his thick skull that backing up the toilet and overflowing the tub is a no-no? Even a two-year-old understands the word "no" and understands cause and effect. Jake knows too. I swear he does. He understands simple commands, and when his mother or Sal talk to him, he seems to be able to connect the dots. He doesn't say anything but the same string of curse words over and over. He lets it be known what he wants.

The once-a-week water seepage has caused a large, unsightly hole in the water-stained dining room ceiling, a giant black eye staring down at me from above. The place is drafty. Two winters after having complained about the drafts of cold air coming in through the rotting wooden windows, Josie's brother finally came to fix them.

His solution? The windows are now painted shut, forcing me to buy an air-conditioner at a yard sale and have it installed into the dining room wall because we couldn't open any of the windows in summer. I think about hiring a workman to come in to fix it but realize it would be costly and pointless because of Jake upstairs. Josie won't or can't stop him from flooding the bathroom once a week.

"How can she stop him after the hole is fixed?" Josie's brother Philip stares at it one month on the seventh when he's collecting the rent.

"That's her problem. Mine's the hole in the ceiling. I need it fixed," I say.

"No point. The cause ain't structural or from the pipes. The cause is human," Philip says.

"The cause is your nephew. How about you fix the hole and read the riot act to Josie about teaching that lump of a son of hers to shower instead?"

"I'll see what I can do," Philip says, stuffing the envelope with the rent check into his back pocket.

It's a roof. A roof over our heads—even a leaky one—in such a good neighborhood is better than no roof at all or a place in a crappy one where drug dealers ply their trade. After the Charmless Prince vanished, we lived in worse places for twice the rent, and Josie's brother hasn't raised the rent much over the years. He tries. I point to the hole in the ceiling.

"When will that be fixed?" I ask. "How about we revisit the rent thing when the hole is fixed?"

Still, I daydream about more money and apartments with dishwashers, intact ceilings, and no Jake. Mostly, no Jake. Haphazard freelance income lends itself to daydreaming and raises adaptability to high art.

I'm a graphic designer, though honestly, I haven't been working much. My client base is drying up gradually. I need to get a day job. This I also know, but I can't bring myself to answer want ads, to rush the girls and me out of the house every day, to give up my independence from the nine to five, the intellectual challenge of a variety of projects for a variety of clients. My office—a Mac computer, a light table, a printer, a bookshelf, a wax machine for the pasteup work, and a small white desk—sits in the corner of the dining room—the farthest point away from where the ceiling leaks.

Aside from the dining room, there are two slightly smaller bedrooms, a living room, and a full bathroom off the kitchen— and the highlight, a roomy backyard large enough to fit a large plastic pool in summer. Josie's second-floor apartment has a small porch that overlooks the yard. Her small porch acts as a roof for our porch, where we store onions and potatoes in a three-tiered metal hanging basket, some outdoor toys, and my plant collection. A garden borders the yard where JoAnna, Rachael, and I usually plant flowers in one section and vegetables in another. The yard is peaceful. In the summertime, we cook outside on a dime-store hibachi and eat dinner outside on our small picnic table next to the plastic swimming pool.

Sometimes when we're swimming, Jake sits on the upstairs porch, grinning like a rabid ghoul and gawking down at us. The girls call him Mr. Beast. Mr. Beast stamps his huge foot continuously, mumbling, "Son of a beetch, Jesus Christ, shit-shit-shit" under his breath, loud enough for us to hear. He leans over the porch wall and leers down at us. That's when we get out of the pool and scurry back inside, worried that his weight and stomping will cause the porch to cave in.

I never have a hard time getting my girls out of the pool then because we are all afraid of Mr. Beast. Sometimes he's grinning quietly when he gawks down at us. JoAnna usually feels his presence first. She'll swim over to me and quietly whisper, "Mr. Beast" in my ear, then in Rachael's. Then when we look up, he's there, standing on the porch, wearing that stupid grin, watching us as we get out, gather our towels from the picnic table, and scurry inside. Damn him. Mr. Beast.

When we first moved in, Josie said he was born normal, that a three-day-long high fever left him that way, that she didn't know what caused the fever, that her family was cursed. The fever may have fried his brain, but his body matured into that of an unusually large man—Mr. Beast easily towers over all of us, including Sal. Even with his husky build, I bet he's close to six-four. His mother considers him as a perpetual child, speaking to him as if he were a toddler, referring to him as "Jakie-boy." And I can see it sometimes, too, flashes of innocent facial expressions under his shock of curly, brown hair, which his mother keeps long and full rather than barbered like a grown man.

When they're outside on the corner bench, "Jakie-boy" sometimes licks her face with his fat pink tongue, and the old-timers look away disgusted. Josie just sits there with her arms folded over her ample breasts and acts as if it is all normal, childish behavior. She ignores "Jakie-boy," who touches her constantly. I've never known any toddler who does that, but maybe it's normal for the impaired. And maybe he gains real satisfaction stringing multicolored beads onto shoestrings, if that's how he spends a portion of his day. And maybe chickens can fly, but when he stands on that porch, his face loses any hint of innocence, and when he gawks down at the girls and me when we're in the pool, his expression raises the hackles on the back of my neck because it doesn't look like a toddler's gaze to me.

Compared to Mr. Beast, Josie's oldest son, Sal, looks like a wimpy man with Elvis gone-wrong hair, but he is the only one who controls that giant idiot brother of his—something he proved about six months ago when I let my guard down.

The girls and I were carrying groceries into the apartment when one of them left the door ajar. I told JoAnna to run her bathwater, while Rachael and I put the frozen vegetables away. Rachael was looking for a missing box of butter, while I stacked the fat cans of crushed tomatoes on the countertop.

"Son of a beetch, Jesus Christ, shhhit-shhhit-shhhit." Jake, his head tilted, stood in the middle of the living room. Grinning stupidly, he walked slowly through the dining room toward us. "Shit-shit-shit." Eyes as big as moons, Rachael looked up from her search, then stood up, dropping the grocery bag.

Fingertips in her mouth, she whispered, "Mr. Beast."

"Rachael, go into the bathroom with JoAnna. Lock the door behind you. Stay there until I tell you to. Go now!" I said through clenched teeth.

Rachael's little body darted behind me. Relief flooded my senses when the bathroom lock clicked, but my stomach somersaulted and my head pounded. I heard the girls whimpering through the bathroom door.

"Go home, Jake," I shouted. "Your mother's looking for you."

Grinning, he moved forward, toward me in the kitchen. Extending his arms as if he wanted to touch me, he cursed as he moved one gigantic leg in front of the other. He stuck out his tongue, and I could tell he wanted to lick my face the way he licked Josie's.

"Go home. Go back upstairs, home, home, home!" I screamed, hoping that Josie would hear me. There was nowhere to run, except out the back door, which leads to a dead end. "Go home, Jake," I yelled and looked around the kitchen for something to hit him with and spotted the wooden meat mallet in the jar of oversized utensils on the counter near the stacked tomato cans. I grabbed it and braced myself against the counter, waiting for him to get close enough. He placed his huge hands on my head, and, pinning me against the counter with his body, he stepped closer and attempted to lick my face. I could feel he was hard against me, and I pushed him back. He didn't move, so I hit his side with the meat mallet. He looked stunned.

"JAKE!" Sal's voice boomed just as Jake's expression changed into anger. Maybe no one had hit him before.

"Jake, come on. We need to go upstairs now," he said. Still looking angry, with his eyebrows linked and his lips stretched over his teeth, Jake turned toward Sal. Sal grabbed his brother by the elbow and led him outside.

Shaking, I dropped the meat mallet and slid down the cabinets to the floor. I could tell that Jake was angry that Sal had interrupted him. His eyes, flashing anger or rage, held mine for an instant before Sal led him away. I kicked the door shut, and my fingers shook as they fumbled with the locks.

"It's okay now, girls. You can come out now," I yelled through the bathroom door. The three of us sank to the kitchen floor in a huddle and rocked.

* * *

Maybe in some aspects Mr. Beast really is like a small child, given his mysterious intelligence level and his mysterious handicap. Maybe Josie still mourns the normal child lost to a high fever. Maybe that fever killed a part of her when it maimed Jake's brain. No matter.

Those damned creaking sounds continue. Working at home makes it hard to escape them, especially deadline time when a poster or a brochure or a magazine design is due. I concentrate on my X-Acto knife and on the light table, where 50 tiny drawings, all of shoes, are piled for a poster project due in two days. The stereo doesn't drown out the rhythmic eek-ee-eek-ee-eek-ee. Lately, the sounds interfere with my work schedule, and I've been working late into the night after the girls are in bed. Sometimes they carry on at night, and then I can't sleep even with the radio on. They pick up frequency after Jake's attack.

"Come on, girls, let's go take a swim." JoAnna and Rachael are playing with their collection of Barbie dolls in the living room and jump up and down, happy for the unexpected water play. I want to get them out of the house before they ask questions about the creaking noise again. I let them leave Barbie's considerable wardrobe littered all over the living room floor because I don't know how to explain the noise and want to escape it. Last time they asked, I told them Josie sits in a rocking chair and knits, or maybe Mr. Beast jumps on his bed. They laugh.

"Can we jump on the bed, too?" Rachael asks.

We put on bathing suits, grab towels, and head out the back door to the yard. Playing in the sun-warmed pool, we don't worry about Mr. Beast gawking at us from the porch or stamping his huge paws, because he's never outside on the porch when the creaking goes on. And neither is Josie.

Sometimes I imagine flipping him the bird, but I don't. He's always with her, like a shadow. Sometimes he places his mammoth hand with his fingers spread over the top of her head. Sometimes he fondles her nose as if it were a hook on her face, and her cheeks with his fat fingers, letting them sit there. Arms folded across her bosom, Josie says nothing, does nothing, as if it weren't happening when he licks her face. When he sits next to her like that, he seems content enough listening to his mother commenting on the weather and what the neighbors are doing. I look at Jake's eyes, and they look as if they understand. Jake understands a lot more than his mother lets on. Or maybe Josie isn't aware that Jake understands? She sits, her arms crossed over her huge tits, while Jake, his bandana-ed head tilted to the side, occupies the bench's edge. He grins at women who walk by the bench where they sit together every summer night. His mother simply ignores what he does to her.

And though everyone else pretends not to, they watch him carefully. When Jake sees a woman he likes, he honks loudly like a goose and mumbles, "Son of a beetch, Jesus Christ, shit-shit-

shit" loudly under his breath. He stamps one of his huge feet, and, arms stretched outward, he claps his chubby hands. Sometimes he leaps up from the bench and begins pacing up and down the length of the sidewalk, next to the brick wall of the building next door. Sometimes he smacks the brick wall with his hand and honks loudly with each blow.

"JAKE! Stop!" Josie yells, only when he gets extremely loud. She doesn't look at him when she yells and simply bellows the words into the air in front of her. Sometimes he stops and returns to his seat on the edge of the bench. Most times he doesn't. Ranting, he just keeps right on looking at the women and honking or stamping his foot loudly on the pavement. And he sits on the bench, annoying the neighbors with his honking, stamping, clapping, cursing, and sticking his tongue out with his mouth wide open most of the night before somebody tells her that he's being a nuisance.

"I do my best with him," she says.

As soon as he starts, JoAnna, Rachael, and I edge away from the bench. Sal's gone a lot lately. Who in the hell is going to stop him? His vacant-eyed mother?

"That Jake is something else, ain't he?" says Mealie. We all leave after Jake starts an outburst. "Ain't you afraid living in the same building?" She shakes her head.

I don't answer.

"I don't know why Josie don't do something with him. At least she could send him to a special school during the day. Then he won't be around so much of the time, and he can learn something useful," Rosa says.

"Terreeible," Blondina says.

I think about those creaking sounds. "He's her life," I say, finally. "He's her child. Just not right up in his head."

"You live there. Maybe you can talk some sense to her about a doin' something wit dat boy of hers. We sure tried. Over the years, we tried, and each time, she gets mad at us. He's gonna end up doing something terrible one of these days," Blondina says.

"She ain't no spring chicken anymore. What's gonna happen to him if something happens to her? Somebody's gotta get her to think ahead. Especially with Sal working and going out now," Mealie says.

"Her husband used to take the boy out at night and give her a break. It's hard for her, I know. Asia, can't you say something in nice way? She might listen to you," Blondina says.

They want me to say something because I'm the outsider, not someone who grew up with Josie, who knew her husband, who knew Jake before the fever robbed him of his wits.

"Isn't this something you had better do yourselves?"

"It might sound better coming from you—a stranger," Mealie says.

"I don't think so," I say, hurrying up with the girls to the house.

That night, when JoAnna and Rachael undress for their baths, they pretend they are Mr. Beast but act like Godzilla instead.

The next day the creaking begins after lunch. We go outside to the pool until the sunshine falls. We get out of the pool for dinner, though I, feeling annoyed that my shoe poster will take an all-nighter to finish in time for the deadline, cover the pool with the blue tarp. Inside, the girls change into dry clothes, and I start dinner.

That's when we hear the loud knocking at the door. The rapid succession of the knocks makes it sound urgent. I think of Mr. Beast right away, banging on the door with his fat hands. My stomach jumps. What if he has decided that gaping at us over the porch wall isn't enough anymore?

"Who is it?" I ask through the door. My heart pounds.

"It's Josie. I need to talk to you right away. It is an emergency."

"Is Jake with you?"

"No. He's upstairs. I don't want him to hear what I have to say. Open the door."

I let her in. It's the first time she's been in my apartment since we moved in, and I can tell she's surprised.

"It's nice in here—so bright," she says, looking around. I motion her to sit down while I lock the door. "You got it fixed up pretty nice in here, Asia," she says, "just like *Home Beautiful.*"

"Thanks." I turn around to see JoAnna and Rachael peeking out of their room.

"I got to talk to you about something important. It's Jake."

"Oh?" I say, wondering if she is going to tell me about that creaking bed. I feel my face flush. "What about him?"

"Blondina, Mealie, and Rosa called this morning. They said nobody likes Jake. That he's dangerous and they want me to put him in a home. I can't do that to poor Jake. I just can't."

"Maybe they're looking out for you, too," I say. "Maybe they want you to think about the future. Jake needs a lot of attention, and you could use a break, couldn't you?" I ask.

"NO!" she says. "How can you say that? Would you put one of your children in a home if she was like Jake? Jake has a home, and it's with me."

"What if something happens to you?"

"Sal will take care of him then," she says.

"What if Sal doesn't want to?"

"Just like I don't have a choice, Sal doesn't either. Jake is not a dog. He's a boy. My boy."

"Others may see him as a man," I say. "He's big enough to be a man."

"The fever done that to him. Left him like a three-year-old. In his mind, he's only three."

I picture Josie sitting on the bench without Jake licking her face. I picture her wearing something besides a snap-on housedress and dirty terry cloth slippers. I picture her with red lipstick and big hair, walking to the harbor with Mealie, Rosa, and Blondina.

Josie stands up. She looks around the apartment, and for the first time since I've known her, I can see wheels turning in her head.

"Families take care of each other no matter what. I ain't putting Jake in a home," she says. "Jakie-boy is not dangerous. He ain't going to attack ANNNNY body!" Josie yells and gestures with her entire arm. "Mealie, Rosa, and Blondina are wrong ... dead wrong ... because, because ... well, because I do what needs to be done. Understand?" Her eyes bulge in her crimson face.

"But Jake attacked me!"

"No. No, he did not. He was just down here trying to visit with you, but Sal told me you just screamed at him to go home. You didn't even give him a chance to have a simple visit. You could've given him some cookies and milk and invited him to sit down and watch TV with your girls or something nice like that. You ain't nice."

"Sal lied to you," I say. "Jake did attack me. He pinned me against the counter, and I hit him with a meat mallet. But he wouldn't get off me. So you're wrong, Josie. And he isn't a three-year-old anymore. He's a man."

Josie moves toward the door. "If those ladies come here and ask you anything, you'll tell them. You'll tell them that everything is peaceful here, and that Jake ain't a problem."

"Are you threatening me?"

"I'm protecting my child from vicious people like you and those three busybodies," she says. "You got a pretty nice apartment here. It could get much nicer, too." She gestures widely and points to the hole in the dining room ceiling. "I'll have my brother come over and fix that."

I don't answer.

"Rents around here and in other nice neighborhoods ain't getting lower, you know. Another apartment round here'll cost you a pretty penny, a lot of pretty pennies. You can't touch a place downtown for what you've been paying. Just keep that in mind, Asia dear." Josie waddles to the door, grunts in disgust when she spies all the locks. "Who you trying to keep out?" The door slams behind her like an exclamation point.

The girls and I eat dinner. JoAnna plays with her noodles.

"What's going to happen, Ma?" she asks, looking worried. "Will we have to move?"

"I don't know," I say.

"I wish Mr. Beast was dead," says Rachael.

I wince. The next day we stay inside. We avoid the convenience store. We avoid the bench with the old ladies. We swim in the morning hours. Jake sits on the porch. Tongue sticking out from between his fat lips, he leans over the wall, stares down at us. He mumbles, "Son of a beetch, Jesus Christ, shit-shit-shit." He's grinning, and I know his huge paw is going to start crashing down on the tile-topped porch fence. Just as the sound of the first crash echoes off the porch floor, we flee inside without bothering to grab our towels off the picnic table. Who do I hate more? Jake or Josie? Or myself?

The girls change into dry clothes, leaving their swimming suits on the bathroom floor. Ten minutes later, the crashing sound outside stops, and the creaking begins. Again.

I turn on the stereo, but the rhythmic eek-ee-eek-ee-eek-ee competes with the music.

In the dining room, I look up at the ceiling and imagine how it will look without the hole. I wonder if a new dishwasher will help drown out the creaking sounds. I picture new, oversized kitchen cabinets and a new ceramic black-and-white tiled floor in there and new windows. I imagine new plaster on the walls and delicate plaster reliefs of leaves, vines, and flowers decorating the ceiling. I picture a new sofa. My mind's eye has transformed the dump into a layout from *Home Beautiful*.

Eek-ee-eek-ee-eek-ee. The creaking sounds wilder, faster, louder, louder than the stereo. I remember Jake gaping, his head tilted as he advanced into our shabby kitchen during his "visit," and wonder if he grins like that when he's upstairs on the creaking bed. With Josie.

Eek-ee-eek-ee-eek-ee. I shudder. We can't escape into a loud stereo or hide in new, oversized cabinets if Jake visits again. And the beauty of delicate plaster reliefs of leaves, vines, and flowers cannot calm frayed nerves or protect little girls or unlock imprisoned minds or free misguided, imprisoned souls from their self-imposed hell.

I snap off the stereo. The creaking old bed thumps against the wall, my teeth clenching with every boom. Finally, I hate this life. More than the pair in the apartment above me. Enough to reach for the phone book and flip to the blue-edged section with government listings and dial.

DADDY'S SHOES

The shoes—covered by a light layer of dust—must have sat in neat rows arranged on the shelves in the overflow closet for the last few years. He must have been too sick in the recent years to clean and polish them, as was his habit. Some of the shoes, perhaps the ones he'd worn most recently, shimmered with a sheen from a distant polishing, despite the dust. Shoes with tassels decorating the toe caps, with buckles, no longer shiny silver and glittery gold, some squared-toed, others with a rounded point; all bore the names of Italian designers—Gucci, Balenciaga, Dolce & Gabbana—and other names, unrecognizable as designers but definitely Italian, older, ordinary shoes, outdated pairs he must have bought during his few trips back home to see his parents and siblings. He must have never tossed out or given away a single pair, and he must have rotated wearing them so that they all appeared gently worn.

Organized by color—browns with browns, blacks with blacks, tans with tans, whites with whites—some pairs appeared worn with uneven heel tops, creased leather throats, and worn tongues, while others looked nearly new. A few never-worn pairs still retained price tags showing prices marked down several times from sales. Several pair of sneakers lined the opposite shelf; their worn toe caps faced forward like soldiers, untied shoestrings loose in their eyelets, frayed here and there. He must have attached the electric revolving belt holder on the wall near the light switch so that he could easily match a belt to the shoes he would wear. He touched them all, placing them neatly in color-coordinated rows on shelves he built himself. He would not have included his work boots and shoes, which he kept in the basement.

He must have been proud of the sheer abundance of these shoes after having told stories of an impoverished childhood with only one pair to his name to wear at any given time, whether they fit or not. He must have worked hard to never be without a pair of shoes. He once spoke of how, as a teenager, he accidentally dropped one of his shoes into one of the harbors of his birth city on an island and was forced to dive into the water to rescue it, not for fear of the beating he'd get at home for having lost a shoe, but from the terror of having no shoes to wear to school.

I had come to pack his clothes, to help my mother sort through his garments, when I came across the closet chock full of shoes on the third floor, where she couldn't go because of a steep staircase. He must have been proud of this shoe closet, concrete evidence that he would never again be without a pair of shoes. He must have polished them all methodically, even after he stopped going to places where he could wear them and found himself restricted to running shoes, sandals, and slippers, housebound footwear after a series of ischemic strokes forced him to stop driving. In the basement, I retrieve black contractor garbage bags and sprint up three flights of stairs with them. I'll drop the shoes into the bags to be passed along to the non-profit for homeless veterans, down-on-their-luck men who once cleaned, polished, and buffed boots as part of their military lives, men who knew how to coax these Italian beauties back to their previous luster, a dead man's shoes to become useful for other men's unshorn feet.

I stand in his shoe closet, marveling at the collection of stylish footwear, seemingly forgotten during his battle with strokes that killed his brain centimeter by centimeter and the dementia they bought. The shoes looked lonely and abandoned under the thin film of dust, remnants of a life now passed. He must have understood that the strokes would steal his memory by degrees, a gradual erasing of his personality, his pride, his power of basic choice as to what shoes to wear each day and why not wear stylish dress shoes under jeans or pajamas.

I considered carefully dusting them before dropping them into the black garbage bags but chose not to. Instead, I peered into each shoe, searched for gems hidden inside, as he was known for hiding things in unusual places, before placing them on the floor and gingerly stepping into his treasured footgear as I once did as a small child. And now, even as an adult, his shoes remain too big.

A NUT JOB

Let's get something straight right at the beginning: I don't make trouble but I don't take it lying down either. I give zero fucks about what happens to people who piss on a rope and try to tell me it's raining. Far as I'm concerned, they get what they deserve, and I can tell you something else: The harpy next door got what she deserved. The battle with the harpy next door started with that goddamn tree, the one over there, the black walnut tree. Let me tell you, those trees can drive anyone to the brink of hell and back. It drove both me and my neighbor to hell and back. Its branches severely overhung my yard, dropping large walnuts from high up in the air—twenty or thirty feet or so—like mini bombs, silent explosions all over my yard that left ugly stains all over the place. Only luck prevented them from knocking my head off and killing me. What if a kid—let's say, for shits and giggles, one of my grands—if my kids weren't assholes and actually came around with my grands—was playing in my yard when those suckers dropped?

They pocked my yard with indentations and holes, making it hard to mow. I spent a fucking hour picking all those damn nuts up before mowing. It robbed my yard of sunlight, killed my herbs, my prized roses, my fig tree. But that damned black walnut tree overgrew wild into my yard because that old harpy refused to prune it. If you looked up, all you'd see was that damn tree, a canopy wider than the moon. No sky. Not a speck of sky anywhere in my yard. At night my yard looked darker, creating a safety issue. Anyone could've climbed down that tree into my yard and robbed my house.

At sixty-nine, I'm not about to let some damn harpy's negligence put me at risk of being robbed when I'm supposed to be retired. I'm like that Johnny Cash tune: I've been everywhere. And I've done a boatload of things. I taught French at a Philly elementary school back in the late '60s before quitting and getting the hell out Dodge. I can tell you the education system wasn't worth a damn then with all the stupid rules, and that was fifty years ago, and the same goes for now. Nothing changed. Different faces, same old story.

I moved to Baltimore in the late '70s to work as a cop in the police department there. After a fourteen-year run, those motherfuckers sacked me when I was the best damned cop on the force. Stupid rules again aimed at the sheeple tripped me up. I confiscated an illegal automatic firearm from an informant. So what, I didn't turn it in right away? Doesn't mean I intended to keep it. I just didn't get around to submitting it to the Evidence Room fast enough for the Brass. I do admit to hanging out of my patrol car window waving a medieval sword, threatening to stab perps in the ass if they got out of line. Yes, I did that on the city's west side, the worst sector with the highest crime rate, but those pork chops respected me and kept their hoodlum asses inside when I was on duty. Nobody had a sense of humor back then. The Brass Asses didn't like it. They spread the news that I was a nut job—do I look like a nut job to you? The stats spoke for me. Hoodlums and pork chops didn't want to be out on the streets on my shifts. Some numbnuts—probably a pinko commie bleeding heart liberal—complained about due process, civil rights, and all that, and dropped a dime on me to the Internal

Investigation Department. Those IID motherfuckers had a field day. I do admit to mocking a captain who couldn't speak English properly. How the hell do you get to be captain if you can't speak proper English? How the hell was I supposed to know that he had a speech impediment and just wasn't a stupid fuck, saying "pacific" instead of "specific?" Let's just say the corrupt-assed PD and I agreed to a mutual parting of the ways down there in that podunk mini city that thought it was a German Shepherd when it was only a Chihuahua.

Even before I went to podunk Baltimore, thanks to my parents I possessed a wider view of the world than most of those bozos in that teeny-tiny city with their stupid, ignorant accent of which they're so proud. My squad, those stupid fucks, would say "pockeybooks" for "purses" over the radio. I'm serious as a heart attack.

After the PD, I poked around awhile, trying out this and that: sold insurance but didn't make a cent; worked as a cook in a country restaurant for not enough money, especially for a guy with two bachelor's degrees; and then I went back to school to become a nurse. In 'Nam they called me "Doc," so becoming a civilian ER nurse, a piece of cake. When on the PD, I showed my squad my left arm, scarred from my wrist to above my elbow, a gunshot wound. From 'Nam. Fighting gooks. Can't feel anything hot with my left hand to this day, which suited me fine, especially when cooking. I'll let you on in a little secret: I've never been to 'Nam even though I told everyone, including the batty dame next door, that I spent time in the Army.

Regarding that tree, the old harpy dished up enough excuses to feed an army of hopes. She loved that tree so much, she couldn't bear trimming one branch, which might be how it came to overtake my yard. I got tired of her neglect and sick of listening to her billions of excuses. I got a chainsaw and started sawing from the bottom. She heard the chainsaw and came running out. By this time, I had already sawed off a good portion of the bottom branches. When she realized I wasn't going to stop chopping those branches, she called the cops.

The limb—thick and fat with age—required serious effort, and God damn, my mood turned lousy because even with a chainsaw, it proved to be hard fucking work. Two Boy-Scout cops arrived. They looked twelve years old, playing dress-up in their daddy's clothes, and when they hollered up to me from the harpy's yard, I ignored them and just kept sawing. I knew, and they knew, they can't do a fuckin' thing about my trimming the overhanging nuisance branches trespassing on my property.

"What's going on, Mr. Thorne?" one of them shouted above the noise of the saw.

What a stupid thing to say. Obviously, what was going on looked plain as day with me up on a ladder sawing those branches off.

"Nothing to see here, boys. You can move along now."

"Maybe you can shut that thing off, and we can find a better way to resolve this," the other one said.

After waiting for months for that harpy to trim her damn nuisance tree, resolving the issue, in my mind, translated to cutting it back to the property line.

"Why?" I asked, climbing down the ladder.

Tweedledee and Tweedledum shrugged.

"It would be more neighborly," Tweedledee finally said.

"Noted. Material for the circular file. Thanks for dropping by, boys," I said. I climbed up the ladder and turned the chainsaw back on.

Months ago, when I rang that old harpy's doorbell to complain about the tree branches, she shut the door in my face. Never met a ruder, more disagreeable woman in my entire life. Always a shrew—complaining about one thing or another—after her husband kicked the bucket, she specialized in being a bitch. She could have snagged herself a new man, one who would take care of the damn tree. Her sour personality and attitude worked against her. Sending her a bill for services rendered crossed my mind. I tossed offending limbs over the fence into her yard on the other side of the cops, the unripe green hulls of the nuts quivering on the branches.

"Whoa, Mr. Thorne," Tweedledum said.

I kept sawing. My hands began to cramp from clenching the weight of the saw, forcing me to take a small break and flex my fist. I turned it off. The old harpy dragged an aluminum ladder behind her that she leaned against the fence separating our yards. Tweedledee and Tweedledum explained what I already knew: Nuisance overhanging branches can be pruned by the property owner of the yard in which they're trespassing. *What was the bigger nuisance, the tree or the harpy?* I wondered.

Tweedledee and Tweedledum moved on because the harpy refused to understand the concept that I can cut the branches in my yard all the way down to the property line, marked by the fence.

"Mr. Thorne, I thank you to leave my magnificent tree alone," she said, her mouth barely moving, as if she was sucking on marbles. Plain as the nose on your face, she considered herself superior without knowing anything about me.

"You're murdering my tree. A beautiful and majestic life form," she said, waving her arm theatrically in circular motions.

"And please stop tossing those branches over the fence. Someone could get hurt."

Who would get hurt? I wondered. She lived alone. She didn't even own a pet. She climbed up her ladder to tell me this in a scolding voice. Well, fuck her.

"I'm returning your own shit back to you."

At this point, I sawed off many of the thinner limbs that had extended their fingers into my yard as if they wanted to pluck something out of it. The heavier, thicker ones extended their arms into my yard, looking ready to capture one of my cats, which never go outside.

"You're destroying my tree!" she shouted. "It'll die! You're butchering it!"

"It's destroying my yard. Look at all those indentations in the ground. It looks polka-dotted."

"I never complain about your cats," she said. "They ruin my rosebushes, dig up my herb garden, and shit in my seed beds."

My cats never go out. They stay inside, safe from chicken hawks, safe from foxes, safe from coyotes, and safe from poisonous people like the harpy who probably sees them sitting in my windows, plotting against them. I turned the chainsaw back on to finish off another branch, tossing it over the fence. Then I thought about it and turned off the saw so she could hear me loud and clear.

"My cats don't go outside. Ever."

"Do you specialize in being a dick? Did you take special how-to-be-a-dick classes?"

Her eyes, twin blue chips, glared at me from her prune face, no doubt dried up from all the sun beaming into her yard, which her tree robbed from mine.

"How kind of you to notice," I said, forgetting that my short sleeves exposed my scarred arm, its length and depth looking like a white river and its tributaries. Part of me for more than half my life, I forgot about its initial effects on someone seeing it for the first time. Gunshot wound. 'Nam. All that.

"No doubt some brave woman somewhere who got tired of your bullshit did that," she said, pointing to the exposed scar. "Stabbed your sorry ass. Too bad she missed anything vital." She climbed up a few rungs of her ladder and started pitching hard, green walnut hulls at me.

"Maybe if you had a man in your life, you'd have a better attitude. Maybe you need a good boner to set you right," I said, tossing more limbs into her yard.

Her face turned crimson with anger, and I knew I must have hit a nerve.

It was true: I got shot. But not in 'Nam. It was also true a woman shot me but not how the harpy thought. Those 'Nam stories about taking and retaking Hamburger Hill? Also true. They happened. But not to me. I read every book about 'Nam I could find and then combined and retold stories to my squad when I was a cop while those fuckers feasted on my beef stroganoff, pilaf, and beer. Stories about gooks and Bouncing Betties, stories of calling in air strikes on gooks, about Agent Orange stripping foliage clean, about "doctoring" wounded before loading them up on helicopters, about guts hanging out of the dead and beautiful Mama-sans. Nobody doubted my stories, regardless of what job I held. Not one of the dumb fucks at any job ever bothered looking up anything, or they'd have discovered that I lived in Quebec City, Canada, during the war, finishing college at Laval University after getting tossed from the military one in Philly after I got shot and after the draft notice fell into my parents' mail slot. Marching in dress grays and fighting mock battles on a military college campus and marching into combat anywhere consisted of two different kinds of marching. I'd gone to 'Nam, no problem, but my parents embraced a different notion—one that included me taking over my dad's company, which I desperately wanted to avoid. I loved wearing the dress grays, the light-blue trousers of the military college's uniform. I can still fit into it. Maybe if those fuckers at the military college hadn't expelled me in sophomore year, my life would have unfolded differently. Maybe I would have shipped out to 'Nam and died there, or been one of those poor bastards struggling with PTSD, homeless and addicted, kicked to the curb by a country that sent them there to die but killed them in other ways instead when they came home.

I got expelled along with another cadet. We commandeered a ferryboat that crossed the river bisecting the town. We suffered a small accident—not with the ferry but with a small derringer, a .22 caliber that I gave to my date to hold in her purse after the Coast Guard boarded the boat and ended our adventure. It proved to be a helluva joyride. Yes, other passengers were on board but nobody got hurt. How hard is it to pilot a ferryboat across a river, for Pete's sake? I gave my date the gun—a tiny thing with pearl handles—because I knew I'd be in less trouble with it safely hidden in her purse. Only nineteen at the time, I was a kid. I still own the gun, a true beauty, after a huge legal battle that my parents and I waged to get it back. My date, whom I never saw again after that night, had not seen or held a gun before, and especially not one as pretty as that pearl-handled derringer, so small it fit in her hand like a toy. Instead of dropping it into her purse, she held it, admired it, and when the ferryboat lurched due to my friend's inexperience as a ferry pilot, she accidentally shot a .22 into my left arm. Small-caliber bullets do a lot of damage.

It took a long time to recover, a shit ton of surgeries, but my arm functions normally thanks to my parents' money. The doc gave me the misshapen bullet, which I kept for a while but then lost along the way.

The harpy fired those green walnut hulls at me, but I ignored her and the nuts and kept on sawing.

"Mr. Thorne, enough. Stop chopping my tree," she shouted over the chainsaw, continuing to shoot those unripe green balls at me, trying but failing to hit my head.

What a lousy shot! I wondered if she was totally sober. It pissed me off that she correctly assumed that a woman injured my arm. I contemplated telling her to fuck herself but said nothing. I contemplated hurling those green walnut hulls back at her and imagined taking out her eye, or her nose, or seriously injuring her pruned-up face, which would be doing the world a favor, a favor lost on the likes of Tweedledee and Tweedledum, who'd only return to haul me off for assault. As a nurse, I couldn't do it. So I just kept sawing those fucking branches.

"Do you have to cut every blasted one?" she shouted, her indignation turning her face red. She nailed me with a green walnut hull, one for every word. I turned off my chainsaw.

"Yes," I said calmly.

I descended my ladder, chainsaw in hand, and set it on the ground before moving the ladder closer to the fence but further away from that harpy and started sawing the slightly thicker branches closer to the trunk. I carefully sawed the branch right at the property line to keep things legal, yelling, "Tiiiiimber!" just to piss her off as I tossed the branches into her yard.

I hadn't noticed that she moved her ladder closer to mine on her side of the fence. That old harpy fired another unripe walnut hull at me, this time hitting me hard in my face, gouging my right cheek, which started bleeding. I dropped my saw to the ground and held my face, which hurt worse than getting shot in the arm.

"Son of a bitch," I yelled, my cheek bleeding into my hands. "What the fuck is wrong with you?"

I looked up just in time to see her arm reach over the fence, trespassing into my yard just like her tree limbs. She pushed the ladder over with all her might, saying how sorry she felt that I fell off the ladder, and what a terrible accident it was. This time I called Tweedledee and Tweedledum. When they arrived, I lay flat on the ground, unable to move, my cheek still bleeding, my ankle swollen. They referred to me as "Old Man" when they called an ambo. I wanted to tell them I wasn't an "old man." Before I could speak, I heard the harpy describing how she witnessed me falling off the ladder. Technically true: She watched me fall. Also technically true, she pushed the ladder while I was on it; in my old cop brain, that translated to attempted murder, which was what I told Tweedledee and Tweedledum, and yessiree, you best believe I filed a complaint for attempted murder.

After I got home from the hospital with all these casts, I called a few buddies over, and for a couple of cases of brewskis and delivered pizza, they fed my cats, cleaned all the litter boxes, and sawed every branch of that tree that took up air space in my yard. My new neighbors—cat lovers—pruned and cared for the tree so that its branches no longer hogged my yard. Every now and again, I mail that old harpy some picture postcards of the tree at her new digs at the state penitentiary, her vacation place for the next few.

TRAINING WHEELS

Three generations of Jerome Porteras lived in one small Baltimore house, and all three— father, son, and grandson—shared the same nickname: "Romey." The two elder Romeys, called Big Romey and Romey Jr., sat on the bench in front of their house watching Little Romey, now six, ride his two-wheeler, training wheels attached. A Saturday afternoon, the older Romeys, in shorts and white tank undershirts, sipped bottled beer while the boy sped up and down the block, taking his hands off the handlebars and yelling, "Look at me, Dadio! Look at me, Poppy! No hands!"

Romey Jr. watched the back of his son's head, the wind caressing his dark brown hair, causing it to fly behind him.

"Hey, son, slow down and hold on, or you'll end up killing yourself," he yelled to the child who had already reached the pear tree that comprised his north boundary four houses down. "And don't go past that tree." Watching the boy, feet spread apart, ready to spring into action if he took a spill, Romey Jr. sprang off of the bench to make sure the child did not pedal past the pear tree. He sipped his beer. Big Romey watched the boy, too, though he, relaxed, remained seated.

"Why don't you take 'em training wheels off? That'll slow him down," Big Romey said. "He's ready to ride without them anyways. By the look of it."

"Too little," Romey Jr. said. "He'd only get himself all scratched up. Break a bone even. Six ain't big enough."

"Bullshit. He's taking his hands off the handlebars. If that ain't showing he's bored with that bike now, I don't know what is," Big Romey said. "It ain't going to be the end of the world if he takes a fall or two, gets scraped up. Hell, he's a boy. He ain't no hothouse flower. All you and Ant do is coddle and baby him, sissifying him. He needs some scraped knees, for Pete's sake." Big Romey sipped his beer. "For his own good," the old man added. "And you gotta learn to let go. Give the kid some kind of room."

"Not at six, Pop," Romey Jr. said.

Big Romey shrugged. "If you had another kid you wouldn't feel that way because you wouldn't have a choice."

"Ant been talking to you again?" Romey Jr. asked. His wife, Ant, short for Antoinette, had been begging for another child for a year, saying her window of opportunity was about to snap shut. Romey Jr. remained ambivalent, both about the evaporating time frame his wife worried over and about another mouth to feed. He hadn't wanted Little Romey, not really, but the boy, who looked as if Big Romey chewed him up and spit him out, had a funny way of growing on him. And now Romey Jr. found himself so attached, he worried about the kid's future, paralyzed by an astonishing and endless array of "what ifs": What if the baby got a terrible disease and died; What if Romey Jr. himself got a terrible disease—after all, he wasn't a young guy at forty-five anymore—and died, then who would take care of the kid? What if someone stole the baby away or, worse yet, tortured or molested him? The thought alone caused Romey Jr.'s heart to pump furiously, turning his face and ears red, and he gritted his teeth, picturing the pain he'd inflict on the individual who'd dare harm Little Romey.

"Nope," Big Romey said. "But I agree with her. You still refer to the boy as 'the baby.' He ain't a baby no more. He's ready to ride a two-wheeler. Without them training wheels," his father said, pointing to the child now standing up and pedaling furiously toward them. "Look at him. Blink, and he'll be gone before you even know what hit you. Ain't nothing pleasant about being alone, which is what he's gonna be if you turn him into a mommy's boy, afraid of every little thing."

Romey Jr. regarded his father, his now gnarled hands that once laid beautiful brick walls holding the beer bottle, his dimpled cheeks and soft brown eyes peering out from a face with thinning skin growing ever thinner and topped by a head of thinning gray curly hair.

"He ain't going to be a mommy's boy, and you ain't alone, Pop."

Big Romey shrugged. "My friend Pietro had a boatload of children, and to this day, his house is noisy. The kids all had kids, and every day every week Pietro's got something interesting to do with a different person. You gotta admit, our house is a bit on the quiet side."

"Whatta ya saying, Pop? I'm boring to you now?"

Big Romey laughed and shook his head. "Not at all, Junior. Ain't saying that at all."

Big Romey, almost seventy-three-years old and a widower, had sold his house to move in with Romey Jr. It was Romey Jr.'s idea, a way to fill up the extra bedroom and keep an eye on his father at the same time. Much to his surprise, Big Romey went along with it without much protest. After his wife Stella had died, Big Romey banged around alone. Alone in his own house where he had had a heart attack and stumbled outside, knowing he needed help. If it weren't for Big Romey's next-door neighbor, who heard a thump and the sounds of glass breaking when he'd fallen on the porch, Romey Jr. would have lost his father, too.

Now the old man tended their backyard garden, a city garden, his gnarled hands covering the two fig trees in winter and planting Cucuzza vines in summer so that figs and squash came in abundance, along with plum tomatoes, basil, rosemary, and other herbs. He resuscitated the old rosebushes, too, and talked about filling half barrels with dirt to plant some flowers. The old man had kept himself busy, too, doing odds and ends around the house, easily including Little Romey in whatever he did, bringing him to the neighborhood bocce courts where he taught the kid the game, feeding pigeons and wrens bread crumbs and seeds with the kid every Sunday morning, reading him stories, telling him stories about Stella, about the old country, about growing up during the war, stories that he had heard before and that the old man let out slowly like fishing line to the child who absorbed it all like a sponge. Romey Jr. liked the fact that his kid and his Pop had become close buddies.

His own grandfather had been back in the old country, and Romey Jr. had never met the man or missed having a grandfather around. His father had never been much into tossing around a baseball or football, but the two of them had spent every Saturday and Sunday together, building a train garden in the basement, his father's patient, thick fingers demonstrating how to make tiny trees using yarrow found by roadsides and then dipped into tiny vials of yellow and green paint. Together they had fashioned tiny houses, lakes, beaches, movie theaters, churches, stores, and sundry buildings and topography that comprised a town with a railroad track. When not working on the train garden, they operated a ham radio out of the attic, their handles being "Big Romey" and "Romey One," chatting up people all over the world, and they also built and flew fuel-driven, remote-controlled helicopters and airplanes. Romey Jr. smiled, remembering their shared fascination with things that moved and his mother's loud concerns over Romey Jr. being too young at age ten to be around the gas, the airplanes, and especially the helicopters with their thwaping blades.

"Those blades can cut him to shreds if they fly off the model or if the thing crashes and falls on his head," she had said. Big Romey had waved away her concerns with promises of being extra careful, while winking at Romey Jr., anxious to be with the men, his father, and the amazing models in the park.

"Your mother couldn't have any more," Big Romey sniffed. "Or you'd been one of a flock, a huge goddamn flock," he said. "One child by himself ain't good, I tell you," he said. "We were lucky to have you. Why don't you toughen up that boy and teach him to ride that bike without them goddamn training wheels?"

Romey Jr. placed his beer on the stoop. When the boy turned around at the pear tree and made his way back to the stoop again, Romey Jr. called him over.

"How about you ride that thing without them training wheels? You wanna learn?"

Little Romey's eyes lit up. "I can ride like the big boys," he announced.

"Go sit with Poppy while I take off the wheels," he said.

Romey Jr. pushed the bike on its side and pulled his Swiss army knife out of his pocket before he sat on the pavement to unscrew the training wheels. He glanced up at his father and son and noticed that the old man and the boy shared more than a name. They resembled each other: Both had the same color root-beer brown eyes, the same thick curly hair, except Little Romey's was the color of ink and his father's gray, and they shared the same olive complexion. Romey Jr. resembled his mother's family with fair skin, dark straight hair, and blue eyes. Big Romey hoisted Little Romey onto his lap.

"When you were a baby only this big, I used to wheel you around the neighborhood in a stroller, and now you're going to be a big boy riding a big boy's bike. Pretty soon, you're going to be wheeling your Pop around in a car." The old man laughed and stroked the boy's head.

"When I'm bigger I want to drive a motorcycle," the boy said and began to make motorcycle rumbling sounds.

"A motorcycle?" the old man asked and laughed. "We'll see about that when the time comes," he added and kissed the top of the boy's forehead. "Meantime, you're gonna do good learning to ride the bike like a big boy, right?"

The boy nodded his head.

Ant hadn't been home from the hospital for one day before Big Romey and Stella came bringing clothes for the baby and pans of lasagna and chicken wings. They had come daily, too, drawn to the baby like magnets. Stella had tidied the house while Pop fed the baby, giving Ant a much-needed rest and telling Romey to stay with his wife. They'd run interference with the phone, kept the army of relatives at bay, and when they left each evening, a hot dinner waited for them on the stove. Stella massaged Ant and taught her how to bathe the baby and look for signs of cradle cap. When Ant regained her strength, Stella, who kept her job, visited once a week, but Big Romey, who'd been retired, arrived daily and strolled the infant around, beaming over his first and only grandson. When Stella died so unexpectedly, Ant went along with the idea of Pop living with them, almost as if it'd been her idea.

"Okay, sport," Romey Jr. called his son. "Let's have a go at it."

Little Romey slid off his grandfather's lap and bounded to his father holding the bike—now minus the training wheels—steady.

"I'm ready, Dadio," the boy said. Fearless, he climbed onto the bike. Romey Jr. winced a little seeing that the child's feet didn't easily touch the ground.

"It's a little too high for you. I'm going to hold the seat here in the back and you pedal," Romey Jr. instructed and ran to keep up with the child's pedaling. "You gotta steer right so you don't go into the street," Romey Jr. said, running, out of breath but refusing to let go of the bike's seat.

"I know, Dadio. I won't go into the street. I'll go around the block."

"You can do it. I know you can," Big Romey shouted from the stoop and waved.

Much to Romey Jr.'s surprise, the kid took off like a rocket, building enough speed that Romey Jr. couldn't keep the pace and was forced to let go of the bike's seat. Little Romey didn't notice that his father no longer held the seat, and though a bit wobbly, the boy, grinning widely, steered the bike around the corner at the top of the block, a busy intersection, which prompted Romey Jr. to sprint after his son on the bike. Frantic that the bike was no longer under his control, Romey Jr. ran, praying that the kid would not lose balance and fall into the busy street.

At the top of the next block, fifteen yards ahead, Little Romey faltered, and Romey Jr. could see the bike leaning right toward the street. Envisioning the child falling into oncoming traffic, his child being hit by speeding cars on one of the city's main arteries, his heart raced faster, and he sprinted faster to catch up to the child.

Little Rooooomey," he screamed, the sound coming out of his chest like the yelp of a wounded animal.

The bike fell and the child toppled over, but not into the street. Before he could reach Little Romey, the boy got up, wiped himself off, picked up the bike, mounted it, and took off again. Romey Jr.'s heart pounded in his chest and in his head, the beats echoing in his ears like a steel drum. The child's confidence surprised and humbled him.

"Slow down, son," he called. Little Romey didn't hear, or pretended not to hear, and sailed onward toward the top of the block.

"Don't forget to use the hand brakes to slow down," Romey Jr. called as he ran behind the child. Little Romey didn't look back. He nodded that he'd understood his father's cautions about the hand brakes, and Romey Jr. could tell that the child had slowed some, but not much. Romey Jr. chased his son on the bike, certain that calamity lay around the next corner, but the child steered the bike and rounded the corner like an expert, and all Romey Jr. could see was the back of his son's head as he pedaled down Stiles Street now, past the old men on the bench who called, "Atta boy, looka at heem go!" and chuckled knowingly as Romey Jr. gave chase.

"You're the one who's got to slow down," they called and laughed as old men do.

Around the last corner, son rode, and father ran, Big Romey, beer in hand, still sitting on their stoop watching for them to appear.

"Look, Pop. I rode all the way around the whole block. I only fell once!" The boy laughed, but neither slowed nor stopped, and continued on for another ride around the block.

"I told you you could do it," Big Romey said, smiling while Romey Jr., huffing and puffing, ran on. On the stoop, Big Romey chuckled.

"Junior, this is just the beginning," he called to his son, whose legs pumped as if he were running the Baltimore marathon.

"One more time, Dadio," Little Romey yelled without looking back at his father. Following his son, unable to breach the fifteen yards between them, Romey Jr. ran and wondered what it would be like when he'd watch the kid ride into a different world, leaving his parents behind, and he wondered if another child would work like a set of hand brakes, slowing the flight away from home, or if he or she would function like a gas pedal, speeding it to double-time.

A BEAUTIFUL DEATH

Margherita Castelabate Smith inhaled the salty ocean tang and watched waves crash. Wearing Jackie O sunglasses, she occupied a beach chair, observing seagulls congregate and compete for small fish and crabs at the water's edge. She envied them, their indifferent circles around the kites dotting the sky like speckled paint. The kites reminded her of Xander, but then everything did. Everything pointed to him, his absence.

She'd forgotten about the young families at the beach at the first crack of summer. She hated them, all the parents of healthy, living children, children yelling, laughing, crying, squealing. Xander died five years ago, the loss still fresh, the wound raw. Margherita kicked the sand with her toes, created a sand fountain, imagined his chubby baby hands holding plastic yellow water wings, buckets, shovels, and windmills. She traced Xander's name in the sand with her big toe. These beach devotees with playpens and coolers who spent most of the day at the water's edge irked her. How careless they were with their babies, confident in their futures! None of them were forced to say, "Ph+ALL," or to sit endless hours in PedMedOnc. She pursed her lips, remembered Dr. P's lips moving, saying Ph+ALL to her and Randy, saying, "a particularly aggressive form that is fatal for those who have it despite receiving the maximum therapy available." Xander's days? Numbered at birth. Why my child? Genetic. Not hers. Randy's.

She gathered a pile of rocks and pitched them one by one into the surf.

"I hate you," she whispered with each pitch, three stones, each assigned a word, tossed into the sea, an angry prayer on her lips.

A chorus of children's laughter tormented her; she sucked in her breath, throwing the rest of the rocks as far as her arm allowed. Why did she come to the beach with Janey anyway? They'd come to Ocean City together since kindergarten, Margherita forgoing the annual trip after Xander died, and this, her first since—at Janey's suggestion—unnerved her.

She tossed flat stones into the surf, watched them skip before disappearing under the surface, a game she'd played with her father and not played with her own son. Her gray sweatpants soaked by the sea, its chill biting her skin, the odor of dead fish assaulting her nose, she stared at the horizon. She'd left Xander's pillow at home, and she missed its scent, its comfort.

In her chair, Margherita rolled her wet pants to her knees and sipped her now tepid, flat diet soda. And she ate a large chocolate bar, hiding the wrapping at the bottom of her tote bag. She allowed the candy to sit on her tongue for a few seconds before she swallowed it, hiding it from Janey. Comforted, she wiped sticky fingers on her pants.

"Aren't you hot?" Janey asked.

Startled, Margherita wiped chocolate from her lips on her sleeve. Janey glistened with sweat, her body toned and muscular in black spandex exercise clothes. A black headband circled her blond head. Janey grabbed a bottle of water from their cooler and gulped half before stretching, bending her left leg backward at the knee and holding her foot to her butt. Janey's frenetic activity fatigued Margherita. She yawned.

"I didn't see you coming," Margherita said.

"I ran all the way to old OC and back," she said. "Let's go in. The water looks fabulous." Janey removed her running shoes and socks and set them on the corner of the beach blanket. "Come on, Reet. Just down to the edge."

"Did that," Margherita said, pointing to her wet pants.

Janey shrugged. "Do it again."

She waited for Margherita, who failed to budge. Janey frowned and headed for the water, first to her ankles and then to her knees, then past her thighs. In her exercise clothes, she dipped into the sea and jumped waves. Flashing a wide smile, she motioned for Margherita to join her, but Margherita shook her head no. Janey disappeared under the water. Margherita looked away from Janey's bobbing head, remembering how as young girls, they'd jumped waves, loathing the moment they had to come out, remembering how easily she'd plunged into the water as a young married. Randy had laughed at her on the same beach when a cold, rough wave had skewed her bikini top, rushing her toward the shore, one boob showing.

"Beware the one-eyed sea monster," he'd yelled, cupping his hands around his mouth so she could hear him. Everyone looked, and she'd been laughing too hard to be embarrassed, staying low in the water, retying her top. Afterward, anytime either of them said "one-eyed sea monster," they'd dissolve into giggles, even when they were arguing. The endless nights at Mercy's PedMedOnc robbed the phrase of its humor. When Randy had whispered it to her there one night, she'd wept instead. They'd both wept.

Cold water cascaded over Margherita. Holding a large, empty yellow bucket, Janey was standing over her and laughing, the broken-glass sound of it cutting Margherita.

"If you won't go into the ocean, the ocean will go to you," she said. "Don't you feel cooler, better? We're at the beeeeaaacccchhhh. Now you have to take off those sweats. Come on, Reet. It's so refreshing. And healing!"

"Why'd you do that?" Margherita asked. She couldn't remove her wet clothes with no bathing suit underneath. Her old ones no longer fit, and she refused to buy a bigger size for one trip.

Janey tossed Margherita a towel. "Um…people get wet at beaches. HEL-LO!" Janey grabbed a second towel for herself.

"Not funny," Margherita said, careful to keep her tone neutral.

"Can't you try to have some fun?" Janey sighed. She dropped to the blanket with a thud. "What were you thinking about all zoned out in zombieland?"

"Randy," Margherita said, setting the folded towel atop her tote bag. Her wet hair hung around her face, past the chair's armrests. It felt foreign, heavy, as if it weren't hers. She felt foreign to herself.

"Raaandy?" Janey rubbed sunscreen onto her arms. "That's all you've done since we've been here. Talk about Randy," she said. "And Xander. Xander's gone. You and Randy are kaput! He's had the same girlfriend. Lots of other fish, you know," she said. "Huge sea out there." She nodded to the people around them, not the ocean.

Margherita closed her knees; her right leg bounced and jerked. Janey was plucking her nerves. She drank herself into a stupor at the Seacove every night, and then spent the mornings like a penitent, jogging, sucking up protein drinks, and lifting weights at the condo gym. She ate tiny portions of cottage cheese, tuna salad, and egg-white omelets, saying, "Food is fuel. You're clogging up your engine with bad fuel."

"Let's talk about those insidious liquid calories," Margherita had said, in between bites, her mouth full of pancakes with whipped cream. "We both pick our poisons. I get it," she said, uprighting an empty beer bottle on the breakfast counter to punctuate her point.

Margherita folded her arms. "Not interested in other fish. We raised a son, and then we watched him die. Nothing compares. Randy is attracted to Stripper Girl's son. Not to her. Father envy," Margherita said. She gazed at the sea, avoiding Janey's face.

Janey laughed. "De-Nile ain't only a river in Egypt," she said. She slathered her legs with tanning lotion. "I saw them a week ago at FoodShopper."

Margherita pursed her lips, shut her eyes behind the sunglasses. She couldn't bear Randy after Xander died, much less touch him, allow him to put his hands on her. She'd wept every time she saw Randy's hands, larger versions of Xander's with the same tapered fingers and flat nails. She'd blamed him, his "piss-poor gene pool." But she didn't want to hear about him and Stripper Girl either.

"Children aren't like cats," she said. "Randy refused to get tested. He'd have us endure the crappy ordeal again with another baby. He's a gambler. Let him be happy with Stripper Girl. I don't care." Margherita's right leg bounced with fury.

From her tote, Janey pulled a plastic shake bottle filled with brown powder. She grabbed another water bottle from the cooler, poured half into the plastic shake bottle, and shook it vigorously. Her post-run protein drink.

"Ha!" Janey said.

Not knowing if she felt more angry at Randy or Janey, or herself, Margherita clenched her jaw. She kept her face a mask, tried to look indifferent.

"Maybe mothers and fathers grieve differently," Janey said in between sips. "Maybe Stripper Girl allowed him to grieve his own way. Maybe she doesn't want any more kids."

Margherita winced. "Randy does." She paused. "What does she look like?" she asked.

"Cute—dark, spiky, short hair, huge black eyes. Not trashy if that's what you expect. She only dances on the side. You know, to augment her real estate income," Janey said. "Survival. I think she quit doing that now."

Margherita squeezed her eyes shut. Picturing Randy with Ms. Body-Beautiful-Enough-to-Take-Off-Her-Clothes-and-Dance-in-Front-of-Men twisted her stomach into a knot. She swallowed more soda. Her face and her neck tensed, and she folded her hands into tight fists, fingernails digging into her palms.

"She sells lap dances and houses," Margherita said, careful to keep her voice calm, also careful to swallow the word *bitch*.

Janey laughed. "That's hysterical!"

"It's the kid," she said. "Reminds him of Xander."

Janey chugged the last of the drink and stuffed the shake bottle into her tote. "Doubt it. The kid doesn't look a thing like your towheaded Xander."

"It's the kid," Margherita insisted. Both of her legs bounced now. She wondered if the kid loved Matchbox cars and trucks the way Xander did. If he squealed "naked baby" at bath time before jumping into the tub the way Xander did. If he loved Spiderman underwear and shirts and toothbrushes the way Xander did. Xander's Spiderman toothbrush lay tucked in a plastic bag in her bureau drawer.

"He's got this magnificent smile. Quiet, held his mother's hand. Randy was pushing the shopping cart. I said I'd babysit if they ever needed one."

"Judas!" Margherita said. She fixed angry eyes on Janey, who'd been her best friend since kindergarten. "How could you?"

Janey sighed, shook her head, lay back on the beach blanket. "He's a baby. He didn't do anything to you. Reet, forget it, forget Randy. Move forward. Come to the club tonight. We can go shopping and get an outfit," Janey said. "It's June. You're dressed like February, and we're in OC for God's sake."

It promised to be a long, torturous week. "Let's find something else to do," Margherita said.

"Like what? Putt-putt? No thank you! The boardwalk with all the teenyboppers and tourists? You, Dancing Queen, used to love the Seacove! You were the one entering us in wet T-shirt contests in college. I miss *that* Reet. Where is she?"

Janey looked earnest, wanting an answer. Margherita knew that look. But Janey had never been a mother, never pushed a child in the world, never suffered through that child's death.

Margherita narrowed her eyes. "Dead. All that stuff? Happened B.X.D. It's A.X.D. now."

Janey sat up. "B.X.D.? A.X.D.? What the hell is that?"

Margherita's bouncing legs jerked the chair. "Before Xander Died. After Xander Died."

Janey laughed with her mouth opened so wide Margherita, stunned, could see her perfect row of teeth. Janey snorted even. "Must you be so dramatic? B.X.D. and A.X.D.?" she asked.

"Don't you think you're carrying this too far?" Now she sounded serious. She patted Margherita's shoulder as if she were a child. "You're drowning, Reet. I'm throwing you a lifeline."

"Lifeline? Nothing will ever be the same! Nothing will ever be the fucking same anymore!" Margherita shouted.

Sunbathers, vacationers tanning on beach blankets, stared at her. Her face and neck tense, she folded her beach chair, collected her tote bag, and stomped through the sand, away from Janey, back toward their condo. Janey had no right. Margherita rounded the pathway from the beach, knocking into a blonde, cigarette-smoking woman pulling a small crying girl by her arm and yelling, "Shut the fuck up, you little snot head." The girl wailed.

"Watch it, you idiot," the blonde woman snapped at Margherita.

"Excuse YOU!" Margherita said. "You're the one who should watch IT. And stop abusing that child or I'll call the police and file a complaint for child abuse."

The woman pulled a drag and breathed smoke into Margherita's face. "Who the fuck do you think you are?" the woman said, puffs of smoke streaming out of her nose.

The cigarette danced in the woman's mouth as she spoke.

Margherita smacked it into the sand. "You don't deserve a healthy child. Maybe she'll get lucky and *you'll* die from cancer," Margherita yelled.

The girl stopped crying, watched Margherita through frightened blue eyes. Trembling at the sight of the slight child, a tiny thing, her arm still hoisted like a doll's, Margherita fought the urge to grab the child and run.

"Crazy-assed bitch," the blonde woman said, staring at her cigarette smoldering in the sand. She bent to pick up the butt, but Margherita stepped on it before the woman could reach it. They locked eyes, and finally, the woman pushed her way past Margherita, pulling the child's arm.

"Crazy-assed bitch," she repeated.

"Troglodyte," Margherita said, elongating the word.

The woman, right hand on her hip, turned toward Margherita. "What did you say?"

Margherita imagined strangling the woman but ignored her and strode past the condo entrance.

"Fat bitch," the blonde woman yelled.

"Tell me something I don't know," Margherita said without stopping. She crossed Route One and headed for the convenience store. She needed chocolate. She'd been avoiding mirrors and she hated her fat self, but chocolate soothed her. Nothing would ever be the same. Not even her body.

Margherita paid for the pile of chocolate bars and swept them into her tote. Outside, she reached for one. Slightly melted, the candy stuck to the foil and to her fingers. Margherita devoured it, inadvertently spreading the melted chocolate into her hair, onto her chin, onto her hands, and subsequently all over the frame of her beach chair like a chocolate virus. Walking toward the condo, she ate a second. Chocolate coated her tongue, her lips, her mouth, her fingers, but she couldn't stop and ate a third before wiping her hands on the sides of her damp gray sweatpants. She raised a sticky, thick finger to press the elevator button and, at the condo, washed chocolate from her wet hair, her hands, her face. She felt sleepy.

Janey was cleaning the chair frame with ammonia spray and paper towels. Margherita had forgotten about the mess on the chair.

"Candy isn't going to bring Xander or Randy back," Janey said, wiping smeared chocolate from the living room wall and doorknob. "Maybe you need to see somebody. A shrink. A priest. Somebody."

"Thanks for cleaning up," Margherita said, her face flushed red at the evidence of her chocolate binge.

"So, shopping and Seacove tonight?" Janey asked.

Margherita bristled. "Don't you want to paint or something?"

"Are we going shopping or not?" she said, an edge in her voice.

Margherita shrugged. "Not."

Janey shook her head. "I bet there's a store with stylish clothes that fit you."

"Not exactly in the mood to try on clothes."

"I'm going to freshen up. Maybe you'll want to do the same," Janey said, pointing to Margherita's chocolate-stained pants. "If you find something flattering, promise you'll go to the club. If you don't, I won't bug you about it anymore." Janey smiled. "I'd forgotten how lovely your hair looks down. It'd look great down tonight." Janey looked hopeful.

Certain no beach stores would carry fat people's clothes, Margherita slipped into clean gray sweats—the color and cloth of failure—and an oversized, short-sleeved T-shirt. She stepped into flip-flops and pulled her damp hair into its usual haphazard bun. Staring at nothing, she waited on the sofa for Janey. Ten minutes later, on Route One, they passed the mall.

"Where're we going?" Margherita asked.

"The new outlets on Fenwick and Rehoboth. The club should be fun tonight," Janey said, glancing sideways at Margherita.

Margherita shrugged and flicked on the radio. "How's Pauly?" she asked.

"Super. He's been super letting me move back home 'til Jeff and I can sell the house. I missed the signs. I should have figured it out ten years ago. Time to find someone new."

Margherita flicked the radio buttons. "Not at Seacove," she said.

Margherita liked the stretch of road just before the Delaware border. Undeveloped, huge sand dunes rose like mountains on both sides of the highway; it looked moonlike, solitary.

"When your husband loves someone else, and that someone else is a man, that's not exactly how things were supposed to work after sixteen years," Janey said.

Margherita sighed. "Nothing turned out the way either of us expected."

Neither said anything for a while.

"I'll need a new place soon. Pauly wants to marry Beth. I don't want to intrude on them."

"Maybe Pauly will move. Maybe Beth doesn't want to live in your childhood home," Margherita said. "Why don't you buy Jeff out and keep your home?"

"Is that how you stayed in the house?" Janey asked.

Margherita clutched her purse. "You can crash in my guest room if you need a place to stay," Margherita said, surprising herself. "We're not divorced. Or legally separated. We're just in a holding pattern for now."

"For five years? That's a helluva holding pattern," Janey said. She merged into the right lane and turned into the Fenwick Center parking lot. "Fenwick Woman," she said, pointing to a storefront showcasing a cardboard advertisement featuring a plus-sized woman wearing light blue cropped pants, a matching blue shell, and chunky wooden jewelry.

"A fat clothes store at the beach!" Margherita said.

"Seacove or bust!" Janey sounded like a flight attendant.

"Oh joy!" Margherita said, her voice flat.

"You agreed. I want the real Reet back."

Margherita stared at Janey. "I didn't go anywhere. I'm still me."

"Let's go see what they have," Janey said, waving away Margherita's words like gnats.

Fenwick Woman's racks of pastel and jewel-colored clothes overwhelmed Margherita. Janey approached her with Chinese red cropped pants.

"What size are you now?" she asked.

Eyeing the red pants, Margherita refused to respond. She didn't want Janey knowing that she now surpassed a 22, and she wouldn't be caught dead in red, turning her into a giant target. Janey pulled her toward the back.

"These will fit, too," she said, holding a garish blue and yellow muumuu up to Margherita's body.

"Really? A muumuu?" Margherita said.

"They look beachy," Janey said. "You can dress it up, give it sex appeal with accessories. Some strappy shoes. You love shoes!"

A closet full of her too-small, sexy, come-fuck-me pumps collected dust. Her now fat feet could wear flip-flops and rubber shoes. She'd look ridiculous trying to balance on high heels anymore.

"There's nothing appealing or sexy about a muumuu," she said, keeping her voice even.

"Ditto for those gray sweats," Janey shot back. "You used to be bold."

"B.X.D. This is A.X.D.," she said, heading for the exit. Janey held the loud large-print muumuu in her hands. At the exit, Margherita considered chocolate ice cream and saltwater taffy. She considered waffle cones with gelato and jimmies.

"You promised, Reet," Janey said, following her. "Don't think you're getting off easy. I'm not letting you. You're going to get out of the condo tonight."

The shop door window reflected her image, and Margherita barely recognized the fat woman looking back at her. Margherita realized that though she'd preferred to have died soon after Xander, her stubborn body with its obstinate flesh held its own wishes and desires, neither dying nor disappearing among them. She wanted to shuck off the obstinate flesh the way she used to shuck off clothes. She wanted to vanish, disappear. Margherita climbed into the back of Janey's car, curled into a fetal position, and slept, awakened later by the car's motion and Janey singing softly to the radio. Margherita feigned sleep.

* * *

Janey had found her an outfit. Black slacks, black knit overblouse, black kitten-heeled sandals. They fit, too. Black felt right. Not as comfortable as failure gray, but it echoed her mood. Astonished by Janey's perseverance, unnerved by the thumping bass rattling the walls, Margherita sat in her new clothes alone at a booth at the Seacove, sipping diet soda and munching on bread sticks. At Janey's insistence, her too-long hair hung like a sheet of black curls around her shoulders and past her waist. She couldn't pull it into her usual bun because Janey had kept the elastic band around her wrist from when she'd applied makeup to Margherita's face. She used to wear makeup all the time, but now her glossy red lips and her coal-lined eyes all dramatic made her feel like a clown.

With its thick wood railings, bamboo chairs, palm trees, and ugly painted-over plastic tiles, the Seacove remained unchanged from their college days. It looked like a cross between a home improvement project gone awry and a tiki bar. She and Janey had hit the Seacove during summer breaks, entering and winning bikini and dance contests, drinking and flirting. Now Margherita fingered the menu. She and Janey planned to eat dinner, stick around a bit, but Janey was now dancing with a Pew Hefner doused in Old Spice. Margherita peered at the dance floor, looking for Pew Hefner's neon shirt to find Janey. She ordered fish tacos, sweet potato fries, refried beans, and nachos with guacamole and melted cheese.

"An extra plate, please," she told the waitress, who raised eyebrows, insinuating Margherita had invented an extra person.

Why would Janey drag her to Seacove then abandon her? The waitress brought the appetizers, set them and two plates down on the table, smirking, glancing at Margherita's two plates. Margherita imagined smacking the smirk off the waitress's face. Janey and the Pew Hefner appeared when the fish tacos came. Laughing, Janey plopped on the other side of the booth, Pew Hefner sliding next to her.

"I'm famished," Janey said, scooping black beans onto the nachos. "Thanks for ordering," she said. "Have some, Glenn. Reet, this is Glenn," she said, pointing at the man with her thumb. The man looked preserved, plasticized, with his eyebrows unnaturally arched and dyed.

Glenn, who barely registered her, ordered Janey a Long Island iced tea and a beer for himself. "You want anything?" he asked Margherita, not looking at her.

The waitress registered surprise that not one but two others had joined her. Margherita declined Glenn's offer, while Janey ate Margherita's fish taco.

"Great choice," Janey said in between bites, sharing it with Glenn. The waitress served the drinks, Janey sucking hers down like punch. "This is great!" she said. "Reet, have some!"

"Keep 'em coming," Pew Hefner told the waitress.

"Janey, do you want another drink?" Margherita asked.

"Course she does," Glenn said.

"Course I do," Janey said and giggled. "This tastes great!" She drank it fast.

Janey allowed the man to put his arm around her. She allowed him to kiss her arms, elbows, and neck. The waitress served the next round.

"Three's a crowd," Margherita said. She folded a paper napkin into triangles.

"What are you? Some kind of lesbo?" Pew Hefner asked. "You're a crowd all by yourself," he said, laughing.

A buzzed Janey laughed, too. "Oh, Glenn, you're baaaaad." She sounded flirty, not outraged.

"It's too bad you feel that way," Margherita said, angry with Janey and wanting to leave. "What's up with the Pew?"

"I don't want to be alone," Janey said. She finished the next round. Margherita ordered another diet cola and fish taco.

"You're a twin," Margherita said.

Glenn kissed Janey's neck and ears. He kissed her throat and worked his way to her cleavage. Glenn pulled Janey out of the booth and onto the dance floor, and Margherita knew she couldn't leave her alone with Pew. The smirk now absent from her face, the waitress served the second fish taco and cleared away the dirty dishes. She returned with a fourth set of drinks.

"Take those away, and don't bring any more," Margherita said.

"The gentleman said to keep them coming," the waitress said.

"Okay, keep the beers coming, but not the Long Island iced teas. And add all the food to his tab," Margherita said.

Eating the taco, angry with Janey for turning her into a wing woman, Margherita watched Glenn unsuccessfully attempt to shuffle Janey to the other side of the room. She caught Janey's eye, and Janey staggered back to the table, Glenn behind her.

"Parched," Janey said, grabbing Margherita's soda. She slid into the booth; Glenn followed.

Margherita finished her taco. Glenn ignored Margherita as if she were invisible, touching Janey's arm, kissing her hair, and working his left hand toward Janey's crotch.

"The room's spinning," Janey slurred, ignoring Glenn's advancing hand. She leaned her head against the booth wall and moaned. "So dizzy."

"I'm dizzy for you, Jane-baby," Pew Hefner said.

"I'm taking her to the restroom so she doesn't throw up here," she told Glenn, ordering him to move out of the way. Margherita gathered their purses and led Janey away from the table, away from Glenn, his Old Spice cloud, and his Long Island iced tea plans.

Moaning, Janey leaned against the restroom wall. Margherita fished the car and condo keys from Janey's purse and slipped them into her slacks pocket. Margherita guided her through the exit toward the car.

"I didn't say good night to Glenn," Janey slurred.

"I already took care of that. Left him with a big thank you to remember us by, too," she said.

"Since when do you drink Strong Islands?" Margherita asked when they reached the intersection two blocks from the condo.

"Tonight," Janey said and laughed. She sat slumped sideways in the passenger seat. "They're soooo good."

Once they were back in the condo, Janey sank to the foyer floor and vomited the fish taco. Margherita shuffled her to the bathroom, where Janey puked again before passing out. Margherita removed Janey's stained blouse, cleaned puke off her chest and arms, her face and hands, out of her hair. She'd grown accustomed to cleaning noxious bodily fluids. Nauseated from chemo, Xander had vomited frequently, his body growing frailer, his perfect little round head becoming bald. She half dragged, half carried Janey to her clean bed, slipped an oversized T-shirt over her head, removed her shoes and skirt, and covered her with a light blanket.

Her new black clothes soiled, smelling like puke, Margherita stripped, piling hers and Janey's clothes in the bathroom corner. She found a bucket, rags, and bleach. She'd cleaned so much vomit from floors, walls, beds, and clothes when Xander was dying, it seemed mechanical, even in her underwear. The smell of it, the ghastly, horrible smell of it reminded her of Xander's weak voice saying, "Don't cry, Mommy."

Margherita cleaned the mess, tears dropping onto the floor just as they did when she'd cleaned Xander's. It gave her something familiar to do, a small mercy against the now empty world. Afterward, she showered, slipped into clean gray sweats, and crawled into her own bed, missing Xander's pillow but missing her child more.

* * *

Janey drove toward the Dulaney Valley Beltway exit, toward the house she shared with Pauly. Margherita stifled a yawn.

"I feel gritty," Janey said, breaking the hour-long silence. "And sticky."

Tired of the car, tired of Janey, Margherita longed for home, even empty, minus Xander and Randy. She imagined sitting in the polished rocker in Xander's room looking at the photo albums documenting his four short years from birth to death. They crossed the Loch Raven Dam Bridge.

"Me too," she said. "Can't wait to be home."

"You'll be alone," Janey said.

Margherita shrugged. "I don't mind it."

"You want to stay with Pauly and me?" Janey asked. She took the hairpin loop exit onto Dulaney Valley Road north toward Phoenix.

"No." Margherita shifted.

Janey turned right onto Blenheim Road, gunning the car to power it up the hill before turning right at its crest and into the twins' driveway. A sturdy purple Victorian with a steel-blue wraparound porch inherited from their parents, their house sat back from the road far enough for Pauly to landscape the front yard around Japanese maples. Azalea bushes lined the perimeter and both sides of the steps. The three-foot-tall Blessed Mother statue stood on the lawn in the exact spot where their mother had placed it, surrounded by Pauly's colorful blooms. He'd planted impatiens, violets, black-eyed Susans, and other flowers Margherita couldn't name along the edges of the driveway and around the statue in honor of their late parents. He'd repainted the bench his father had positioned next to it.

Janey parked behind Pauly's blue Nissan and Margherita's silver Acura and climbed out of the car, slamming the door, causing the blue glass rosary dangling from the rearview mirror to sway, its beads tinkling against each other. Margherita heaved herself out of the car and transferred her suitcase to hers. Janey reached the front steps, where her black cat, Max, was stretched vertically across two steps in an odd position.

"Maxie! Did you miss Mama?" Janey said in a loud voice. Still as stone, Max didn't move. Pauly, half awake, appeared at the front door.

"Hey," he muttered, stepping outside. "Good trip?"

Setting the bags with Pauly's gifts on the top step, Janey bent, petted the top of Max's head, but quickly withdrew her hand.

"Something's wrong! He's dead!" Janey said. "Look at him. Didn't you feed him? Didn't you notice?"

Margherita noticed the cat's clouded, vacant eyes looking fake, his mouth open, his tongue hanging out. Flies buzzing around him, Maxie's hind legs were on the third step, his front paws on the fourth. His black fur, stringy and thin, indicated his advanced age.

As a child, Pauly had caught spiders and centipedes in the house, setting them free outside, one of the qualities Margherita's loved about him.

"Shit, man! He was okay yesterday morning," Pauly said, examining the cat.

"Couldn't you see that something was wrong?"

"I thought he liked that spot."

"How could you not notice Max being sick? Or dead? How could you *not* notice something that basic?"

"You asked me to feed the cat. I fed the cat. I also did his litter like you asked. I took care of your cat," he said.

Margherita smiled.

"You didn't notice he looked weird?" Janey shrieked.

"I'm sorry! Sorry! He's seventeen. What do you want?" Pauly said. "A miracle?"

"Poor Maxie died all alone on the steps, and you didn't notice," Janey said, her voice cracking. "He didn't have a beautiful death." She blinked.

"He had a beautiful life," Pauly said. "What's better? A beautiful life or a beautiful death? It's not my fault your old cat died." Slamming the door behind him, he disappeared inside the house.

Margherita laughed quietly. Not about the dead cat, but at Pauly's oblivion. Although she turned away and laughed into her armpit, Janey saw her.

"It's not fucking funny! He was alive when we left. You'd be pissed if I'd laughed when Xander died."

Margherita's face burned. "Max was an old cat," she said, annunciating each word slowly. "Don't you ever compare a cat to a child!" Margherita breathed hard. "I'd give anything for seventeen years of Xander. Anything! I got four."

Without waiting for the twins to move their cars, Margherita maneuvered the Acura around their vehicles and crossed the lawn, smashing Pauly's flowers—something she regretted—onto the road. Janey sat near Maxie.

Pointing her car homeward, Margherita pulled a chocolate bar from her tote—slightly melted from the four-hour trip. She peeled off the wrapping and stuffed half in her mouth. The sweet comfort, chocolate, coated her tongue. A.X.D. The dusk sky, devoid of birds, looked empty, naked, wintery, despite June's white heat, the lush tree line, the endless road before her. Margherita tried to fling the remainder of the candy out the window onto the road, but it stuck to her gooey fingers, and she stuffed it and her fingers into her mouth, weeping as she drove home.

CHOCOLATE LEARNS MARKETING

I knew it. Soon as she walked in the door like she's all that and a bag of chips, like she owned the dang-on world, I knew the girl meant trouble. I mean, this was Club Pussy Cat, not Club Prissy Cat. Here, big-booty girls danced and stripped for about $150-$200 bucks a night, and this joint ain't for girls like her. It ain't for girls like me neither. I came from what you'd call a good home with a Christian mother and father and five brothers and two sisters. But me, I was just chillin' at the CPC trying to decide what I wanted to do with my life. And so far, nothing came to mind and nothing beat the Benjamins from dis joint.

Plus, I never told my parents how I made my dough. They ain't never gonna find out, neither. Far as they concerned, I work as a receptionist in a law office. Five years from now, I ain't gonna be strutting around for my bread. I tried to get one of 'em prissy jobs riding a law firm desk, but none of them bitches would hire me. I needed fast cash, and dancin' paid more than being one of those Walmart sale associates jobs where a girl is stuck hanging up bras and underwear for eight hours at a stretch for no kinda serious cash.

But I understood me working a joint like this for the money. With all them seven brothers and sisters running around, my parents ain't got no moolah to send me or any of us to college or vocational school. I hated school anyways, so I quit and got me a

GED. I ain't doing so bad, either. I paid for my ride, my man, and my two pit bulls.

But this bitch was single and free. What's a bitch like that doin' dancin' at Club Pussy fucking Cat? Her clothes screamed dollars and cents in a big way, and her 'do looked like one of them expensive salon cuts and not a crappy ten dollah joint from Snip and Run. Dark brown hair in one of 'em evenly cut bobs just like you see in magazines around a face with skin clearer than the Ivory Soap baby. Big, cow-brown eyes looked like black diamonds and a killer smile with them big white teeth. She looked like she stars in a fuckin' toothpaste commercial. She carried a black duffle bag with "ALE" in fancy letters on the side in silver thread. Yeah, dis bitch got some dough or she came from some dough—well, more dough than my family and all dem kids running around with bad habits like wanting to eat three plus times a day. Dis bitch just slummin', taking dough that she ain't due.

The girls dancin' in this club—any club in this skanky-assed town—have stringy hair, muddy skin, and crooked teeth, not them perfectly straight white teeth that looked like they been in braces for half a life. Except for one or two, most of them what you call professional druggies, not real dancers. I was doing it to get my financials together. Course, I always kept my 'do up in right with extensions colored and highlighted down to the middle of my back. I was born lucky with good hair and always keep a good 'do. Dis uptown bitch with her bob and perfect straight white teeth asked me if it was my own hair.

"Whadda you think?" I told her. I mean, I bought and paid for these extensions, so it was mine alright. I ain't going to tell her my secrets or how much I paid to make my hair look fuller.

I ain't a real dancer with fly girl training, but I ain't no druggie neither, and I worked out my routines. I took it serious, you know. I fell into this job cause I have the looks, and the money was solid, man, a good solid temporary money-making job for someone like me. My stage name was "Hot Chocolate," though sometimes I went by "Café au Lait" because it sounded tight. You just gotta check out my crib, man, cause it's hooked up, especially for a girl barely past nineteen. Dutch, my man, cleaned it and walked the dogs. It looked like he was a bum 'cause he stayed home all day, but he sold some junk on the side, bred them pups which bring in about $700 bills each, and sat around to think some big thoughts. When he wasn't taking care of them dogs, flim flaming, or painting dem portraits he hung all over the walls of our crib, he built a fine entertainment center out of pine from Home Depot. He made specially-measured places for the TV, VCR, stereo, and PlayStation and compartments for movies and CDs, and painted the whole thing black. Nice furniture, no bugs, no noise, no fingerprints from seven brothers and sisters. Yep, I loved my crib and my man just the way it was.

Anyhow, Little Miss Prissy walked into the club and walked her ass right over to Lil'Man, who sat behind the bar, and asked for the manager. She acted like a fuckin' cell phone executive about to cut a deal. She didn't look nervous or nothing. She acted like she didn't care if she got the job or not. Lil'Man told her he was the manager. Without missing a beat, she extended her hand, shook his, and said her name was Amy and how could she go about applying for a "dancer position." Now you got to understand a dancer in this place ain't like none of that Demi Moore stripper shit, and there ain't dancer "positions." And another thing, dancers in this place ain't shaking Lil'Man's hand.

We danced three dances and then mingled with customers so they buy some booze for them and us. But we didn't actually get booze. Well, the girls older than twenty-one got real booze if they wanted it, and some of them left the club at night drunk and high. The younger ones got cola drinks that mimicked the drink we ordered. We collected a commission off each drink and tips from dancing. On a good night, we pulled in more than three bills. Some nights, man, I went home with six bills. We tipped Lil'Man though. Nobody minded cause he took care of us right.

Lil'Man told Amy she had to audition. She acted like she knew the score and asked if "now" was an okay time. Lil'Man nodded his big head, and she rummaged through her bag and pulled out a CD.

"I like my own music," she said.

"Kay with me," said Lil'Man, who, underneath his burly shoulders, big Santa Clause beard, and ugly-fugly plaid-shirted fat belly, had a heart the size of a roast beef. He managed the bar, and he oversaw the girls like a mother hen, even if half of them didn't know their heads from their asses cause they so high sometimes. He also worked overtime trying to keep the roach population down to a bare minimum by spraying some nasty-smelling potent bug killer twice a day, but he didn't make no connection between them and all the grime and dirt in the place.

Amy gave him the CD. "Where's the dressing room?"

With that, I liked to die laughing. "There ain't no dressing room for dancers here," I yelled from across the bar and smirked. "You think this's the Ritz?" I laughed so hard I almost fell out of my shoes.

Dancers changed in the ladies' room, the drab, battleship-gray dressing room with dirt and mouse turds stuffed in corners and a blurry mirror attached to a dirty wall, and that was that. Lil'Man pointed her in the direction of the ladies' room. She came out in a slinky purple number with a black chiffon-looking overdress down to her ankles with two side slits up to her knees. She wore clear, plastic, strappy shoes with Lucite platforms and stiletto Lucite heals. She lined her eyes in black so they looked catlike and big under the lights. She had a genuine bubble butt and a little waist and decent-sized tits. She's had one of them curvy figures, and when I saw her looking more like a fucking fashion plate, even in dancing clothes, my heart shrank two sizes. I knew right off that she'd hog up all the tips without even trying. A money drain. From my pocket into hers.

Lil'Man watched her sashay over to the stage area where there were two dancing poles. She nodded, and he inserted her CD in the player, smacked the play button, and damn if a rap song didn't start playing. A rap song. What dis bitch know about rap? But the beat was good and slow at first, perfect for dancin'.

The bitch danced like a fly girl, had some moves I planned to steal, stripped off her clothes nice and slow until she was down to blue thong underwear like she done it a million times before, and I knew she passed the audition. A tattoo of some kind of elf decorated her right breast, and two silver rings dangled from each nipple. A fancy-ass stone on a silver ring circled her belly button. Another tattoo of a yellow sun with a lion's face the size of a small tangerine decorated the left side of her back near her shoulder. She flaunted her flat belly; with them money ball muscles in her arms, it didn't take no rocket scientist to figure out she lived at the gym, a regular ol' gym rat. Shit. When Lil'Man told her she was in, she didn't act surprised, or happy, or grateful, or anything.

"Thank you. Here, I'm 'Cupid,'" she told Lil'Man and extended her hand again. "'Round here, please use only my stage name."

"Welcome aboard, Cupid," said Lil'Man. "When can you start?"

"Let's talk money first," she said.

Lil'Man's eyes got a little wide but he explained the deal.

"How about tonight?" she said, and that was about two months ago.

Right away, the other dancers didn't like Cupid. First, she didn't do no drugs, not even weed. She smoked cigarettes but spaced them out so she held on to a pack for about a week. Instead of drinking colas like everybody else, she brought in some fancy-sounding Eye-talian water—Saint Pellogreeni or something like that—for water with a lemon in it, but ordered a gin and tonic in front of customers. She also brought in her own special glass with Cupid written on the bottom in pink nail polish. She took that glass home with her every night and brought it in the next time she worked—something about running it through her dishwasher to keep it clean. She said she didn't drink sodas because of the eighteen tablespoons of sugar in every eight ounces and preferred to keep her complexion clear with the fancy-sounding water.

"Look at that! Dis ho don't want no water from the faucet. It ain't good enough for her," I said out loud to no one in particular one night before the rush. "She wants water that gets imported all the way from Italy." I snatched the bottle from behind the bar and took a swig and spit that bad shit out. "Shit, man. Dis bitch not only don't want water from the faucet, she *pays* for his shit-tasting stuff." I dropped the dark green bottle that looked like it contained white wine instead of water in the trash and smiled at her when it landed with a ka-thunk.

Cupid shrugged. "Different strokes," she said, looking at the inside of the trash can. I could tell she was pissed I sipped her precious H-two-O and then threw that bad-tasting crap in the trash where it belonged.

Right away, customers took to her like she had some magic up her ass and bought her drink after drink. Lil'Man liked her ass more and more every day, especially when he saw cash flow like a green river into the register each night she worked. Me and the other girls felt like stinking seven-day ol' cheese when she was on shift. She acted like Miss Personality Plus, cracked on customers who laughed and appeared to like it even though she insulted them big time.

Miss Personality Plus's personality extended only to customers. She ain't had no personality for the rest of us dancers. Cupid pretended a big plastic wall stood someplace between her and the rest of us. She sucked all the tips from us like some human vacuum cleaner and expected us to sit around and take it like she some celebrity. She talked to Lil'Man mostly when there weren't customers in the house, and Lil'Man didn't talk about her behind her back. Her uptown self acted like she walked on water, and the rest of us, nothing but sewer rats. She dissed Angel Pie one night when the kid offered to share some new Mary Kay makeup with her. Angel Pie's nothing but a seventeen-year-old kid, six months pregnant but not showing too much yet. All the dancers—even the skankiest ones—try to look out for Angel Pie, who don't belong at CPC but who's just down on her luck.

"Listen, Bitch…you might think your shit don't stink, but you in here with the rest of us taking off your clothes for money," I told her when she snorted her nose down at the kid's offer. "You're no better than any one of us, and you sure as shit ain't no better than Angel Pie."

"Whatever," Cupid said, shrugging her shoulder like she brushing away a gnat, walking away like I was invisible.

"Hey, you! Where you going? We ain't finished here," I said. "And you ain't dissing Angel Pie like she's a dirt pile under your feet." Well, dis bitch just snorted and turned around to walk away. "And you sure ain't dissing me either, bitch."

I shoved her ass and she went flying in those Lucite stiletto shoes, flying like she was running from Godzilla. She fell, too, and when she did, all the girls, except Angel Pie, laughed. Only Angel Pie, her belly protruding slightly, walked her skinny bird legs over to where Cupid sat on the ground and helped her up. Angel Pie, gullible Angel Pie with her innocent blue eyes and her brown hair pulled back into a ponytail, the only one who looked like she belong at a high school mixer and not at the CPC, the dancer who's only guilty of believing the lies of a boy who said he loved her, treated like a dirt pile under Cupid's feet, showed that uptown bitch how a real lady acts. Cupid didn't even say thank you.

"What can one expect from a pig, but a grunt," she said in my direction when she got up onto her Lucite shoes. She straightened out her dress, threw me a look that would wither the skin on a fresh orange, and sashayed herself toward the bar.

"Takes a pig to know a pig, bitch," I hollered after her, but she didn't turn around to face me. She just kept walkin'.

One evening, she came in with a road map. A simple fucking road map.

"Hey, Lil'Man. Can I talk to you a minute?" she asked in a sugary voice.

He nodded. She floated up to the bar before she even changed outta her street clothes and handed him a map while words like "proximity," "message," "marketing," and "win-win" floated out of her mouth like yellow butterflies. When it came time for her to change, she left the map on the bar. I walked over to peek at what the big pow-pow was all about and saw two red circles drawn around parts of the interstate. Big whoop. Two red circles around the interstate. So what. Big fuckin' deal. What so special about the interstate except that it can take you from here to there without having to stop for a bunch of red lights.

Next day, when she came in, she pulled a red folder out of her bag, and then, using that cell phone executive voice of hers, she and Lil'Man worried over the stack of papers in it as if they was reviewing the peace treaty between Lincoln and Lee. Fat belly touching the table and sagging between his thighs, Lil' Man moved his hand around the papers, and they sat down for about fifteen minutes, looking like they negotiating before they shook hands.

"It's a deal," Cupid said and smiled her big-toothed, perfect, white smile.

"Deal," Lil'Man said. He nodded his head up and down in appreciation of the deal.

"I just need you to sign here," she said. Damn if Lil'Man didn't sign that piece of paper Cupid had.

Cupid didn't come in the next night—a Tuesday—even though she was scheduled, but she called and talked to Lil'Man. He didn't seem to mind she missed one of her nights. She missed the next night, too. Whatever she was up to, Lil'Man was in on it. Cupid finally hauled her ass back in the club on Thursday. When she did, she headed straight for Lil'Man and pulled a sheet of papers from her bag and handed them over before she changed.

The papers were fliers—lime green, lemon yellow, neon pink—with a silhouette of a girl wearing a top hat and a tailcoat with her leg raised in a dance step, advertising "Club Pussy Cat Club" and offering a $5 off coupon on the first $20 spent for any Friday night. In order to get the discount, the coupon had to be presented. Cupid had made them on her computer and spent two days leaving stacks of 'em in all the truck stops on the interstate within a certain radius from the club. She also had somehow kept track of how many fliers went where.

That Friday night, a flow of truckers with them fliers in hand streamed into CPC and asked for the $5 off the first $20 spent. They packed the club. We all did pretty good that night, too, even the skankiest, fucked-up ho in the joint. But it don't take no mental giant to figure out that Cupid made off with the most because she, no doubt, collected another commission off every customer who brought in a coupon. So already she wasn't workin' a month and figured out how to have two days off with pay and how to get some extra moolah in her pockets when she did work. Shit, it didn't take no genius math-head to figure out she pulled in some hefty tips since she usually now pulled in more tips than anybody else, including me, who used to haul in the biggest load before her ass showed up.

Ignoring us, Cupid talked to Lil'Man when there weren't any customers in the place. She plucked everybody's last nerve the way she looked down her nose at us. She plucked everybody's last nerve, that is, except Lil'Man and the customers, who couldn't seem to throw enough money at that ho. She plucked everyone's last nerve when she fucked over Princess Ice. Big time.

Princess Ice, strung out as usual, barely sat in the chair at the table near the stage. A skinny-assed chick with dyed yellow hair that looked like straw and blue eyes that looked like the color leaked out of 'em, Princess wore her dance costume, a black and brown leopard number that looked like nothing, and she was bent over with her head between her knees like she gonna puke. When she got the energy to push herself in an upright position, her eyes, underneath them big, long false eyelashes, rolled to the back of her head like they had a will of their own.

Wearing a flouncy, pink, ruffly number for the sickos out there, Baby Doll, another ho already on stage, finished her dance when Cupid walked over and took a long look at Princess Ice bent over in the metal chair. Princess Ice, up next, didn't look like dancing was the top item on her to-do list. With her head between her knees, her hair covering up her skinny legs with red sores on them, she moaned and groaned like a dying dog.

"Hey," Cupid hollered at her. "Hey, if you're gonna dance, then dance," Cupid yelled at the top of Princess's head. She sounded like a fucking queen. "If you ain't gonna dance, I'm taking your turn," she added and strutted away in her purple and black chiffon number, acting like the queen bee.

When Baby Doll climbed off the stage, Cupid took Princess Ice's place and got the rest of us pissed at her.

"Hey bitch, who you think you are anyway? You can't just take Princess's place without first running it by the rest of us," I challenged her.

"I'm here to dance and to make some money. Nothing else. If Princess Ice isn't dancing her number, I don't have to ask your permission to take her place. Nothing personal. I saw an opportunity and took it," she said matter-of-factly. Course, she didn't look at me when she talked and concentrated on buckling the straps of those damned fancy Lucite stiletto shoes.

"We don't work like that here," I told her.

"Now we do," she said and then pulled up that plastic wall.

"I say we don't."

"Right, like you HAVE a say…. This is nothing but a job for me. A business. A way to make some money. Princess Ice didn't dance, so I'm taking her place. No fuss, no muss. Don't expect me to ask yours and anyone else's permission for what I do or don't do," she said, working her other shoe and not even giving me one glace in the eye. When she finished buckling her shoe and put her foot down, she stepped on a roach. We both heard the crunch. "Fucking insects," she said. She finally looked me in the eye and said, "Nothing personal, just business."

"Listen, bitch. What makes you think you so goddamn special? This ain't nothing but a job to the rest of us, and we don't much like you coming in, taking over the joint and stealing dances."

"That's too bad for you." She sniffed and walked away.

Later, I overheard her talking to the bouncer, and they mocked Princess Ice and Baby Doll. The bouncer—Jimmy Junga—told Cupid about Princess's side business of selling blow jobs for a buck in the back of the club. From that point on, the two of them, in cahoots, referred to Princess as PBJ—short for Princess Blow Job—and they laughed and smirked. Jimmy also told her about the scams the other hos pulled, like Baby Doll selling junk, MistyRain selling a fuck for a dime and two—that's twelve bucks—so she can buy her fix. He told her about the night Big Mama, called Biggie, whose fat rolls make the Pillsbury Doughboy look like the poster child for a diet plan, was wearing nothing but a thong and lifted up one of her giant fatty legs and one side of her even grander ass and let off a fart so loud and stinky it cleared the bar for about ten minutes. Jimmy Junga had laughed so hard telling Cupid about it he hardly got the words out. He didn't say nothing about me. Good thing, too, cause I'd have busted him one.

Then, I suspected Cupid for a cop. She acted too cool to be a girl trying to make a buck, plus she one them health freaks. Lil'Man might be tight-lipped, but Jimmy, his long-time friend, got a mouth like Niagara Falls. Jimmy Junga, a big-muscled brother who shaved his head because his hair was almost gone and he felt too proud to admit he was going bald, pretended his shaved head made him a badass. He packed on the pounds, too, a little chubby in the waist, so he didn't look so much like a badass as like a pile of lumpy mashed potatoes. He and Cupid both thought their shit smelled like Avon Emeraude, but I knew Lil'Man didn't pay him as much as he'd make in a regular job that paid regular taxes and benefits.

So Jimmy Junga, shady in some off sort of way, took a liking to Cupid even though Cupid only used him and his stupid ass was too dumb to see it. If she a cop, Jimmy Junga better watch his back.

One day, I first asked Jimmy about his son to get on his good side, and he talked his head off. Then I asked him about Cupid and that's how I learned she got herself a son, too, fathered by a brother, and that's how she got herself kicked out of her fancy, highfalutin' house. College girl, too. Well, not anymore. Bad enough to get knocked up in one of those uptown homes, worse when the baby's father was a no-count, drug-dealing brother. Now I understood why she so money hungry, but she still rubbed us other dancers the wrong way acting the way she do.

Lil'Man didn't give a rat's ass about the way Cupid carried on because ever since she dreamed up that flier idea, business boomed, his cash register clanged, and his heart sang. After the first go-round with the fliers, Cupid and Lil'Man sat at the bar again with a stack of newspapers and about six pieces of white typing paper.

"Lil'Man, you got to spend money to make money," Cupid said with authority, the be-all, end-all of the business world.

"Yeah, Lil'Man, you got to spend money," I mimicked her. Cupid shot me a killer look. Lil'Man said nothing but studied the sheets of white paper spread out before him in a fan on the bar. Next to the fan of white papers, which featured some kind of design similar to the high-stepping woman on the flier, sat an index card with numbers in a row, like them multiplication tables from grade school.

"From what I know, the rule of thumb is that it takes three times to get a message out. I recommend six so you can get a deal on the price. All with the coupon, so we can track 'em," she said, using her uptown voice. Lil'Man studied the line-up and then he nodded his head. "Next go round, we skip any outlet where no coupons came back," she said.

Next thing, an ad in the local weekly appeared for the Club Pussy Cat billed as a "Gentleman's Club" with dancing and music. Also, the ad said there was a happy hour from six p.m. to nine p.m. every Wednesday and Thursday and to bring the coupon for a $5 discount on the first $20 worth of drinks. When Cupid came to work the Wednesday the ad appeared, she brought a stack of the weeklies from other neighborhoods and plopped them down on the bar for Lil'Man to peruse. Looking pleased, he stared at the ads—in six different weeklies. When I looked at the ad, even I wanted to come to Club Pussy Cat even though I knew it was a skanky-assed place with roaches, mice, and customers who sometimes liked to fight. The excitement in the ad just made you want to be part of the whole Club Pussy Cat scene.

"Wait 'til they come here expecting a gentleman's club and they find this skanky-assed bar with peeling paint and mouse shit in the corners," I said out loud, trying to burst Cupid's little bubble. "They'll think this place is real fiiinnnne."

"Week one," said Cupid. "Don't expect anything special. Maybe one or two."

Lil'Man nodded. I wondered how Cupid knew all this shit.

Sure enough, one guy came in holding the ad and gave it to Lil'Man when he ordered two drinks, one for himself and one for Baby Doll. The next night, a Thursday, two more "gentlemen" came in with the same ad and coupon. I saw Lil'Man put the coupons in a cigar box behind the bar.

The next Wednesday and Thursday when the second ad ran, six new customers came in with the coupons from the paper. The week after that, it was nine, and so on. By the sixth week, an extra two dozen people came in, and between the Wednesday night specials from the ad and the Friday night specials from the fliers, the joint was jumpin' with people wearing preppy clothes and blow-dried hair. Cupid convinced Lil'Man to keep running the ads offering all kinds of specials for things like bachelor parties and over-the-hill fifty-year-old birthday parties and brokered him a deal with the paper since he was running more ads. Ideas floated out of Cupid's head like diarrhea and all of them seem to work cause she had some powerful magic in her ass.

Except for Lil'Man and Cupid, nobody liked the changes at CPC. Lil'Man joined the local businessman association since his joint was now a popular spot. Cupid got a cut of the extra business she brought in. The ol' regulars, customers who been coming in for years, looked uncomfortable and out of place with the rowdy bachelor party patrons and the obnoxious fifty-year-old birthday party groups. The regulars still wore dirty, torn-up jeans and wife beater undershirts, and the newbies slinked around in shiny penny loafers and knit shirts with alligators on them, acting like the regulars were just "local color."

Baby Doll and Princess Ice quit complaining because of the extra dough in their pockets. Big Mama stayed long enough to make $300 and tore out of there faster than a metro liner, and

Angel Pie, who cut out the dance routines because of her baby, picked up decent cash waitressing. The rest of the skanky-assed dancers didn't give a damn one way or another so long as they made money between the time they got to the club and the time they left. One big happy family, you'd think. But Cupid's uptown bullshit, her foreign water bottles, her Miss Personality Plus act, irritated the shit outta me, especially when she treated the rest of us like three-day-old eggs.

Lil'Man and Cupid put their heads together again, a sure signal something was up. Then Sunday night, at closing time, Lil'Man looked over at Cupid and announced that we all have a paid day off on Monday. Shit. Something big was up. He paid all of us about $100, better than a slow night, which Mondays usually were, but crap for a good night. I wondered what Cupid and Lil'Man had cooked up next, especially since Miss Personality Plus stood there, all-knowing, and she didn't get any of the extra moula.

Tuesday night, the place looked different. Light fixtures on the ceiling shone, and instead of a smell of stale cigarettes and booze, the place smelled like oranges. A fresh coat of turquoise paint covered the walls that needed painting. No more chips hanging off any walls. No more mouse crap in the bathroom corners. No more dirt anywhere. The bathrooms smelled fresh and orange-y. A fresh coat of bubble gum pink paint brightened the small ladies' room with all kinds of Barbie stuff glued to the walls. Also painted bubble gum pink, on the front door of the ladies' room hung a plastic box with a Barbie inside, the word LADIES freshly painted in white above the box. The Barbie in the box wore a pink and red polka dot bikini and pink high heels, and that outfit matched the color scheme inside the bathroom. A basket of plastic pink flowers sat on the toilet tank, and a new full-length, clear-as-day mirror hung on the wall next to the door.

A new toilet paper dispenser like the kind you find in office buildings with one giant roll to a stall hung from the wall. Shit, the fucking floor tiles were new, shiny ceramic numbers, a seafoam green that contrasted nicely with the pink. I never would have thought to pair those two colors.

In the men's room, the same story. The front door of the men's room had the same plastic box glued to the door with a Ken doll in it. Ken wore a black and white cowboy outfit. I peeked inside, and a fresh coat of tan paint coated the walls, and the stalls were painted some kind of burnt red. All kinds of Ken doll stuff were glued to the walls with an overall color scheme of black, tan, and white. The same kind of new toilet paper dispenser hung in there next to a new machine that dispensed condoms, and a new tile floor in there too, roasted pepper red or maroon.

The wood floor of the stage, polished to a high gloss, looked like it had been sanded with a satiny new finish on top. A totally new room was created by the stage that said DRESSING ROOM with the same hot pink paint that said "Ladies." Inside the dressing room, which didn't have a ceiling, sat a wall of beat-up, dented lockers with all the dancers' stage names painted in the hot pink. Inside the room, cameras hung from the ceilings. The dancing poles look new, too, but they had just been polished to a supreme glow, and they looked slippery. I thought of Princess Ice trying to sail around those polished poles while she's a tiny bit high and sailing right off the new satiny-looking stage.

The old sticky black floor in the bar looked reddish. The black must have been the never-cleaned-up dirt because somebody scrubbed and waxed it. Light from the streetlamp shone through the cleaned multicolored windows of the bar. All the liquor bottles had been wiped off and the place looked like

Mr. Clean and his brother Mr. Fix-it spent the day and night touching the place with magic fingers in a contest to see who could outdo the other.

So us dancers now had a dressing room. No more changing in the drab ladies' room, no longer drab, and Cupid and Lil'Man, sitting at the shiny, newly-polished, cleaned bar worried over a new set of papers. I wished I had thought of a makeover for the place.

"We're targeting another demographic that will bring in twice as much…" Cupid said, Lil'Man nodding. "But we have to have something to deliver when they get here. Aside from the discount on the coupon, I mean."

Lil'Man's head bounced from side to side like he understood the butterfly words floating out of Cupid's mouth. Cupid gathered the papers and stuffed them into her bag, which she then placed inside the locker with her name painted on it. She attached a lock, but no one else did because we didn't know we were getting any lockers. When I went to stash my stuff in my locker, I noticed an extra row of lockers with no names painted on 'em.

Next day, a never-ending stream of tight-assed, muscled, hunky-looking men, the Chippendales on parade, came to see Lil'Man. He asked them a few questions, and the word "experiment" came trippin' outta his mouth. Finally, Lil'Man shook hands with three. One was a brother that was so built he looked like the Hulk, except Black instead of green. The brother had dreads and wore a diamond-like stud earring in his right ear. He was hot, let me tell you. The second guy looked like a cocktail, half this and half that. This guy had black hair in a thick braid that fell straight down his back above his waist. A barbed wire tattoo circled around the bulging bicep on his right arm. Real simple black tattoo. The third guy, white, with short, military-cut, sandy hair and blue eyes, looked like a bicycle cop. The three of them had clear complexions like Cupid's, and I could tell right off they weren't no druggies; they looked too healthy to be druggies. All gym rats, probably into protein drinks. And steroids. Or undercover cops.

In the dressing room, the unnamed lockers on the bottom row now had names painted on them in bold black letters, the same color as the letters that said MEN on the men's room door. TOMMY BANG-BANG, JOHNNY ROCKS, and BLACK DRAGON.

When Tuesday rolled around, the three of them rolled in, too. The brother stuffed his bag into the locker with "Tommy Bang-Bang" painted on the outside. The white guy said he was Johnny Rocks. Black Dragon, the cocktail who wasn't wearing a shirt, nodded in my direction. When he turned to stuff his bag in his locker, I saw the huge, colorful green, red, and gold dragon tattoo painted onto his entire back. Boy, did it look awesome with those colors.

"Tattoo boy," I said with a smile. "That dragon rules."

"Thanks," he said.

That was all he said. Nothing more, nothing less, as if striking up a dialogue with me would cost him a dollar a word.

Tuesday night also brought in these bitches, all carrying those stinking coupons with the $5 off the first $20 spent for the "all-male review" on them. Sickening. These hos screamed at Tommy Bang-Bang, Johnny Rocks, and Black Dragon like they never saw nearly naked men before. Sickeningly, they stuffed dollar bills into the string undies of those gym rats.

That Cupid, she turned a normal, everyday strip club into a circus, complete with three clowns called Tommy Bang-Bang, Johnny Rocks, and Black Dragon. All they missing is the big hair and squeaky red ball nose, but they clowns just the same. The joint jumped and hopped with new male customers, some of them trying to hook up with the ladies there to see the all-male review, and some of them trying to hook up with each other. CPC turned into a regular three-ring circus with Cupid, the ring leader, and Lil'Man, seeing the register grow fat at the end of the night, happier than the only ho on a battleship. Cupid must be raking in the dough. Pretty soon, she gonna be Lil'Man's partner. I could see the handwriting on the wall. I don't mind working for Lil'Man. I do mind working for that bitch-ho.

All night long, Lil'Man smiled behind the bar, watched the action with dollar signs in his eyes. The regulars looked thrilled to see a bunch of bitches walking into the club, even if they did look like plain office ladies trying to forget their boring-assed jobs and their boring-assed lives. And the new male customers who came in to score with each other proved to be a trip to watch. And like I said, us regular dancers—me, Princess Ice, Baby Doll, us from south Baltimore—all left with a sizeable chunk of change in our pockets.

I hated all the changes to the club. Them changes came too fast, and the club turned into Club Prissy Cat. The handwritin' on the wall, except Baby Doll, Princess Ice, Angel Pie, the other girls, nobody noticed it. Neither did Lil'Man. So long as they went home with fat pockets, nobody cared to see what was happening. But I saw it: Cupid aimed to be the fucking boss. She aimed to be the new owner of CPC.

Wednesday night was the regular night, no male review. Cupid, Baby Doll, Princess Ice, Big Mama, Angel Pie, and I danced our regular schedules. Cupid's dance came after mine. I was in the dressing room changing into my mingling clothes while Cupid danced out her routine. That's when I saw her Lucite stiletto shoes sitting on the floor instead of in her locker, which she kept a lock on. She started this dance in her French maid costume but I knew the stilettos were her favorite shoes and that she'd probably wear them for her next number. Nobody was in the dressing room but me. I snipped at the elastic of the T-strap on the left shoe. Then I changed in a hurry and scooted out of the dressing room before she finished her number.

The night dripped by. I couldn't wait for my next number because I knew Cupid was up afterward. When the time came for her dance, sure as shit, she had on those Lucite stilettos, and I waited for her to walk out of her left shoe unexpectedly at any minute and humiliate herself by fallin' on her face mid-dance. That woman must have a horseshoe up her ass because she was prancin' in between poles when the left shoe gave way, but this bitch saved herself by catching onto one of the poles, swinging around with two hands like a fucking ice skater or gymnast and kicked off the shoe into the area just below the stage. She made it look like it was just a new step in the routine. Later in the dressing room, she examined the shoe. She said nothing to nobody about it, and I said nothing to her either.

Thursday, before the crowd filtered in, I accused her of stealing my "I-dream-of-genie" costume. Aside from illegal drugs, the other thing Lil'Man didn't want in his club was a thief. He don't care if we come in high or go outside to get high, but he didn't want no drugs inside the joint or in our bags. And he can't stand stealing of any kind. Those are the two things that got a dancer fired.

I belly-ached for all my worth that Cupid stole my $180 costume, ordered special from Fredericks of Hollywood.

"Chocolate, here's a news flash: I can buy my own."

"Well, it's gone. I left it in my locker, and now it's gone," I said.

"What makes you think I took it? Why not Baby Doll, Princess Ice, or Big Mama, or any one of the other dancers here?" The left corner of her mouth turned up like she ready to laugh.

"Because Baby Doll already got herself a genie costume of her own, and Princess only wears animal prints, Big Mama can't fit into it, and Angel Pie's too pregnant to look like a genie," I said. "So that leaves you."

"Maybe you misplaced it. Or left it home and forgot that you left it there. Or maybe one of those pit bulls you're always bragging about tore it to pieces. I don't have your costume. And another thing, I'm no thief," Cupid said matter-of-factly in her uptown voice.

Cupid wasn't heated by the accusation. She just shrugged her shoulders and acted as if I said, "It's going to be a ball-buster of a hot day today." She didn't even get the least bit indignant or try to get in my face with denials. If somebody accused me of stealing something when I didn't, I'd be in their face big time and threatening to bang them upside the head.

Later, I saw her talking to Lil'Man. Then after she walked away, he made a phone call. In the middle of the shift, right before my second dance, Lil'Man pulled me aside and handed me a bag.

"You left your costume at home. Thought you might want to use it for your next number," he said, extending his hand with the bag with my costume.

I promised myself that Cupid would be gone by the middle of the next night. That would be Friday, when the joint was jumpin' with all them truckers from the fliers. One less dancer sounded like lots more moolah for me.

Friday, I had a plastic bag of ecstasy pills, about a dozen of them. Es or Xs, as Princess called them. They looked like cute little buggers with colorful cartoon characters on them, and, positive they were going to be Cupid's ticket out of the club, my stomach did somersaults when I had them in my hand because I knew these babies in Cupid's fancy-assed ALM bag would be an instant goodbye. I watched for every opportunity to stuff the pills in her bag and was tickled with joy when she was in a rush for her third dance and didn't shut her locker lock all the way.

When she was on stage, I whispered to Lil'Man that I saw Cupid with a plastic bag of Xs. Lil'Man looked at me hard. It took every ounce of strength not to smirk.

"I see," said Lil'Man.

"I saw the bag of Xs in her hand. Maybe she don't use, but I bet she sells."

"We'll check it out."

Cupid finished her number and sprinted to the dressing room while the music changed and Baby Doll strutted onto the stage. It took forever for Lil'Man to complete a drink order for Princess Ice, but when he did, we walked over to the dressing room together. He rolled in and grabbed Cupid's bag and dumped the contents out on the floor. She didn't even protest.

Nothing. No bag of drugs. Cupid, with magic up her ass, must have seen the Xs and plucked it somewhere else.

"What's up with you?" Lil'Man said, looking right at me.

"I swear, I saw a plastic bag with Xs in it in her bag!" I defended myself.

"Riiiiight," Cupid said.

"Check her person. I bet she is hiding them on herself somewhere," I said.

"Right now, we're going to have a locker inspection."

Lil'Man ordered Cupid to open her locker, and he took everything out. Still no plastic bag of Xs.

"You next," he turned and said to me. Open your locker."

Lil'Man pulled all the stuff in my locker and placed it on the floor. There wasn't much, a purse, the genie costume, a bag of makeup and my 100 percent navy blue nylon bag with my regular clothes and shoes, some perfume. Lil'Man rooted through my nylon bag and didn't find a thing. Ditto for the purse and the genie costume, which he unfolded and refolded with the precision of a dry cleaner store owner. But he overlooked the make-up bag until Cupid pointed it out to him. He dumped all the makeup on the table in the dressing room, and sure enough, out came the plastic bag with the Xs.

"What's this?"

"They're not mine," I said.

"Riiiiiiight," Cupid said.

"Ho, I said they ain't mine!" I stamped my foot.

"They're in your bag," said Lil'Man.

"But they ain't mine!" I shouted.

"Well, they're not mine either," Cupid said.

"They belong to somebody," Lil'Man said. "There's an easy way to solve this." He went over to the fucking camera I forgot all about and pulled out the cassette. He disappeared into his office for about half an hour.

"You're fired. Get your shit and get outta here," Lil'Man said to me.

"What? You can't fire me."

"I just did," Lil'Man said.

"Bitch," I screamed at Cupid. She smirked, looking triumphant.

I knew that girl meant trouble soon as she walked in the door like she owned the place; it would be a matter of time before she did own the place.

The Wagon Wheel needed a dancer. I walked into the joint like I owned the place and shook the manager's hand. Copies of Cupid's fliers sat in the bottom of my bag, and I knew the Wagon Wheel would be in for some big-assed changes once I passed the audition.

NOTHING FALLING APART IN THE HOUSE

Aunt Frankie and Mother screamed at each other in the downstairs bathroom, their angry voices rising up through the pipes. Jeannie and Katie crept into my room and the three of us listened by the vent on the floor near the window. The girls were scared, I could tell.

"Jody, you're going to have to get it together. I'm leaving in three days and you're not making any effort at being a parent or being the adult in charge. These are your kids, and they need you to be living in the now, in the moment, and not the past," Aunt Frankie shouted. "Ted is dead, but you're not. And neither are they."

"Why do you have to go take care of some fucking kids that you aren't even related to? What's in Chile? Why can't you stay? I need more time," Mother pleaded.

"I have my own life, Jody. This is all about choices, yours impinging on mine. You're perfectly capable of stepping back into your life. Shit happened. Bad shit happened. You have the opportunity to make some good choices. You know what you need to do, dammit. I want the opportunity to live my life as I see fit."

"I can't," Mother said, her tone flat.

"You have to. As long as I'm around, you'll use me as the easy way out, the way to check out of your life. Last night you totally zoned out on us. You'll dump your shit onto me. I helped when you needed me, and now it's time to help you help yourself."

We could hear by the footsteps that Aunt Frankie left the bathroom. Through the hallway window, we saw her get into her blue Taurus and drive away.

"Aunt Frankie doesn't want to take care of us anymore," Katie said.

"It's Mother's job," I said. Something happened to Mother when she was in jail for shooting father. She wasn't the same.

Downstairs, Mother attempted to make Saturday pancakes. They burned, sticking to the frying pan.

"It's been a while since I've cooked anything, kids," she said, scraping the mess into the trash.

"We don't need pancakes today," Katie, fidgeting with her hair, looking up at Mother with hopeful eyes, said. "We can have cereal."

Mother put the large, yellow box of honey oats and three bowls on the table.

"Get the milk," she said. "Help yourself. Help Jeannie, please," she said.

In the living room, the TV went on.

Jeannie couldn't pour the milk herself. Katie got her situated in the chair and served her cereal, remembering her special blue-handled dinosaur spoon, pouring the milk so that it wouldn't spill. Jeannie picked out the oats from the bowl with her stubby fingers and Mother didn't see it to scold her the way Aunt Frankie did. Aunt Frankie was right. Katie shouldn't be the one taking care of Jeannie.

"I wish she'd go back to jail," Katie whispered. "I don't like her anymore."

* * *

When Aunt Frankie came back at dinner time, she and Mother yelled at each other again. We had mostly spent Saturdays cleaning. We'd help Aunt Frankie after breakfast. Then we'd go to the grocery store and to other stores. Sometimes she'd take us to the park. Mother hadn't done any of these things on this Saturday morning. Instead, she laid on the sofa, staring at the wall, even though the TV blared. She hadn't noticed that Jeannie pulled Aunt Frankie's make-up box down from the shelf in the bathroom and dabbed a spot of red lipstick in the center of each white tile, painted her face with shades of green and pink, and dropped powder and lotion all over the floor and rug. I had tried to clean up some of the mess, but when I wiped the lipstick on the tile, it simply smeared. She hadn't noticed that Katie had left the house to play with friends and hadn't yet returned, way past the time that she was allowed to be out. Afraid to leave the house, I lied, telling my friend Jimmy I was grounded when he knocked on the door asking if I wanted to come out. Mother hadn't fixed any of us lunch or dinner. Jeannie's toys were strewn about the house. We ate cereal all day.

"Jody, what the hell happened here? Did your brain go on vacation? This isn't fair, Jody. To the kids or to me," Aunt Frankie yelled, upset at the makeup mess Jeannie made and the cereal spilled in the kitchen. She yelled for Mother to get up from the sofa. She switched off the TV. She ordered Mother to clean the bathroom properly, to take a bath. Mother acted like a robot. In the kitchen, chopping potatoes, eggplants, and onions, Aunt Frankie cried. Maybe the onions made her cry.

* * *

Later, Father Pete, the pastor from our church, and Grandma Costa came over, Grandma opening the door without bothering to ring the doorbell. Katie stayed in her room, punished by Aunt Frankie for having gone to a friend's house without permission. Jeannie was in bed.

"Yoooou who…." she called. "Frankie? Jody? Where are you?" Grandma led Father Pete through the house to the kitchen. She motioned him to sit down and opened the refrigerator.

"How about something to drink?" she said to the priest before calling Aunt Frankie. Grandma stirred the pot with the simmering eggplants and potatoes.

"Thanks for coming," Aunt Frankie said, coming down the steps, wiping her hands on her pants. Whispering to Father Pete, she said, "Jody's upstairs. She'll be down. How about something to drink?"

Aunt Frankie gave Father Pete a glass of red wine; Grandma, lemonade. She gave me sliced oranges and told me to go watch TV. Waiting for Mother, the three of them whispered in the kitchen.

When Mother finally came down the steps, Aunt Frankie winced. Mother had taken a shower but wore the same clothes. So far, she'd worn the same clothes for five days. Grandma told Mother that she'd look great after she put some meat on her bones and air kissed her. Father Pete and Mother left to take a walk while Grandma and Aunt Frankie whispered in the kitchen. They set the table.

When Father Pete and Mother returned, she looked as if she'd been crying. Father Pete blessed her, the house, us, Grandma, and Aunt Frankie. He commented on the beautiful bookshelves, shelves that Father built on his days off. The house was filled with things that he had worked on, touched with his hands. Like the cocktail table that he had made and wrote "Tommy and Daddy worked on this" with the date underneath. The walls also had marks from holes in the walls that he put there when he was mad or hitting Mother. Mother shuddered. I wondered if she remembered the good things like the table or the bad things like the holes in the walls, now repaired.

We ate Aunt Frankie's spicy eggplants and potatoes. Mother moved food around her plate. She pretended to listen to Father Pete, Aunt Frankie, and Grandma, who talked about Mother's new life and Aunt Frankie returning to her old one. She was a Sister of Mercy at an orphanage in Chile, tending to children whose parents got lost and never came back, she had once told me. I could tell that Mother had zoned out again.

"I'm looking forward to getting back to work in Chile, Father. There's so much to do down at the mission. I can't wait to see the new changes at the convent," Aunt Frankie said.

He glanced at Mother. "Maybe God's plan for you has changed, Sister Aloysius."

Aunt Frankie frowned.

* * *

"Father Pete's blessing didn't work," I told Aunt Frankie later. "Mother still stares at the wall and doesn't eat."

"Don't worry, Tom. She'll get there. Once I leave, it's do or die. She'll have no choice. But you know I will always be in touch with you, only a phone call or a letter away."

Aunt Frankie was wrong. I could feel it. *She's not the one who'll die*, I thought. *Mother already killed father. What if she kills us, too? Not with a gun the way she killed Father, but slowly, in small steps.*

* * *

"I don't need happy pills," Mother said when she and Aunt Frankie came back from the doctor's. Mother puffed on her cigarette. Aunt Frankie glared, but didn't say a word.

"You need something. An attitude adjustment. I leave in two days, and you'll need to get with the program sooner or later," Aunt Frankie said. "You need to get a job, too."

* * *

No onions in my pockets, but I couldn't stop crying. Quietly. Even though boys don't cry. Katie and Jeannie followed Aunt Frankie up and down the stairs asking her about Chile. They didn't cry. Aunt Frankie was going away for a long time. I kicked her luggage standing guard at the front door waiting for the commuter van to haul them and her off to the airport. The suitcases fell over like dominoes. I ran upstairs and slammed the door to my room.

"Tom?" Aunt Frankie knocked on my door. I grunted, and she pushed it open.

"Tom?" She came in wearing her traveling clothes and a big wooden cross around her neck. She had tucked her brown hair into a short white veil with red markings that looked like a huge kerchief.

"Why do you have to go?" I demanded, wanting to pinch her arms.

"It's time for me to go," she said. "Take this," she said, handing me a large rectangular box. "Open it."

Aunt Frankie hugged me, but I pushed her away. The box fell to the floor. A notepad, colored pens, art paper, two books of stamps, and two phone cards spilled to the floor. Inside the box sat a black, yellow, and red crocheted blanket, the colors of my favorite basketball team.

"I made one for each of you to remember me by," she said. She pulled the blanket out of the box and wrapped it around me. "I love you, Tom. I'll miss you so much," she said, sniffing.

"Then why can't you stay?"

"Your mother's job is to take care of you and your sisters. My job is to take care of some children who don't have mothers," she said. "Write to me, call if you need to. I'll send you letters and packages."

The blanket dropped from around my shoulders and I pushed it under the bed. I refused to hug her back. I refused to say anything, not goodbye, not how much I loved her or how I didn't want her to go.

Katie, wrapped in a similar pink and purple blanket, burst into my room yelling, "Look at me! Look at me! I look like a queen!" Behind her came Jeannie dragging a black and white blanket on the floor.

Whispering goodbyes, Aunt Frankie hugged and kissed Katie. She picked up and squeezed Jeannie, swung her to her hip as she'd done a million times over the past four years and planted kisses on her fat cheeks.

"I wanna go with you," Jeannie told Aunt Frankie. "I wanna go with you," she whined. "I wanna be with you."

Holding Jeannie on her hip, Aunt Frankie hugged me close.

"You'll all be okay. Trust me," she whispered in my ear. Tears filled her eyes but Aunt Frankie blinked them back. "I love you, Tom. You're my special angel, and you will be fine. You'll see."

Outside, a horn blasted. Aunt Frankie ran down the stairs with Jeannie in her arms and, at the bottom of the steps, handed her to Mother. Jeannie wailed for Aunt Frankie.

Crying, Mother held Jeannie. "I can't do this without you," she said.

"You can. You did it once before, and you can do it again," Aunt Frankie said.

She hugged mother, who didn't hug her back. The horn blasted again. Aunt Frankie picked up her powder blue suitcases and flew out the door, as if she couldn't dance away fast enough. I wanted to dance away with her, dance away from Mother, from the girls, from the ghost-filled house.

Later, I wrapped the blanket around me like a cocoon, closed my eyes, pictured Aunt Frankie in Chile with those poor, poor lucky children, and refused to cry.

DOORWAYS: ENTRANCES AND EXITS

The Blue Moon Saloon's heavy door slams behind Lucy, Delia, and Nick, a swoosh of cold air following them like a shadow. Lucy likes Nick more than she ought to like any student, and, piqued by his invitation to join the Thursday Night Blues Jam, she relishes the proximity of his body near hers. Dating students is frowned upon, but in the truck, she heard him tell Delia he's a bass and strings instructor at the Peabody, which puts him into a different category. Is she ready to break her longtime rule of never dating fellow employees? Nick intrigues her, and his voice sounds genuinely caring and gentle. She'd ascertained that he's taller during his first lesson when he had to push the piano bench away from the piano to accommodate his long legs. His precision and musicality, his smooth tenor, his silvery laugh impressed her, and now she wonders if he's married or has a girlfriend? Does he have a child? Is he divorced? Is this invitation strictly professional? Something inside her flutters when he's around, and she's started looking forward to his lesson time.

To check herself from leaning into Nick, Lucy instead leans toward the warmth of Gracie's body, the guide dog obediently beside her, and she automatically begins assessing room details. Under her feet, the floor feels hard—perhaps wood or tile that's sticky and worn in places; the dank, faint odor of old, stale beer permeates the air, and judging by the airiness of the space around her and the low hum of voices, the place feels empty. To her right at one o'clock, a bell that sounds as if it belongs on a boat clangs loud enough to startle her. A loud cheer rises, telling her that people must be already sitting at the bar. In a few of the Fells Point bars she's patronized, bartenders clang a bell when they receive a tip.

"Dog's not allowed. It's got to go, and if it don't go, then you both got to go." The man at three o'clock sounds bored, matter-of-fact, accustomed to power and people obeying. He didn't ask for her ID, just dismissed her because of her service dog.

"Gracie goes anywhere I go," Lucy says, trying to keep her voice even, trying to mask the irritation that rankles her at the scrutiny because clearly, this bozo does not know the laws. Gracie's harness clearly indicates she's a "Service Dog," and any low-level idiot should be able to realize Lucy's blindness.

"Then you and your fake service dog have got to go," the man says. He dismisses her and addresses Nick and Delia in a no-nonsense business tone. "You two, IDs."

"Gracie and I aren't leaving," Lucy says in a loud voice, interrupting his ID check.

Lucy's irritation stiffened her. She also felt irritated with Nick for inviting Delia, her private piano student and an underage child, to boot, on what could be a first date. Whatever the night represents, with or without Delia, she's not about to let it begin with being bullied and dismissed by a bouncer. Lucy realizes that Delia may not get in either, but that would be for a legitimate reason, whereas she and Gracie are within their rights.

"You don't look disabled to me," the man says. "In fact, you look like that lady—in the movies—the brunette. What's her name? Whatever, it don't matter. Animals are not allowed in places where food is being served."

Her blindness is not his business. And what does it matter what she looks like? What if she were struggling with an invisible issue like epilepsy or a traumatic brain disorder or even PTSD? And if so, those things would also be none of his business. She says nothing, allowing tension to grow.

"I'm calling the manager. Dogs of any kind ain't allowed," the man says.

"Call the manager," Lucy says, undeterred.

When the manager arrives, he apologizes to Lucy before explaining the bar's no-dogs rule. Lucy suggests the manager call the owner.

"I'll call the cops instead," the manager says.

"Be my guest," she says, thinking that this guy sounds too young to be a manager. Still, he ought to know the laws. How can a simple outing turn into a major problem? Lucy says nothing and waits for the man to capitulate by calling the owner or the cops or simply allowing her and Gracie to enter.

"Dude, she's blind," Nick says, stepping in front of Lucy. "What the fuck is wrong with you? Seeing eye dogs go everywhere. Let's get this show on the road."

"You're just trying to get the dog inside and think I'm gonna fold for a pretty woman," the doorman says.

Lucy wants to scream at the stupidity and also at Nick for divulging personal information. She feels exposed. The manager says nothing for a few moments before finally saying it's okay for her to enter with the dog without calling the owner or the cops.

"My blindness is none of your business. What is your business is knowing that my service dog—any service dog—

legally can go anywhere I go. End of story," Lucy yells at the doorman and manager, her voice rising with each word. "You two bozos obviously don't know shit. I can sue the crap out of your sorry asses and this place to make sure this stupidity doesn't get repeated.

"I'm not staying," she tells Nick, pausing slightly between each word for emphasis, but now she must stay to make a point. "What's the point of being in a place that serves up humiliation with its drinks?" However well-meaning, Nick shouldn't have blabbed her vision issues to the idiot manager and doorman or talk about her as if she weren't in the room. She decides she won't see him again outside his lessons. "It's nobody's business why I need a guide dog," Lucy says, her voice sharp.

"It's done. You're making a scene, and now people are looking at us. Let's just get the table near the stage," Nick says, sounding impatient, nudging her forward, trying but failing to neutralize her anger.

"Are you for real? People are *looking* at us?" she says, her voice more curt and sarcastic than she intends. Still, why should she care that people are *looking* at them or at her? As if she could see them? Let them look all they want.

At the table, Lucy fumes and keeps her coat on, deciding how long she'll need to stay to make a point because the night is ruined. She commands Gracie to sit at her feet.

"I am not staying long," she says, wondering if she should just cab it home and bring Delia with her.

Nick ignores her tone. "Gracie saved our butts. If they'd actually checked Delia's ID, we'd be in a bigger world of hurt right now," he says.

"Unlike Delia here, I'm not a child. My mouth and brain work fine. You blabbed my medical information to a damned door bouncer? And you should have thought about Delia being carded before you invited a child to a bar."

"It's not like it's a big secret that you're blind," Nick says. "And Delia—you know—looks older. She can easily pass for eighteen."

"I'm not a child either," Delia says in a low voice.

Silence drapes the table. On stage, musicians introduce themselves before playing the opening notes of what sounds like one of the first pop songs Lucy learned, an old blues tune—"House of the Rising Sun." An exceptional bass voice sings the words to "Amazing Grace" instead of the Rising Sun lyrics, and the fusion enchants her. She loves what she's hearing. This jam session ranks among the more special musician gatherings, one she shouldn't miss, despite idiotic Nick. She decides to return next week on her own, without Nick.

"My ID says I'm eighteen," Delia adds over the music, her voice matter-of-fact.

"What? You have a fake ID?" Lucy asks.

She wonders why the kid came to her house this evening, something Delia hasn't done before. On stage, the musicians continue their fusion of the two blues tunes, yet as much as Lucy loves the rendition, she's debating whether she ought to leave and take Delia with her to talk about why the kid came to her house and why she has a fake ID.

"I have two," Delia says, as if reading Lucy's thoughts. "Everyone at school has two or three. I've never used mine before tonight." Delia exudes excitement.

"Don't get any ideas. You're here to play," Nick tells the girl. "You need to play your best whether you're playing in a concert hall or in a room with just one person. Isn't that right, Lucy?"

Still smarting over the door bouncer debacle and Delia's presence, Lucy agrees with a grunt, but she refuses to further buttress his point.

"What are you having, Lucy?" Nick asks.

Lucy decides she needs her wits about her. "Colas for both Delia and me," she says, reaching in her purse for her wallet.

"Not for me," Delia says. "I'll have a rum and Coke."

"No you won't. I'm not getting into trouble for giving alcohol to a minor," Lucy says. "What do you know about rum and Coke?"

"It's what my mom drinks," Delia says.

"Nick, if you bring this girl a rum and Coke, I'm out of here right now."

"The bouncer and manager know you can't see. You could say it's yours, and I must have switched the glasses," Delia says.

Lucy feels her cheeks and neck flush with anger at Delia's sudden cheekiness. Nick puts his hand over hers.

"On me. I can buy you both the colas," he says. "Kiddo, nothing doing, even with your fake ID."

Musicians on stage end their set, call for a break, and house music fills the room.

"Well, well, well. Two pretty ladies at a table alone," a voice says, twelve o'clock high. "I'm Sledge. Nick always comes waltzing in here with the finest-looking ladies ever. Do you mind if I join you?"

Lucy recognizes the voice as belonging to one of the vocalists just on stage, and she can tell that Sledge is already sitting based on the location of his voice.

"Loved the fusion," Lucy says.

"Yeah, we talked about doing some kind of fusion like that at our last jam session. We didn't know how it would turn out. It ain't our idea to fuse those tunes, though. Chester, the dude on drums, heard a band outta Alabama singing it that way," he says. "What do you play?"

"Piano," Delia answers for Lucy. "We both play piano."

Lucy's irritation mounts. Delia's answering for her now? Before she speaks, Nick returns with the drinks, colas for all. Other musicians join them at the table, including all members of the Dawgs, a band that also includes Sledge, she learns, and with which Nick performs every weekend.

"We're looking for a keyboard player," Sledge says.

"Can I audition?" Delia asks.

"Tell you what," Sledge says. "You jam with us tonight, and we like your sound, you're in. Your jam is your audition. Let's shake on that deal," he adds.

"Whoa, whoa there, Sledge," Lucy says. "Delia's not in. She's too young."

"I want to add Lucy to the roster," Nick says. "She's the teach."

"Delia's too young," Lucy says. "She won't be able to get into the gigs."

"Wait, wait, wait. How young is young?" Sledge asks.

"Fifteen," Lucy says, now answering for Delia.

"We can try," Delia says. "I got my ID."

"You're not even driving yet? How are you going to get to and from gigs? You're not ready," Lucy says, knowing the kid has the chops for the music but not for being around a bunch of grown-assed men.

"It's not as if you drive either, Lucy. Do gigs pay? How much?" Delia asks Sledge.

"You can make a little something-something extra. Augment your day job," Sledge says, laughing. "What's your day job? Don't tell me it's something boring like an accountant. You in college, or what? What's your name again, Mama?"

Sledge is flirting! She listens for Nick to chime in, but he's engrossed in another conversation with another musician.

"She's not interested, and she's not ready," Lucy says. "And she's too damn young for you to be considering other thoughts, Sledge," she says, unable to stop herself from making an exasperated sound.

"I'd rather get paid doing music than my job," Delia says, a pleading tone in her voice.

"It's not major money, and it could interfere with your grades," Lucy says, shutting down the conversation.

"My mom doesn't care as long as I'm bringing in some money," Delia says.

Lucy fumes. She turns the conversation away from Delia's joining the band, and soon the chatter around the table begins to sound more like a musical salon. And although she's not thrilled about Delia being along in the first place, she's glad the girl is present to hear discussions on technique, on music as a business and as an art. Despite her youth and innocence, Delia asks good questions and even surprises Lucy by asking more about the business of music. Lucy slips off her coat, deciding to stay after all, and when it's time for the next set, all the musicians at the table find their way onto the stage. Gracie sits under the table.

On stage, they improvise at least a dozen blues tunes, and Lucy's excited to hear Delia's facility and musicality. Sledge and Nick sing, and Nick also plays his standup bass. When she hears Delia, who's playing Sledge's keyboards while he plays flute, she realizes that of all her students, Delia would be the best candidate for the Peabody scholarship audition in the fall. The bar crowd screams, whistles, and claps its approval, and Lucy's unease about her earlier humiliation begins to evaporate.

Later, when Lucy checks her watch, it's after midnight, long past the time she planned to stay, and she tells Nick that she and Delia need to leave.

"I promised to get you home," he says. "Let me get my stuff. We have to wait 'til the set ends."

Lucy frowns. "That's another fifteen to twenty minutes. Delia and I can cab it back."

"No way! I'll take you and just come back for my stuff," he says.

Squeezed into Nick's truck again for the short ride home, Delia sits nearly atop Lucy.

"It's a school night, Delia. How on earth will you get up in time for school?" Lucy asks.

She can feel Delia's shoulder rise and fall in a shrug, and for the first time since she's been teaching Delia, she wonders about the kid's home life, why Delia's not worried about her parents being upset that she's out so late. Lucy touches her watch. It's nearly one a.m.

Nick slows when he approaches Delia's house. The girl thanks them before she hops out, and Lucy notices that Nick waits for the girl to disappear inside her house and shut the door before taking off. Lucy realizes that they must be approaching her house when she feels the car slow and grabs her house keys from her purse.

"I'll help you get in. May I come back after I pick up my stuff?" he asks.

Lucy gathers her equipment. "What for?" she asks, remembering Nick's interference.

"A nightcap?" he asks.

"Maybe another time," she says, exiting the truck, knowing she will never invite him into her house for anything. Or even agree to join the band or see him again outside his weekly piano lesson. "Thank you for a wonderful evening. Can you please hand me my keyboard?" Gracie jumps out of the truck and takes her place by Lucy.

"Lucy, wait! I said I'd help you get your stuff in," Nick says.

She hears him move the gear shift, prompting her and Gracie to step away from the truck. Seconds later, the driver's door slams, and Nick is beside her, his woodsy, spicy cologne causing her stomach to lurch. He sets the keyboard down on the pavement beside her stoop.

"I'm going to make sure you get in okay," he says.

Lucy unlocks and opens the door, then commands Gracie to enter. She steps inside and turns to ask Nick to hand her the keyboard. He's right behind her with the instrument in hand. He gently shifts her out of the way.

"I am setting the keyboard down, handle up, on your sofa," he says.

"Thank you for your help," she says. She's standing by the door, the storm door open so that she can lock up after Nick leaves.

Nick positions himself close to her, and she can feel his breath on her face.

"Lucy—I'm sorry. None of this evening went the way I wanted it to go. I've never been around a blind person before and don't know the dos and don'ts. I just wanted the ID check to move along because I knew that Delia's would be an issue. Let me make it up to you with another date. A normal one—at a restaurant and some dancing, if you're game. Do you dance?"

"I'll think about it and let you know," Lucy says, nudging him through the doorway toward his truck outside.

"That sounds like a 'no' to me," Nick says from the top of the stoop, facing her as she blocks the doorway with her body.

She says nothing, knowing he's right and knowing she failed to anticipate that their height difference means that they are now face-to-face, and his woodsy, spicy cologne is making her heady.

For a long time, Nick says nothing either. They breathe nearly in unison. Then, without any warning, Nick leans forward, and on the threshold with her inside and him outside, he kisses her on her lips, tender and sweet. Unable to stop herself, she kisses him back, raising her arms to begin exploring the contours of his face and the unexpected and strange corkscrew-like ropes of his hair.

BOOM-BOOM BECKY'S BAKERY RISES

I watch her gather ingredients on the table: She measures two cups of sugar and pours it into a clear bowl. She breaks eggs, using her hands to separate the yolks and whites into two porcelain mixing bowls. She melts chunks of butter in a small pan and pours the golden liquid into a smaller mixing bowl, scraping it all with a spatula. She pours milk into a glass measuring cup, water into another, heavy cream into yet another. She's efficient as she unwraps six more sticks of refrigerated butter, dumping them naked into another, still larger bowl, carefully setting the wrappings next to it. She grates graham crackers into crumbs in a small blender, dumping the light-brown mix into another bowl. She unwraps cream cheese from its silver paper and presses her fingers into the substance to test its softness.

I don't know what she's planning to make but realize that she's intending to make several cakes, maybe a cheesecake and something else. Maybe cookies. I anticipate licking the bowls, especially if she's making whipped cream or something with chocolate, but she doesn't see me watching or waiting and places the bowls into the dishwasher. It's as if she's in a trance, channeling her inner Betty Crocker, her body moving on automatic pilot while her mind has escaped elsewhere, away from the tiny, cramped kitchen with its ugly, avocado-green tiles and matching refrigerator. She keeps an eye on the clock.

She's following recipes handwritten on a paper, barely glancing at them because she knows them by heart. Whatever she's making is both for a baking contest and for a customer. The first prize is a mega amount of money and a new kitchen renovation. She told me she doesn't care about the kitchen renovation and hopes to win the money.

"Nothin' like cold, hard cash right here, babydoll," she says, smacking the palm of her hand.

Who knows what the customer wants or when she wants it, but I know that Ma intends to finish this cake before Dad comes home from work. He fails to appreciate the baking contests, says they are a waste of money due to the cost of the ingredients, and he doesn't get to eat any of the goodies. Except he's deadly serious when he says it, his tone the opposite of joking. He fails to appreciate the effort she makes at the contests, and he fails to realize that she's been baking and selling cakes out of her kitchen for months now. I don't know where she hides the money, but I do know she hides the cake and pie orders in plain sight in a black-and-white marble notebook, written in shorthand, a skill left over from the days she worked in an office. The pages look like lines of scribbles with doodles. While she's on the phone discussing things with customers, she doodles feet, high-heeled shoes, faces, flowers, plants in pots, cats and dogs. He looked inside once and tossed it at her, shaking his head as if only a dolt would fill a notebook with nonsense.

"This is what you do all day?"

"I see you are still filled with so much joy and light today," she said, knowing the opposite was true. She flashed him a wide, fake smile.

"More like piss and vinegar," she told Aunt Mary later on the phone.

For months Aunt Mary has been urging her to leave and move in with her and her cats.

With Ma's network of friends and church ladies, she's a wizard at hiding all kinds of things: bags of flours and sugars, boxes of powdered sugar, cases of eggs and butter. I heard her on the phone telling Aunt Mary that she doesn't want the right hand to know what the left hand is doing at the moment, especially when the wrong hands mistake her for Muhammad Ali.

"I'm thinking about it," she says when Aunt Mary suggests we come stay with her.

She puts the phone on speaker so she can talk to Aunt Mary and still bake, which is how she spends every morning.

"I just want the bad parts to stop."

"Whatever happened to the Boom-Boom Becky in you?"

I want to know about the "Boom-Boom," too, but I don't ask.

"Time to resurrect Boom-Boom, MoJo Mary," Ma says and laughs her head off.

The last time I hear him mistaking Ma for Muhammad, like always, the sounds of cracks and thuds race up the stairs like horses stampeding. Usually I hide under the covers, trying not to tremble, though this particular night something changes; something different happens. After the slaps, instead of her whimpering or crying like usual, she roars like a lion. Her voice booms from her belly, loud, and reverberates up the stairs.

"NO! YOU! DON'T. I'm NOT your fucking punching bag."

Glass crashes and breaks, and something else thuds, a different kind of thudding, like balls hitting the sides of the wall, the thudding repeating itself in quick succession—*thud-*

thudthudthud—thud. I hide deeper under the covers and pull the blanket over my head. Will she run up the stairs and order me to get dressed like she did the last time when we went to Aunt Mary's for a week? That night, electricity energizes the air in the house, a crackling as if the house were rising like a helium balloon. No one runs up the stairs. After the thudding ends, silence drapes the house, rushing through it like the wind, quieting everything except the sounds of my heart beating wingbacks in my ears.

The next day, an aluminum colander filled with peeled, boiled potatoes sits on the counter, leaning forward on a crooked foot and wearing dents along its sides like a series of dimples. A large bowl overflows with peeled and sliced apples covered with cinnamon and sugar. On the kitchen table stands a large, dusty trophy, a shiny, blue column taller than my wooden ruler holding up a golden girl with her arm pulled back, a ball in her hand. A giant, golden star surrounds the figure, and it's the first time I see her softball championship trophy from her high school years.

"I dug it out and stuck it on the table," Ma says.

On speaker phone Aunt Mary laughs. "Boom-Boom Becky wins the day," she laughs.

"I won't be erased," Ma says.

"Plenty of room for you and Phoebe here with me," Aunt Mary says.

I know Ma really wants to open her own bakery and talks about it all the time when she drives me to and from school, when she warns me not to tell anyone else about her dreams because whispered dreams never come true.

"Imagine being surrounded by cakes and cookies, ice cream and candies all the time," she says.

It sounds impossible. "I love chocolate candies," I say, not believing her dream but imagining chocolate-covered caramels and chocolate-covered pretzels. "Can we stop on the way home and get some, please?"

"Of course not," she says.

From the back seat, I look through the windshield and see a herd of dinosaur-sized, puffy clouds tinged in gold and racing forward in a peacock sky. The sky is beautiful. I love watching the sky, and then I imagine something, too. I imagine sketching and painting the sky, wondering the best way to capture those clouds on a paper. I imagine swirling paints into vibrant colors, the way Ma mixes food coloring into buttercream, and step by step, in my mind's eye, paint the sky. We both dream in colors.

"I love the sky," I say. "I could draw the clouds and the sky."

She places the softened cream cheese in the large, silver mixer bowl, turns the standing mixer on to low. Slowly she adds the sugar, a spoonful at a time, and I see the cream cheese grow as creamy and fluffy as clouds. She moves nonstop, periodically glancing at the kitchen clock as if racing against it. When the phone rings, she wipes her hands on her jeans, answers it, tells Aunt Mary she's in the middle of it and intends to finish up before Mr. Butterbeans gets home. I know she's talking about Dad. Mr. Butterbeans sounds like a happy name, although he's the opposite. Jokes don't make him laugh. But the night after the electricity changes the air in the house, after the sounds of thudding balls hitting the sides of the walls, after the trophy—all shined up—occupies the middle of the table, they both seem different, though Ma and I stay wary.

The mixer rotates the bowl, the cheesy mixture swells. She rolls a lemon between her hands before cutting it in half and squeezes its juice into the bowl. She adds the yolks one at a time until each is folded and blended in, turning the mixture gradually into a sunshiny yellow. She uses the spatula to help blend the eggs before she grabs a dark bottle and, without measuring it, adds the vanilla extract. The mixing bowl turns by itself while she focuses on dumping the melted butter into the graham cracker crumbs. She works the butter into the crumbs and then dumps it all into a springform pan, gradually affixing it to the sides. When the springform pan sides are covered by the cracker mixture, she bakes it for a few minutes before sticking it in the refrigerator. She checks the oven, rotates the dial to 350 degrees, and grates lemon zest into the creamy mixture turning in the standing mixer bowl. She watches the yellow shavings disappear into the creamy mixture. Her eyebrows knit together as she turns off the stand mixer, clears the sides of the bowl with the spatula, and inhales before she glances at the kitchen clock and cleans up as she goes. When the kitchen is mostly cleaned, she pulls her roasting pan from the cabinet and fills it with water. She pours the creamy, sunshiny mixture into the springform pan, sets the pan into sheets of aluminum foil, and wraps it around the pan's bottom before carefully setting it into the water-filled roasting pan. She carefully slides it into the oven.

I watch her move—graceful and swift, confident and smooth. Everything is done. The kitchen is clean. She stacks chicken pieces in a bowl and covers them with spices, herbs, and white wine and waits for the customer to come and pick up the cheesecake, packaged in a cardboard box. Ma accepts the cash and slips it into her jeans pocket and hands the lady the box with the cheesecake.

Later, when Mr. Butterbeans arrives home, Ma's busy with the chicken for dinner. Dad's hands overflow with unwrapped presents. It's nobody's birthday and it's not beers. Boom-Boom Becky's bakery rises a few notches with the professional-level cake-decorating tips he hands her, and I step a little closer to painting the sky onto paper with the set of sketchbooks, pencils, brushes, paints, and a how-to sketch book he hands me. I dance around the house, thrilled with my new present.

"Here we go again," Ma says and rolls her eyes. She sets the unwrapped set of decorating tips on the counter and flicks it with her pointer finger toward the wall.

"What's that supposed to mean?"

"Another bullshit gift after you mistake me for Muhammad Ali? It's stuff. Just stuff."

"Can't you just say thank you?" Mr. Butterbeans sounds pouty.

I'm afraid he's going to hit Ma.

"Thank you, Daddy," I shout. "I love my gift!"

It's true. I do love it and skip around the kitchen, but I don't run to hug him. Dad nods at me but Ma acts indifferent, focused on setting chicken pieces into a pan. I wish with my whole heart that she'd smile and show appreciation.

"A little gratitude might be in order," he says, going into the living room to turn on the TV.

"Is that a fact?" she asks.

"What the hell does that mean?"

Ma shoots him a look. "It means what it means. You're still on notice."

"I said 'sorry.'"

Ma gathers a half a dozen potatoes and sets them on the counter near her.

"Sorry doesn't feed the bulldog," she says. "You need help. Get your ass over to the VA. I'm sick of all the I'm-sorry gifts taking up space around here."

She does not wash or peel the potatoes.

"Or what?"

He glances at the potatoes. Then stares at his shoes.

I feel sorry for him. He looks defeated standing in the living room, trying to watch the TV while talking to Ma. Untrimmed, his black mustache hangs over his upper lip as if it's trying to escape his face; whiskers shadow his chin and lower cheeks. He and I share the same dark, almond-shaped eyes, but his go black when he's mad; the same upside-down V eyebrows, except his knit together when he's angry; and straight nose, except his nostrils grow larger and smaller with his breaths when he starts to get agitated. I watch for these signs—changes in his eyes, in his eyebrows, in his nose. I watch his arms and hands, now inert by his sides, knowing they can fly into action like a machine at any given moment. I watch his feet to see if they will start toward Ma in a way that's not good. I watch because I can see that Ma is not acting grateful enough for those cake-decorating tips. Instead, she eyes the chicken and moves pieces around the pan with a large fork and acts as if she doesn't know the man glaring at her from the other room. She glances at the potatoes sitting on the counter and at Dad in the living room.

She holds a long moment of silence. "Or we have nothing to talk about."

Ma continues moving the chicken around the pan. "Look, I'm not waiting forever for you to get your head on straight," she says. "I'm done."

"Who do you think you are?" he asks, sounding shocked that Ma is acting the way she is.

She sets the fork down. "No better or worse than you. I am who I am."

He steps toward the kitchen as if he is going to start something.

"Not one step further," she says. Her voice sounds like the school principal talking to unruly boys sent to her office.

He fails to listen. He steps closer to the kitchen. I want to run upstairs to my room, but my feet stay glued to their spot near the refrigerator. Mr. Butterbeans looks as if he's going to rush at Ma, but before either of us knows what happens, she slips out a potato stored in her apron pocket, lifts her right heel, digs her left into the floor, bends over, explodes off her spot, and pitches that potato straight into Daddy's thigh. It hits with precision and he falls to the floor, hugging his thigh. She grabs another potato and clutches it in her pitching fist.

"Get help or I'm gone. *We're* gone."

She pockets the potato and looks at me. "Phoebe, fill a plastic bag with ice and bring it to your daddy." Her hands are shaking a little; she stares at the chicken in the pan for a few minutes without moving and takes in a few deep breaths before she lowers the heat and finishes preparing dinner.

I listen. Daddy sits on the floor, hugging his skinny leg, the potato on the floor next to him. I hand him the icebag. He moves the potato, pats the spot on the floor, and tells me to sit down next to him. I shake my head and run upstairs to my room. I don't want to be too close in case he switches into the scary man.

When we eat dinner later, no one talks. We eat mashed potatoes and chicken. We eat green beans with almonds. We eat a green salad with fancy dressing, and for dessert, Ma sets an apple pie on the table, which she had warmed up and which we eat with vanilla ice cream.

Things are never the same after that day when Ma pitched a fast potato at Mr. Butterbeans. The next morning, Ma tells him to call in sick to work. They drop me off at school, and later I learned that she dropped him off at the VA hospital "to get squared away." Mr. Butterbeans never came back from the VA, but eventually Daddy did. Not the one whose eyes went dark with rage but the one who sat on the floor with me and who let me sketch his face a bazillion times with that art set he gave me without a single complaint.

Ma doesn't win that baking contest prize money or the kitchen makeover. She says she won something better, more lasting than a one-time prize. Dad invites his friends he met at the VA hospital over to the store on Main Street that Ma rents, and they all work hard remodeling according to plans Ma paid a designer to draw. Before I can imagine it, I'm surrounded by cakes, cookies, and candies and eat so many chocolate candies I can't look at or eat a single one more. Boom-Boom Becky's Bakery rises as high as the skies I still want to paint.

BENJAMIN CAME HOME

FIRST TRIMESTER

Violet Moore seemed to float. Her daughter Mikie, who had stepped away from their restaurant table to take a call, rushed through the dining room as she did as a young girl with a secret bursting out of her. When she seated herself, she placed her cell phone by her plate, fixed her eyes on Violet, and smiled wide.

"Ma! Can you believe it? I found him! I found Benjamin!"

Mikie squeezed her arms close to her body, balled her hands into tight fists, and shook herself in excitement as she did when she was telling Violet she was about to become a grandmother. Violet shut her eyes, elated by the news and at the same time afraid of it.

"My God," she whispered. "My God," she repeated. Her hands trembled.

She had not known that Mikie had been searching for Benjamin. She'd prayed for him every day since he was born, worried about him, sent silent waves of love and light to him. She'd worried if he had enough to eat, if he lived in a good home, if he felt loved and secure, if he knew about her. She'd marked his birthday on the calendar every year and lit a candle for his happiness and health, sending silent prayers for his wellbeing, thanking the universe for keeping him alive and safe and for the Creator of All to keep him wrapped in a sheath of white protective light.

For years, she and her husband, the original Benjamin, wondered about this boy in their quiet talk, a child bound to them through loss and pain. That Benjamin, her husband, and his family had forgiven awed her. Unbeknownst to them, she'd berated herself every day for decades for being bullied into making the most regrettable decision of her life, a decision that changed and marked her for fifty-seven years. Maybe now, things could be set right.

"Is he interested in meeting me?" Violet asked.

She closed her eyes, fearing the answer. A panic rose in her like choking waves, tingling her toes and fingertips. Excitement and fear overcame her. What if he wouldn't want to talk to her? What if he hated her? What if he lived a life bereft of love and blamed her? What if he didn't care about anything that had to do with her or the past?

"Did he ask about me?"

Mikie nodded. "He wants to meet us. All of us. He's flying in, all the way from California."

She could barely finish her dinner. For Mikie, Violet thought, at long last, the search was over. But for Violet, others had always set things in motion in a way that changed her life. For good or bad, what Mikie set in motion would change her life yet again. But maybe, this time, the changes would be good ones. She reached for Mikie's hand, the difference in their skin tones no longer something she noticed. "Thank you. For searching."

Over the years, Violet had thought about it, never mustering either the courage or the money to look. But now her genius daughter found him without paying a king's ransom, and Violet admired Mikie for fearlessness and confidence that astonished her, knowing she didn't possess such qualities at any age. Mikie settled their cheque and squeezed Violet's upper arm in support as they walked toward the car.

"Are you excited, Ma?" she asked as she pointed the car out of the parking lot. "I can't wait to meet him!"

Violet nodded, afraid if she opened her mouth, blubbering wails would fall out.

At home, she set the tea kettle on the stove while Mikie called the twins, her baby brothers Elijah and Van, with the news. On speaker phone, she heard them—now grown men with families of their own—hooting and hollering, congratulating Mikie on her success. Benjamin's absence had never been a secret from them. And now, Mikie explained the particulars to all of them: Benjamin, a lawyer who lived in San Francisco, would fly into Baltimore to meet them all. Unlike them, he'd never married and had no children. They needed to work out the date.

"A lawyer? Talk about poetic justice. I wish your Daddy was here for this," Violet said.

Violet pictured her late husband, the elder Benjamin, dead three years now from an unexpected heart attack. She imagined his happy, full, white-toothed smile she loved so well. She imagined his long, slow whistle when something unexpected happened. They defied everyone around them with their love. Mourning the loss of baby Benjamin bonded them with the same strong cement that kept Greek temples standing for centuries. Even as teenagers when their newborn son came bouncing into the world and then snatched from them within days. Always this hot flashing of shame, the shame of getting pregnant in high school, of being a White girl pregnant by a Black boy in 1964, of being sent to the Hampden's Mothers and Babies home, of her mother's perpetual unforgiveness, overwhelmed her. Over the years, shame diminished but never fully disappeared.

"Your Daddy would be over the moon," Violet said.

"We're all over the moon, Ma. Daddy had asked me to help find Benjamin before he died. We were supposed to do it together."

SECOND TRIMESTER

Fifty-seven years ago, they'd met back in junior year of high school when they spotted each other at a football game while performing in the marching bands of their respective schools. He played trumpet. Whenever a break came to the brass section, he held his horn to the side of his face and flashed her his big, white-toothed smile—she, the only girl in her school's marching band. He'd seen her in the percussion section with the drums, except she hammered her glockenspiel, its bell sounds floating with the melodies instead of beats. His smile electrified her, especially since he followed it with a wink. A Black boy with a beautiful face, his intense eyes above that smile and below the red and gold plumed shako, fixed on her. He often stole the show, playing half-time solos on either trumpet or trombone. He must have played a dozen instruments, and she wondered how many. She looked for him at every game between their two schools. And at the interschool marching band competitions and conferences. They conducted a silent courtship. Their eyes connected them, and she wondered if he were a junior or a senior, knowing that if he graduated at the end of the year, she'd probably never see him again. She didn't know his name.

Then, at the first game of senior year, relieved to him in the brass section, her stomach jolted as their eyes connected. When her band was packing their instruments into their cases after the game, waiting to board the bus to return to school, someone from her own band thrust a package into her hands, then disappeared. She tore it open and found exquisite metal mallets. On the inside of the paper, "From Benjamin Moore, Trumpeter. City High." He scrawled a smiley face with an open smile like his own. Then she saw the rest of the note: "Meet me at the bleachers at your school."

Of course, she would! Her stomach somersaulted. She rehearsed conversations. They'd have to be discreet. White girls did not meet up with Black boys, not even in the modern age of 1964. Being seen together could be fatal for both of them. This made her nervous. Still wearing their marching band uniforms, shakos, and gloves, they met behind the bleachers where they talked for hours, keeping a safe distance between them. He glanced at her, a small cautious smile, told her he planned on college where he'd major in engineering. He named the only all Black college in the city and the names of others she had not heard about. Then he removed his shako and set it upside down on his trumpet case, and removed his gloves, dropping them into the hat.

"Not music?" she asked, knowing that neither of her parents spoke to her about college. They hadn't spoken to her at all about her post-graduation plans. She also took off her gloves, stuffing them into her glockenspiel case, and removed her shako, the blue and gold feathers dancing as she set it on the ground. She unleashed her hair which had been hidden in a topknot under the cap, the bright red mess that her classmates had ridiculed throughout her school career. It cascaded like a sheet around her shoulders. She thanked him for the mallets, pulling them from her glockenspiel case and holding them to her chest. "I love them."

At the sight of her hair, he looked amazed and laughed. She blushed, remembering all the taunts she'd heard every year from stupid kids, "ginger," "firetruck," and "ambo," short for ambulance.

"What's funny?" she asked, embarrassed, pulling it away from her face. '

"'Violet' seems like a funny name for a person with fire-engine-red hair."

She rolled her eyes. Fire engine red. Fire truck.

"I was born bald. Violet is the color of my eyes," she said, widening them and leaning toward him so he could see.

When she leaned over, she touched his hand, brushed his fingers, which, to her surprise, felt no different from her own. Silence hung over them at the unexpected, electrifying touch. As they stared at each other, they explored each other's faces, careful not to touch again. She admired his huge smile. They talked about everything, trading details about themselves. Violet learned that, like her, he played organ for his church. Unlike her, he also sang. His mother, a lawyer, worked in a small firm, and his father owned a barber shop, while her mother stayed at home. Her father worked in the news business. They both earned good grades. Unlike hers, his parents explored post-graduation plans, discussing career options. He glanced at his watch and then began singing a tune she'd never heard. "That's the Way Love Is." When she asked if it was his original song, he laughed.

"Red, don't you ever listen to the radio? 68.7 on the AM dial. All the greats," he said.

He leaned over, grabbed her shako, set it on her head, her hair a sheet around her shoulders and not hidden inside the hat as usual, and helped her up. Its blue and gold feathers clashed with the red of her hair. He produced a long whistle at the incongruous sight. He towered over her, it seemed, as he grabbed the glockenspiel case and handed it to her. His smile took up his entire face.

"Okay, Red. Maybe we can see each other again?" he asked. "I'll wait to leave after you have already been gone for a while."

No boy had noticed her before, not like he did. The boys at her school ignored her with her laughable hair and a zillion freckles all over her face. She knew why they couldn't be seen together. He didn't have to spell it out for her. She knew the dangers of meeting up with a Black boy meant for both of them, but especially for him. Being seen together could bring him terrible harm. Still, despite all that, despite the prohibitions of liking each other, Violet Davis floated home with something shifted inside her.

She remembered the news stories from a few years back of the Freedom Rides in the Deep South that caused mobs of white men armed with sticks and all kinds of weapons to beat Black and White people for sitting next to each other on a bus. Her mother thought the White college students shameful and yelled at the TV news station for them to go the hell home where they belonged. The craziness of the violence baffled her, especially since she hoped to see Benjamin again.

In her room, she searched for 68.7 on the AM dial and listened to the music that inspired him. She wondered why Benjamin's parents had spoken to him about college, while hers had not. She wondered why his parents expressed ambitions about his future, but hers had not. She sensed a chasm of difference between them that had nothing to do with their skin colors.

"What about college?" she asked one night at dinner. "I could major in music."

"Why on earth would you want to do that? You're probably going to get married after school and have a family, like everyone else," her mother said.

"Maybe I want something different," she said. "Maybe I can be a teacher?"

"You don't need college to teach piano. You can do that from home," her father said.

"Maybe I can be a lawyer?" she asked.

"Don't be silly," her father said. "No such thing as lady lawyers."

Violet remembered that Benjamin said his mother was a lawyer. Violet wondered if her parents simply didn't know better.

"Maybe lady lawyers exist, and we just don't know about them," she said. "Maybe I want to do something different."

"You'll change your mind a thousand times between now and graduation," her mother said.

Violet cleared the table and helped her mother clean up.

"Wouldn't you have liked to do something else?" she asked.

"Like what?"

"A profession of some sort," she said.

"It's a man's world," her mother said. "That's all you need to know."

Neither of her parents mentioned college again. She and Benjamin met under the guise of band practice and school-related music activities, and he told her all about his mother going to law school before she got married, pushed in that direction by her father, also a lawyer, to advance civil rights. Benjamin opened her eyes to a bigger world than the one she'd known. He taught her to play the flute. Sometimes, they played songs by ear, the hits she heard on the radio in her room. Sometimes he brought sheet music. They discussed their futures, traded kisses, held hands, explored each other, their flesh softening and hardening against each other, him tall and lean and assured, her paler, shorter, thinner, smaller. She remembered his intensity, his precise finger movements as if she were his flute, his trumpet, his trombone, the warmth of his breath, of his tender words as they lay in each other's arms, bursting with all the love their teenaged hearts could hold. She also held onto the promise of something bigger that Benjamin's parents afforded him, knowing hers presented no real options after graduation other than to get a job as a secretary somewhere until she married.

"Red, marriage isn't the caboose," he said.

In early spring of their senior years, Benjamin showed her his acceptance letters to various colleges, all strange names to her and some far away. Her heart sank.

"Impressive news!" she said, knowing that she had not applied to any colleges. "Are you going far away?"

"Nah. Staying in town so we can still see each other," he said, smiling and taking her hand.

Relieved, she stared at her feet, then looked into his face, held his gaze and told him she'd missed two periods.

"Shit. Ma's going to kill me. She'll know what to do," he said, hugging her.

"I can't tell my parents," she said. "They'll kill me."

"They might want to kill me, too," he said.

Violet began crying. "I'm scared. For both of us."

For a long time after that, Benjamin said nothing. Instead, he held her hand and kissed her under the green canopies of the poplar trees in the glen. She leaned into him, stroked his arm, and kissed him back, reveling in the wetness of his mouth on hers.

A few weeks later when they met, they sat in silence, trying to puzzle a solution to the problem they shared.

"We still can't sit on a bus together. How on earth can we get married?" he said.

"I didn't tell my parents," she said.

"You can't hide us after the baby is born. We got to talk to my mom."

THIRD TRIMESTER

Violet hid her pregnancy. She used diaper pins to hold her pants together and skirts with loose elastic waists and oversized sweaters. She ran the shower and played the radio loud in the mornings to mask the sound of vomiting. She looked as if she put on a few pounds. For the remainder of the school year, she maintained her grades, her school band activities, her piano lessons, and playing the organ at church, grateful to spend as little time home as she could. She and Benjamin continued meeting. He gave her his silver flute to show his commitment. Thankful she didn't look pregnant, oversized sweaters and jackets hid weight gain, one her parents failed to notice, and her navy-blue robe became weekend wear at home, where she stayed in her room saying she had homework. In the mirror, she saw her skin glow; her nails grew, and her hair bounced and looked shinier and fuller. People told her she looked healthy, which surprised her. Behind her smile, in the privacy of her bedroom, she rocked on her bed, afraid of the near future, wishing she could hurry time, wish it away and herself into next year.

Benjamin's mother, Ruth Moore, the only other person in the world who knew she was pregnant, phoned her weekly when her parents weren't home, helped her remain steady, made her promise to tell her parents after graduation, and to be sure to tell them about her baby being Black.

"You got to be careful how you say it. I don't want you telling stories that could get him killed. You understand me, Violet?"

"Yes, ma'am. I want to keep the baby."

"Working that out, girl. That's my grandchild, too, you know."

Violet imagined keeping her baby, continuing to live with her parents for a short time until she and Benjamin could be together, even if it meant moving to Washington DC where they could marry. Except her mother raged. She threw plates and cups at the tiled kitchen walls. Violet watched them sail and then sink before crashing into the floor, shattering into a million pieces. She yelled that Violet was selfish and failed to consider her family. She blamed herself for Violet's veering off the path, a path Violet didn't know she was supposed to be on. She took Violet to the doctor for a pregnancy test.

"How could you do this to me?" her mother asked. "So much for the wanna-be college girl." Her mother's voice dripped with derision.

Humiliation and shame overwhelmed Violet, who chewed the insides of her cheeks, guilty that she'd gotten pregnant and ruined her family. Guilt also overwhelmed her for not applying to colleges herself, not that she could go in her present condition.

"Who's the boy?"

"You don't want to know."

"Why not? We have to talk to his parents about a wedding. I do expect he intends to marry you."

"That's not an option," Violet said. "There won't be a wedding any time soon."

"Why the hell not?" Her mother glared at her, fuming when Violet didn't answer. "Because he's Black," she finally said. "And it's illegal here."

Dumbfounded, her mother stared ahead in shock and then cupped her face and wept. Later that week, Ruth Moore suggested Violet move into her house and that her sister would take the baby. When she told her mother that she intended to move into the boy's house on the other side of the city, her mother began making a series of frenetic phone calls, writing in her notebook. In the middle of Violet's sixth month, her mother announced that Violet was moving all right, but nowhere near the jig-a-boo boy's house—over her dead body.

"We're telling everyone that you've gone to New York to help your aunt, who's ill. You'll come back alone."

"I want my baby."

"You have no idea of what you want."

"I intend to move in with the boy's family."

"You will do no such thing," her mother said, eyebrows knit together in anger. She hardly spoke to Violet for the rest of the summer and near the end of her sixth month, told Violet to pack her bag lightly and that she was moving to the Hampden House of Unwed Mothers and Babies. Of course, Violet alerted Ruth Moore.

"Did she tell the administration there that your baby is Black?" she asked.

"I don't think so," Violet said.

"You don't have to stay there. You're about to have a baby. Time for you to grow up. You aren't a child anymore."

Violet understood, but was afraid to cross her mother more than she had already done. She packed her flute into the nearly empty bag along with the metal mallets Benjamin had given her the year before. On the morning she was leaving, Violet stood on the threshold between the kitchen and the living room, waiting for her mother to look up from the newspaper.

"I'm leaving now," Violet said when her mother failed to acknowledge her.

"Don't come back here with that jig-a-boo baby," her mother said from behind the newspaper.

Violet blinked back tears. She refused to give her mother the satisfaction, but she cried when her father parked outside the Hampden House for Unwed Mothers, a sturdy and depressing-looking brick building that looked like a cross between a hospital and a school. He handed her a large manilla envelope. Inside she found fifty dollars in small bills, some writing paper, and postage stamps.

"Look V, for whatever it's worth, you're not the first or the last girl to get pregnant without being married. It doesn't matter to me what color your baby is. It's still our baby," he said. "Your mom—she's stuck. There's no convincing her."

At the Hampden's Unwed Mothers and Babies Home, Violet and fifteen other girls in their seventh month and beyond of pregnancy learned how to be good hostesses. They learned to follow recipes in the stained copies of the stack of Betty Crocker cookbooks on a shelf in the kitchen. They took turns preparing meals for everyone in the house. They learned how to do laundry, hanging their white maternity panties on the clotheslines behind the house. They learned etiquette, how to set tables, iron and fold sheets and curtains, and other homemaking classes.

Gloria, Violet's roommate, complained loudly, upset that no academics and GED classes were offered to girls not yet graduated from high school. She'd already completed one year of college, something that inspired Violet, who admired her audacity. In the group sessions with social workers, Gloria refused to be shamed when the social workers distributed cheap gold wedding bands and told the girls to wear them whenever they went into the community. The girls' jobs consisted of rehabilitating themselves; otherwise they'd be known as "garbage," "trash," "wayward," "fallen," "hysterical." Social workers told the girls they were "neurotic," "brazen hussies," "psychotic," girls who punished themselves by getting pregnant without a husband on purpose. They acted as if the girls willed themselves to be pregnant, or as if it happened by magic, as if the boys played a minor role. Shame washed over all of them. Except Gloria.

"What crap! Why do we get locked away when the boys get off scot-free?"

She pushed herself out of her chair and paced in front of the group room, her blonde flip- up hairstyle bouncing as she moved and her Doris Day bow remaining firmly affixed to the top of teased yellow hair.

"That doesn't seem right. Aren't they wayward, too? No Holy Ghost came by and made us pregnant."

The social workers ignored her as they distributed samples of the surrender papers the girls needed to sign for their babies to be adopted. Gloria threw the papers in the air.

"I'm here to decide what *I* want to do, and all options are on the table," she said. "It's my baby and my decision. Something people around here seem to forget. It's our decisions because they're our babies. Why don't you explain those other options, too?"

"Because they're unsustainable. You have no resources to keep your babies," Millie, the house mother said. She sounded exasperated. "Girls wanting to keep their babies are selfish, robbing their children of a stable happy home with a mother and a father."

Gloria huffed out of the group room. Later, Violet found her in their shared room on the bed with a yellow pages telephone book making lists of places to apply for jobs after her baby was born.

"Why aren't you keeping your baby?" she asked, her tone accusatory as if Violet's decision did not include her mother's frosty warning to not return with her baby. "We could join forces, you know. Babysit each other's kid and earn enough to support ourselves until we work out something better."

Violet sucked in her breath. Ruth Moore had suggested that she leave Hampden Home to live with Benjamin and their family so Violet could go to college. Ruth's plan seemed elegant and perfect, a plan that would allow Violet to watch her baby grow because he'd be part of the family. But she was afraid to leave. And now Gloria offered her a similar strategy. Violet feared making a decision. She sat on her bed opposite Gloria's, pulled her flute from under her pillow and played to soothe herself. Just as she had no answers for Ruth Moore, she had no answers for Gloria. The next day, she called her father at work.

"I can't tell you what to do, V," he said.

A silence hung between them until Violet hung up the phone. Incoming mail was censored, but she could drop notes to Benjamin and his mother during outings when she and Gloria shopped for incidentals while wearing their fake wedding bands. Neighbors knew they lived at Hampden's. Boys and men threw rocks at them, calling them whores. She and Benjamin couldn't see each other much, although every time she called him, he begged her to come home with him to his family. She didn't want to burden them with the cost of the delivery, which her parents had been paying for in monthly installments. She didn't want to end things with her parents, and going to the Moore's home would forever sever ties with them. Hampden's housemother kept them busy with hostess training as the months slipped by.

"V. V…I'm keeping my baby,' Gloria whispered to her one night. "When I leave, I'm taking my baby with me."

Violet pictured the incomplete surrender papers in her drawer. She envied Gloria's certainty and confidence.

"My baby's Black," Violet said. "My boyfriend's Black."

"Why on earth did you go and do that? Your Negro baby will attract attention. Negative attention."

She stopped pressuring Violet to join forces with her, and Violet remained undecided about those incomplete surrender papers in her drawer, paralyzed and tempted by Ruth Moore's offer, torn between her family and Benjamin's, and the social worker's logical points that a family with a mother and a father could provide a better, stable home for her baby.

BIRTH

Born on a warm afternoon on September 9, 1964, little Benjamin Moore Jr. produced a strong enough wail in the delivery room, one of the midwives said that he might grow up to sing opera. Violet laughed. *Maybe he inherited his father's talent for music?* she thought. The white nurses gave her odd looks, but to her surprise, they allowed her to hold her baby, a tiny thing with a headful of wet hair plastered to his scalp, full lips and almond eyes like his father's, and ears outlined in brown. His nose looked like a perfect button. She fell in love with him.

From her hospital room, she called Benjamin and Ruth to say she had a boy.

"I can't wait to meet him," Benjamin said.

"Are you going to pack yourself up and come home with my grandson?" Ruth asked. "Do you need us to pick you up?"

"I haven't told my parents yet," Violet said.

"Your mom doesn't care one iota about that baby," Ruth Moore said. "She's more interested in what her friends have to say."

She dialed home and both her parents picked up at once.

"It's me," she said. "I have a boy. I want to keep my son."

After a long pause, her father asked if the baby was healthy.

"He's beautiful," Violet said. "A miracle. I'm keeping my baby," she repeated.

"No," her mother said, and hung up. She didn't ask about Violet or the baby.

She could hear her father still breathing on the phone. "I'm sorry, V," he said, offering her no other options, nor permission to move in with the Moore family. She heard the click at the other end of the line.

Violet cradled the now silent phone between her ear and her neck and wondered what would happen if she took the baby to Ruth's. Maybe her mother would never speak to her again. Maybe she'd never see her father again. Her mind empty, her body exhausted, she failed to understand why her mother was forcing her to choose between her baby and her parents. For a week at the Hampden's house, where one room served as a small nursery, she held her baby, bathed him daily, washed his hair as the midwives showed her how to avoid cradle cap, pinned his diapers and pulled up rubber pants over them while trying to sort out what to do. Due any time, Gloria, still swollen, sat on her bed and rocked.

"V, take your baby to the boy's family," she said. "He'd fit in better there."

"My mom said 'no.'"

"Stop being too damned obedient," she said. "Your mom sounds like an A+ bitch."

When she called her father, he said she had to do what's best for the baby. "A baby with two parents in the same house is best," her father said.

"The boy's family wants to keep him," she said.

"Maybe that's not a good idea," he said. "They don't have enough resources to care for a baby."

"But they do. And a bigger family. The baby would be loved by everyone around him, including me."

"Wishful thinking. It's time to sign, V."

"But it's true, Daddy."

The phone clicked in her ear.

At home, her mother nodded and greeted her with a warning: "You'll never talk about what happened to anyone. You'll never mention this sorry episode to anyone. You will never mention that jig-a-boo baby to me or anyone. If asked, you were in New York with your sick aunt. Understood?"

Her mother glared at her. "And get a job to pay us back for the Hampden's bill."

"Maybe you should send Hampden's a bill for stealing my baby. You think people adopting Benjamin get him for free? You think they aren't paying adoption fees?"

Gloria had told her that the Hampden's collected money on both ends: fees from the girls' families and adoption fees from the adopting couples.

"Shut up. No one's paying high fees for your jig-a-boo baby," her mother said. "He'll be lucky to be adopted."

After being home a week, Gloria called saying Benjamin was being neglected, that he was left alone in the hallway, not wheeled into the nursery, that one day, he wailed forever until she picked him up, changed his soggy diapers, bathed him, gave him a bottle. "They don't care about him, Violet."

She begged her father to drive her back to Hampden house to pick up her son. Instead, he called the Hampden's House and raised a ruckus, asking what his payments were for if they were neglecting the baby, and that he was going to call the Governor.

"Why can't we bring him home?" she asked. "Let's go get him."

He stared at his feet. "You signed papers surrendering him," he said. "It's too late."

Later, she heard her parents arguing about her and the baby. A week after her father raised his ruckus, Gloria called to say that some folks had come and taken Benjamin with them. She felt relieved that he'd finally been adopted, but the whole month proved too hard.

Violet lost weight, now lighter than she was before she got pregnant. She kept Benjamin's flute, and they stayed in touch, although his classes and his job kept him busy. She stayed in her room, thinking only about the baby, worrying if he was safe and loved.

Later, when she and Benjamin finally saw each other in the glen at dusk, she sank into his arms.

"Red, you got to do something. My mom says you need to get some help," he said. "You can still come to our house."

Tension filled her house. She and her mother barely spoke, and her parents argued. She and her father talked about nothing important. What no one ever talked about was her absent baby. She stayed in her room, playing blues and R&B on her flute. Because the glock's bells sounded too cheerful, she hid the instrument in the closet, but kept the metal mallets Benjamin had given her close by where she could finger them. Her body remembered that she'd been pregnant, even with no baby around. Her stomach sagged and her beasts looked different even after the shot the doctor gave her to dry up her milk. Her shape changed, and at the same time, was vanishing.

"Holy crap, Red. We lost our son. But you're halfway gone, too," Benjamin said when she sneaked out of the house to meet him at his college campus. "Don't you eat anymore?"

Her eyes wandered nervously up at him. She saw his beautiful face, his wide smile, his perfectly arched brows, the brown of his soft skin, and the love in his eyes. He pulled her hand and then cupped her face.

"Won't you finally come home?"

POST PARTUM

At the Moore family home, Ruth let it be known that Violet had made a terrible mistake, letting her baby go. Unlike her parents, Ruth, Benjamin, and his whole family—father and brothers— mourned with Violet the loss of a baby they'd loved without having met him. She blamed herself. She should have listened to Gloria. She should have listened to Ruth and to Benjamin, who surprisingly didn't hold her cowardice against her. For the first time since having the baby, Violet openly wept for the loss of baby Benjamin.

"I don't blame you as much as I blame your mother. I know you wanted your child," Ruth said, hugging Violet's now bony shoulders to her chest. Ashamed, Violet allowed herself to be enveloped.

"I'm sorry. I'm sorry," she repeated as Ruth held her.

Violet spent her days putting her newfound hostess skills to use when Ruth was at work. She found Ruth's old sewing machine in the basement and completed all the mending piled up in a laundry basket near the ironing board. She woke early, prepared breakfasts and packed lunches for everyone in the house, then prepared supper, ready when everyone came home, but didn't eat much. She helped keep the house tidy and orderly, mindless tasks that enabled her to escape by imaging all the things little Benjamin was doing while his father, Benjamin, attended classes, studied, or worked at his father's barbershop. She played with Rex, the Moore's dog, a little brown mutt that followed her everywhere. Too afraid to walk the dog, she let him out into the yard. She never left the house, certain that everyone in the neighborhood knew her as the girl who gave away her baby. Family weekend music nights, during which she played the flute and sometimes piano, buoyed her. Benjamin and his father and brothers played the horns, trumpet, trombone, saxophone, and she finally understood how he was able to play them all.

After a few months passed, Ruth pulled her by the hand into the bathroom with a long mirror. "What do you see?"

"Nobody," Violet said, averting her eyes from the image in the mirror.

"Nonsense. I see somebody. Somebody stronger. You no longer look like walking bones."

"I made a terrible mistake."

"Yes, you did. You think those other girls told to never speak about it, they're not suffering, too? In this family alone, generations of mothers have suffered over stolen children. Think about that."

"May I stay?"

"If you find something else to do other than hide in the house all day."

CHILDHOOD

Violet bloomed. She and Benjamin took after dinner strolls around the neighborhood's tree-lined streets, admiring well-made brick houses shaded by mature oaks, a neighborhood so green it looked like their glen, or a park, or a suburb instead of a Baltimore City. They studied together after she began classes at the same college Benjamin attended, although she did not declare a major at first. Occasionally, her father visited, uncomfortable in the Moore's distinctive home overlooking the woody Lake Ashburton, where Black families with means lived. She wondered if he recalled saying that her baby would be better off with a family with more resources. She wondered if he harbored regrets, too, knowing that his only grandson existed someplace unknown. Violet never asked about her mother. Clearly, her mother had sent no messages and didn't know her father visited. It baffled her, the way her mother acted, as if she sinned to the high heaven and deserved only punishment, as if giving up her baby wasn't punishment enough.

Her father attended Benjamin's college graduation in 1968, the same year the Maryland law prohibiting them from getting married was repealed. At their tiny wedding, held in the Moore's home, her father shook Benjamin's hand for the first time. When she graduated college, which allowed her to teach public high school, he came alone. He visited after Mikie was born, bringing a savings bond as a gift, and again when the twins were born, but each time, like a ghost, leaving no imprint of his presence behind.

Five decades and change later, three years after her husband suffered a heart attack and died, little Benjamin, now a grown middle-aged man, stepped into the room, a reincarnation of his father. It took her breath away. Only his last name had changed, and he resembled Mikie, Van, and Elijah. They traded details while Mikie served iced teas, coffee, and cake. Little Benjamin studied her through wired-rimmed glasses. He held her hand, told her she'd done the right thing, that he'd had a good life with parents who'd rescued him from foster care and loved him with devotion. He was an only child. He'd gone to law school. Now with his parents dead, he'd thought he'd be alone in the world. Until Mikie called.

"I'm sorry," Violet repeated. What do you say to a child you abandoned?

"Thank you for coming. Forgive me," Violet said, uttering words she'd waited five decades to say. "I always wanted to keep you." Fifty-seven years of shame flooded her, reddening her face under her now grayed hair.

Little Benjamin beamed his father's smile, the one that had enchanted her when she was a teen. All the sounds in the room seemed like buzzing. What a triumph! Benjamin came home. The unexpected craziness of seeing all her children together in one room, the sadness that her husband missed the return of the child whose absence had bound them together. She enveloped her first-born son in her trembling arms, held him tightly, unable to let go for fear she'd lose him again.

PIRATE BURGER

It began in the parking lot outside the Pirate Burger. Wind whipped the leaves covering the asphalt into mini whirling dervishes, twirling along the lower grills and running boards of parked cars, curling around the tires like a frenetic ballet troupe, dancing along the sides and over the curbs. Sitting in her car, watching the leaves and clutching the steering wheel, Beth saw Lou pull into the parking lot. He slid his car into a spot on the other side of the lot as far from her car as possible. *What an asshole*, she thought as she twisted her engagement ring, a ring that, until recently, she felt proud and excited to wear. She knew Lou saw her car, saw her sitting in it because he glanced and looked away, failing to acknowledge her with a wave. He simply exited his car, locked the vehicle behind him with his key fob, faced the entrance to Pirate Burger, and pointed himself like a rocket toward the double doors as if he were programmed like a damned robot.

Instead of enjoying the crisp bite in the fall air, he hunched his neck into his shoulders as he walked. She watched him as if she were seeing him for the first time: tall and slender, almost fine-boned, dark-haired, clean-shaven, slender-waisted, immaculate clothing with crisp creases she knew he pressed and hung with care, white running shoes he kept spotless with special leather cleaner. She'd read that in long term relationships, it wasn't unusual to both love and hate the other, and although she could list qualities she loved about him—his witty one-liners, his penchant for working hard, his artsy photography, his ambition and entrepreneurship—she now leaned heavily in the hate direction. Not an angry person, these feelings discomforted her. But she promised herself she'd focus on the things she loved about him, especially since he would be her husband in a few short months.

She watched him wince as sounds of kids screaming and music blaring from electronic pirates escaped into the parking lot every time someone opened the entrance doors. A giant plastic pirate with green pants and flared jacket with brown patched britches and the requisite wooden peg leg stood guard next to a bush in front of the wooden doors, and Beth smiled at the incongruity of the pirate dwarfing tall Leo as he approached it. She wondered what kind of father he'd be.

"Wait! Wait!" she called, slamming her car door and running toward him, leaves swirling around her feet. Hands stuffed into his jacket pockets, unsmiling, he turned and glared.

"Of all the dumps in the county, why this one?" he asked when she caught up to him. "Is there some favorite item you'd been meaning to steal from here?"

She blanched at his sarcasm, the smug expression on his face when he looked at her, the irritation in his eyes so easy to read.

"Well, aren't you filled with light and joy today," she said and smiled.

They trudged inside and looked around. A trio of electronic pirates with beards, bandannas, stripped britches, and gold earrings sang a dumb sea shanty song from a fake stage, which included a giant flat plastic pirate tall ship oscillating behind the pirates and a huge electronic red and blue crab next to his buddy, a gigantic electronic blue octopus. Beth had always loved the blue octopus with its eight seemingly delicate arms pulling things to it with ease. Only two of the electronic octopus's arms worked, extending and retracting with the beat. Its bulbous head sported a mini, Dixie-cup cap with an anchor in the center, tipped jauntily to the side. She'd never told Lou that she'd worked in a Pirate Burger as a teenager throughout high school, and that the chain provided her with a sense of comfort, regardless of what city in which she lived. Come to think of it, he'd never asked her if she worked as a teenager.

She followed Lou into the large dining room, where tables of kids with birthday parties occupied the area closest to the stage. Overstressed mothers held birthday parties with square-shaped pizzas, burgers, fries, and ice cream for their kids, a three-year-old and family at one table, a seven-year-old party at another. Other family members had always attended and snapped photos of the birthday boy or girl blowing out candles. Serving these families had proved easy since all the servers had to do was place food orders in the center of the tables.

Beth's own family never held birthday parties for her or her sister Yuka at Pirate Burger or any other similar place, considering them extravaganzas, a colossal waste of money for show-off parents, when perfectly suitable parties for milestone events could be held cheaper at home. She remembered, however, that one harried mother had once told her she preferred Pirate Burger parties over the ones at home because it eliminated the need to clean up after a herd of kids, and she didn't want them leaving fingerprints on her walls and furniture.

"Either way, you pay," the mother had said with a shrug. Beth found herself agreeing with the mother. If she had a kid or two, she'd hold their birthdays at Pirate Burger. No fuss, no muss.

"Bad food, too much noise, too many kids," Lou said, crossing his arms. "Is this a fucking joke, Beth?"

"It's neutral," Beth offered a half smile. "We can talk things out sensibly in a place where children are laughing."

"I can't hear myself think in here," Lou said. He set his keys on the table, the mini flashlight key chain rolling into his car key fob.

"We can talk here," Beth said. "No eavesdroppers."

They sat at a table large enough for four. Lou refused to remove his jacket. He frowned at the surroundings and then fixed his eyes on Beth.

"Nothing to talk about. You have some kind of sickness."

"We have to talk before the wedding," she said.

The wedding was a few months away. They had only mailed their save-the-date cards, and Beth had already bought her gown. The bridesmaids were getting fitted, and the catering and venue down payments secured their menu and location.

It had been a week since Beth had confessed to Lou that she had a shoplifting addiction. She mostly stole trinkets and odd bullshit she didn't need. She couldn't help it. Small insignificant things she took every day from every place in which she set foot called her name. They seduced her, these small objects that no one ever missed. Overcome with shame and guilt, sometimes she'd returned the items to the same store. Or donated them. Or gifted them to co-workers, acquaintances, and friends.

Glancing at the mini flashlight on Lou's keychain, she smiled. Lou would never know it matched three others stashed at home, pinched from a gas station. The retro change purse she pinched from a box discount store still sat in her oversized designer purse, price tag attached. Her house contained boxes of ridiculous items she could easily afford to buy, like the mini key chain flashlights, travel-sized toothpastes, plastic lids for pet food cans, salt and pepper shakers, trinkets, and napkins from restaurants.

She and Lou had not yet moved in together, and Beth thought she ought to fess up before they did, before he started wondering about why she was wasting money on junk. Perhaps wedding jitters spurred her most recent urges to walk out of stores and other places with pinched items in her purse. She pinched toilet paper rolls and half-used nail polish bottles from her weekly nail appointments. Greeting cards and lipstick pencils, magnets, and goofy touristy items from the pharmacy chain near her home. Flip flops and socks from the chain shoe store. The most expensive thing she pinched was a designer silk scarf from the same luxury store where she had been purchasing three others. It was easy to confuse the sales lady since she was already purchasing three. The fourth called her name, whispered it, sang it to her, saying she needed it. She'd given it to Lou's mother.

She held this secret about the origin of the scarf but confessed her secret habit to Lou, expecting him to understand. Maybe he'd laugh about it with her. Except he didn't. His jaw dropped, and then he said he couldn't deal with the dishonesty or the thefts before he gathered his wallet, his keys with the mini flashlight, and packed up the few items he'd kept at her house and left, refusing to answer her calls or texts for a week. He exercised what he called "the silent treatment," one of the things she hated about him when he used it upon others, but now this was the first time he'd directed his silent treatment at her, and she hated it more.

What if she walked away, giving him plenty of time to bask in a permanent silent treatment? In fact, the silent week between them prompted her to rethink and refocus things, reevaluate Lou as husband material. She had not yet come to a decision. *What would I lose?* she wondered, then thought of the money already spent on the wedding.

"We don't need to talk. You're the one with the problem. You need to fix yourself. Before the wedding," he said. His voice sounded final, as if there was an unspoken, imminent threat if she'd failed to fix herself. She imagined him lording this secret over her for the rest of her life.

When the server, obviously a high school kid who smiled through braces, delivered menus and two glasses of water, Lou pushed the menus to the other side of the table and asked for a hot, soapy rag to clean the table.

"It's sticky," he said, grimacing while rubbing his fingertips against each other as if to remove imaginary stickiness.

"It's been a struggle," Beth said. "I've been trying to fix it since it started."

She'd hoped that she could finally discuss this issue with the man who was about to become her husband. She wanted to explain that the compulsion started from a head trauma, that she couldn't stop herself from taking things from stores and people's houses, that the stuff she took meant nothing to her, that she'd fought the temptation every time, that after she'd pinched something, the thrill diminished, replaced by shame and guilt. She hoped that Lou would understand, help her manage the problem that plagued her after a softball knocked her down and out in high school. Concussed, she had to be carried off the field, spent a few days in the hospital. It ended her run for a college sports scholarship since she couldn't return to either the softball or soccer fields for the rest of the year due to persistent dizziness and nausea. It changed her in small and large ways, the forgetting and remembering at odd times.

"Brain trauma," the doctor had explained to her parents and her. "Most kids end up with sprained or broken ankles. You're lucky to be alive, young lady. Softball strikes to the face or head are no joke."

Vertigo and nausea eventually faded, sometimes returning unexpectedly to remind her, but then anxiety arrived, bringing with it the impulse to take bullshit items that she didn't want, didn't care about, didn't like from all kinds of places. Therapists, counselors, a parade of medicines helped for a while, although nothing stopped the compulsion.

When the server returned with the wet, soapy rag, instead of handing it to Lou, who held out his hand, the kid washed down the table herself and asked if they were ready to order.

"You see the menus there? We didn't even look," Lou said in a condescending tone. "It's not as if there's a lot of choices here."

Annoyed, Beth sucked in her breath. The server set down the napkin-bundled flatware and paper placemats that said "Pirate Burger" in large, red, pirate-looking script.

"Stop being an asshole, Lou," she said after the server walked away.

Lou stared at her. "You and your joke-y little problem can ruin me," he said. "You can tank my career in one stupid move. It can cost me my job."

Beth rolled her eyes and reached for the menus. She gave one to Lou.

"You own a dry cleaner store," she said, keeping her voice flat.

"Don't you know anything? Obviously not. Customers won't bring their clothing in if they know my wife's a thief."

Beth smirked. Lou left the table and headed toward the ball pit, where he sat on the rim wall circling the area, his legs dangling into the pit. He watched children cover themselves with the plastic multicolored balls. Beth joined him and leaned into the pit to touch the balls, tossing a pink one toward the children.

"Do you want to steal a plastic ball??"

Beth stared at the children, screaming and playing with joyful abandon. "Stop being a dick," she said softly. "I should have told you sooner. I couldn't."

"I hate this place," Lou said.

"It's a safe place for kids," Beth said. "It's a safe place," she repeated.

"Oh? We're kids? We're playing? Is that what we're doing? Playing?"

"Don't be like that, Lou."

"We're together two years and you only tell me a week ago that you're a thief? I can be any way I want."

They'd met at the beach two summers ago, where Beth had gone for an annual work-related conference always held at the same hotel. Beth loved her job working at the state-run zoo in the membership department. She loved meeting up with membership consultants from zoos all over the nation and learning best practices. She loved signing up families for year-long memberships that allowed the kiddos to take all kinds of free classes and time in the petting zoo. She loved the zoo—everything about it, and recently was promoted to working with developing corporate memberships, a position that came with a substantial raise.

On the day she'd first met Lou, she'd gotten up early to walk along the surf because she wanted to see the sunrise, see its light sprinkling the tips of ocean with its sparkling glow, maybe see some dolphins swimming beyond the surf. She pretended not to notice the man with several cameras dangling from his neck approaching her. His red shorts were wet, tight like bike shorts, and his tank top, made from the same fabric, hugged his chest beneath the cameras. His face narrow, cheekbones high, eyes exotic, almond shaped, black and intense in their sockets. He stopped and studied the horizon, the sky, the sea, the birds arcing against the clouds, and snapped photos as he walked along the surf. She was relieved the man had not spoken to her, but then she spotted him again the next morning, and again in the afternoon, dressed in crisp white trousers and a polo, and she wondered if he was at the same conference. When she saw him again a few nights later on, the ocean-facing deck of the restaurant where she and some conference goers went together, he glanced at her and smiled, one corner of his lips higher than the other.

"Beautiful view," he'd said to the group.

She smiled, and he returned it with a wink. She could feel her heartbeat in the barrel of her chest at the sight of the handsome, almost pretty man.

They ran into each other again at the souvenir shop on the last day of the conference, and they began chatting, exchanged phone numbers. Beth had already pinched a lighthouse magnet that she had just dropped into her purse. She was surprised that he lived close to her home. A few weeks later, they met at a coffee shop where Lou showed her the impressive photos he'd taken of the sunrise and one that included her, back toward the camera, walking in the surf. It looked like a fine art photo. He'd framed a few of them for her and slid them toward her, his first gift. After that, they began seeing each other.

Beth inhaled, relieved she had not yet sold her home to share his as he'd suggested many times. She owned her home, loved it, decorated it with art pieces of the animals she loved, and wood and crystal wind chimes. She loved the Buddha in her garden, which burst in summer with cascades of colorful flowers she planted and tended. The photos Lou had given her hung on the walls of her stairway. She just wasn't ready to leave her place, despite it being filled with boxes of evidence of her problem. So far, she'd been careful and lucky to have never gotten caught, although her therapist warned her that legal trouble would become a certainty if her compulsion graduated to bigger things than the useless items she'd pinched.

"I'm not a thief," she said.

"Call it whatever you want. Walks like a…thief, it's a thief."

Panic surged inside her, tied her stomach in knots. She felt anxious. She clenched her hands into fists before sitting on her fingers. She unwound her fingers under her legs and clutched the rim of the ball pit wall beneath her. Oblivious, Lou stared at the screaming children playing with the balls. The sounds of the Happy Birthday song merged with the singing pirates, which turned on every half hour. She knew the panic, lead in her already damaged brain. It would fuse with her anxiety, and then she'd have to fight to keep from reaching for a damned plastic ball and palming it in her hand before dropping it into her purse.

He rose from the wall's rim. "Let's skip this shitty joint and find someplace else to go," he said, a command in his voice. He dusted off his pants, adjusted his jacket.

For a moment, she felt as if he'd expected her to obey. She stared at him. She sold memberships to the zoo, corporate, single, and family memberships, families of all configurations just like the ones who came to Pirate Burger for a few hours of a birthday extravaganza. It occurred to her that Lou had never asked details about her job. He knew she worked in an administrative office at the zoo but it never asked exactly what she did, nor expressed any interest in visiting the zoo. He never commented when she told him about the giraffe calf or lion cubs, or her favorite, the elephant house. His eyes glazed over when she spoke about the magnificent birds in the avian area or the orangutan who seemed lonely. He always talked to her about his store, his issues with employees, his stories about odd customers. He talked about cameras he wanted to buy and lighting accessories. He talked about the boat he wanted to buy to keep at a marina at the beach.

She liked the Pirate Burger. She loved the Asian salad with ginger dressing and other offerings geared toward adults, like the seared tuna and blackened salmon. She loved the happy blue electronic octopus pulling things toward itself without a worry. She loved the innocence of the kids who became immersed in the present celebrations of their birthdays without a thought about the future, without knowledge of how a single accidental softball strike could send them careening in a whole different direction. She loved the fact that this time, she had not pinched a ball from the ball pit, that this time, shedding something felt better than taking something.

As she pushed herself off the ball pit's wall rim, she slipped off her engagement ring, walked toward Lou, and placed it in his hand. She left the ball pit area and hurried toward the restrooms, down the dark hallway, its cheap, sagging paneling smudged by thousands of kids' fingerprints from years of birthday parties. Next to the ladies' room door at the end of the hallway, the exit sign on the back door blinked red.

Lou followed her. "You're leaving me? Don't end it this way!" he shouted.

She turned to face Lou, now hurrying toward her. She shook her head, pushed open the back door, not caring that she tripped the fire alarm, activating the blinking white and red lights and the blaring siren, and ran toward her car, wild, windswept leaves spinning around her ankles.

ABOUT THE AUTHOR

Rosalia Scalia's fiction has appeared or is forthcoming in *The Oklahoma Review, North Atlantic Review, Notre Dame Review, The Portland Review,* and *Quercus Review,* among many others. Her short story collection, STUMBLING TOWARD GRACE released in 2021. She holds an MA in writing from Johns Hopkins University and is a Maryland State Arts Council Independent Artist's Award recipient. She won the Editor's Select award from *Willow Review* and her short story in *Pebble Lake* was nominated for a Pushcart Prize. She lives in Baltimore with her family.

ABOUT THE PRESS

Unsolicited Press is based out of Portland, Oregon and focuses on the works of the unsung and underrepresented. As a womxn-owned, all-volunteer small publisher that doesn't worry about profits as much as championing exceptional literature, we have the privilege of partnering with authors skirting the fringes of the lit world. We've worked with emerging and award-winning authors such as Shann Ray, Amy Shimshon-Santo, Brook Bhagat, Kris Amos, and John W. Bateman.

Learn more at unsolicitedpress.com. Find us on twitter and instagram.

www.ingramcontent.com/pod-product-compliance
Lightning Source LLC
Chambersburg PA
CBHW030001010826
48973CB00007B/2115